BRED

The Dragon's Game
BOOK IV

H. N. Henry

Presse Dragon Libre
Free Dragon's Press

Trois-Rivières, QC, Canada

FREE DRAGON'S PRESS
Huard, Norman Henry
220 B Farmer
Trois-Rivières, Québec, Canada, G9A 3E6
www.hnhenry.com

Publisher's Note: This is a work of fiction. Names, characters, places, and incidents are a product of the author's imagination, except for his use of the Cree language in Roman orthography to number and title chapters and as one of the languages spoken by certain characters; and also for his use of certain Tai Chi exercise names. Locales and public names are sometimes used for atmospheric purposes. Any resemblance to actual people, living or dead, or to businesses, companies, events, institutions, or locales is completely coincidental.

Book Layout © 2014 BookDesignTemplates.com

BRED Book IV The Dragon's Game by H. N. Henry—1st edition

ISBN 978-0-9958419-2-5

Dedication

To my niece, Annie.

Out of suffering have emerged the strongest souls;
the most massive characters are seared with scars.

—KHALIL GIBRAN

CHAPTER

— † —

FROM BANISHED
THE DRAGON'S GAME
BOOK I

Legend tells us dragons fly so high they can see the future.
Reason tells us that to know the future is a curse.
Our hearts tell us the seeds of hope are sown in the reality of
the present.

— † —

FROM BRANDED
THE DRAGON'S GAME
BOOK II

Reality tells us that to lose hope is to welcome death.

— † —

FROM BETRAYED
THE DRAGON'S GAME
BOOK III

Hope tells us light lives even in the darkest places.

— † —

Visitor
Okîhokew

— † —

Darkness tells us it will change us if we venture there.

— † —

Free at last, Danuka, the last dragon in the Land of the Danu, flew above the land, while Nagora, now her Dragon Talker apprentice, guarded and protected her precious eggs.

Nagora gritted her teeth and clenched her fists. "Raynhard, what are you doing here? You agreed not to come!"

She had just come face-to-face with King Raynhard. He was stepping through the crack in the natural stone wall of the bowl that formed the lower third of the entrance to the secret mountain cave where Nagora lived with her dragon.

Raynhard held up his hands. "Nagora, I know, but I had to come. I need to know how you are doing and how Danuka's eggs are."

Nagora stepped toward him and jabbed her finger at him. "But that's not what we agreed to. You agreed to only come when I sent for you. You also agreed to only come at the time I specified. Here you are today, uninvited, come in broad daylight. Someone could have followed you. Perhaps you were followed. You're putting Danuka's eggs in danger. You know what that means. They're the future of your kingdom!"

He pursed his lips and closed his eyes for the time of a breath. "Nagora, believe me. I'm sorry. I was most careful not to be followed. This is not my first time here. I did as I used to when I sought refuge here as Chive. I swear it. No one followed me. I know what's at stake here. Not only are the dragon's eggs precious to me, but you are too. You freed your father and Danuka, and you saved Danuka's eggs. I owe you so much."

Nagora held up her hand and pointed at herself. "If I recall, when I took on the role of Edana and we came face-to-face in the prince's fortress, you didn't think so highly of my actions that night. As a matter of fact, you didn't want me to be one of the raiders to the Isle of Smoke. You thought I would put the whole mission in jeopardy. Well, that's what I think of your coming here today. You're putting Danuka's eggs in jeopardy!"

Nagora turned away from Raynhard and strode past the firepit over to one of the storage shelves cut into the cave wall. She reached for the embossed leather-sheathed royal hunting dagger and stepped back to her king. "Here, you gave this to me as a reminder of my commitment to the role you asked me to take on. Up until today, I've been committed to that role. Not anymore."

Raynhard held his hands together as if to beg to speak, but she continued.

"I've been branded, with this, for a higher cause." Nagora pointed to the Tiwaz brand on her forehead. "Why? So I could reunite with a mother I was led to believe had died giving birth to me. And a twin sister I didn't know I had. I was lied to. Supposedly for my own protection and to protect 'The Cause,' your cause."

Raynhard reached for her hands.

Nagora batted his hands away. I don't care if you're my king. "I helped win the support of the Hundred Best Warriors from the Land of Skulls for our fight to free Da and Danuka.

"I risked my life many times for you.

"I fought alongside Uncle, who trained me to be the warrior I am, and he died of his wounds in that fight on the bridge. Now he's lost to me.

"I've given up being with my da who I longed for all these years because I had been told he was away on a journey of exploration at sea. Another lie to protect me and 'The Cause.'

"I've given up being with my mother and sister, whom I've barely gotten to know. I've given up being with the family I never had, yet could have.

"Here, take back your da's dagger. Take over for me, and I'll get back to those things I gave up for you."

Raynhard held up both hands. "No, Nagora. Don't do that. Keep the dagger. It's yours. You've earned so much more than I could ever pay you. There are not enough words for me to express the gratitude I owe you for all you did and for all you are doing. You know there's no way I could take over for you. You're a Dragon Talker. You have that power. You know it can shape the future of my kingdom."

He shook his head and placed a hand over his heart. "I know you're still dealing with the loss of your uncle Dangor. And I know you're dealing with the task of protecting Danuka's eggs. I know what you're sacrificing. I know what your mother and sister are sacrificing. I know what your father is sacrificing. You are all making sacrifices for me and the future of my kingdom. That is a debt I will never be able to repay. Perhaps, someday, when you see what this country can become, then will you have a sense of reward for the work you have all done."

Nagora swallowed and bowed her head. "I'm sorry. I have no right to scold you. You are my king. You can do whatever you like. It's just that Danuka is worried about her eggs. Every evening when she returns, she goes to them to make sure they're safe. She understands how important they are to the future of your kingdom, but also to the future of her kind. When she returns tonight she'll sense your presence and that will worry her since I did not warn her of your coming, for the same reasons I stated."

Nagora slipped the dagger into the deep pocket inside her sheepskin vest.

Raynhard reached out to touch her arm. "Nagora, Yogari is concerned as well. And your mother and sister want news of you. So does Lars."

"Lars? He's still here? He didn't return to the Land of Skulls?" An ache took hold of her insides. *Lars my savior, my valiant warrior, my lover. You're still here. If only I could run to your side. But that would mean reliving the pain of parting again. It's best you return to the Land of Skulls. I'll have* peace of mind and be better able to carry out my duty as protector and guardian of Danuka's eggs.

The secret location of this cave has to stay so for the safety of Danuka's eggs. Not even Da knows where it is and he too is a Dragon Talker and rides Danuka every day throughout the land.

Every day Danuka leaves the cave before sunrise and returns just after sunset. Even so, I can't send for Lars. I promised to keep this place a secret.

"Yes, Lars is still here. He's in Cairnmase. He's staying with Geirador and Paruline."

Is he waiting for me? I don't dare ask. I'm guessing he is. Though, Nagora had told him she did not know how long she would have to be away from him in her duty to Danuka. It could be seasons or years. I risk losing him.

"Do you know when he might leave?"

"He's helping Geirador and Paruline care for several warriors whose wounds prevented them from continuing on home to the Land of Skulls. When they're fit for that journey through the mountains, he'll most likely leave with them."

Her recollection of the wounds Lars had sustained in his fight to keep his promise to her came rushing back: The image of Lars in Godomor's tent, stretched out on the table as Mina described the wounds she had treated; Lars smiling at her despite his pain and discomfort; and then the moment they had alone in the tent as she helped him dress, when they kissed. These memories made her want him even more.

Nagora pushed those images to the back of her mind with another question. "Where are Mum and Sagora these days? Still in Windhaven?"

"Yes, for now. They've almost finished their work there. They have a last team to train before setting out to towns and villages to verify the decontamination done so far, and they'll help tend to the sick. In Windhaven teams have flushed most of the wells and set up cisterns of uncontaminated spring water. The people are informed and know what to do to make sure the water they drink is safe. Trained teams have already set out to apply the same procedures in the outlying towns.

"The milk test Tagnya devised reassures them. A drop of poisoned well water in a spoon of milk turns it to tiny green curds, a clear warning. Soon your mother, with the help of the people she and Sagora have trained, will travel to towns and villages throughout the land. They'll show the villagers how to test the water of their wells and clean them of the poison."

Mum, I'm so proud of you. "Mum's abilities as a healer amaze me. Did you know that in the Land of Skulls she was a loved healer? Those who she had healed had the honor of calling her 'Tagnuska.' The 'uska' on her name means they recognize her as having the power to heal. It's like calling her 'Tagnyoriva the Healer.'

"To think, the one there who accused Mum of being a witch was the one guilty of poisoning King Godomor, and it was Mum who saved Godomor from that poison, a poison obtained from Hag."

Raynhard had been nodding all the while she spoke. "Coming out of all those years of lethargy Raganora's poison held them under is not easy for many of those folks. You witnessed how it rendered them docile and without purpose. Now thanks to Tagnya, they're coming out that stupor.

"And, I must say, your da's appearances with Danuka are giving them hope once again. Yogari is a great orator.

"When he tells of his years in that cave in the vent hole on the Isle of Smoke with Danuka, and all he did to keep himself in a hopeful state of mind, and how he cared for Danuka, they see that what they have to overcome to rebuild their own homes is not such a dire price to pay. Yogari tells them the People of the Danu will rebuild the land one home at a time. As each family pulls itself back up, so too does our country. It is how it will become great again."

That's my da. He's a born leader. I can see why you've been counting on him. "Raynhard, tell me more about Da. He must be near you most of the time. Do you fly with him on Danuka's back? Is he nearby right now?"

Raynhard's smile broadened. "Nagora, I am with your father much of the time, and yes, I ride with him on Danuka's back. Those who saw Edana free the dragon at the Isle of Smoke Bridge were quick to spread the word of her deed. For those who weren't there to see it, seeing the dragon in the flesh set down on a road leading into their town, with us on her back, is the next best thing. The dragon needs little introduction. They know your father, The Rider. Then Yogari introduces me."

Raynhard stood straight and stuck his chin out. "You should hear him: 'People of the Land of the Danu, thanks to Edana, today Danuka, Mother Dragon, and I, Yogari, Dragon Talker, bring to you your rightful king, Raynhard, son of your once beloved King Bernhard and Queen Julianna.'"

He relaxed his pose. "And then he goes on to lay out all the facts of how and why Raganora, with Hag's help, usurped the throne and all the evil she did to our country from the murder of my parents, to hunting down and killing all the dragons except for Danuka, to changing the name of our land to Innisfhail, to outlawing the word 'dragon' and destroying all images of dragons, and so on."

His eyes sparkled as he spoke the next words. "People cheer when he says: 'Today, we are no longer under her rule. We no longer have to live in fear. We no longer have to live without hope.

"'Today, Danuka, our Dragon Mother, is with us. She has eggs ready to hatch. Soon, as Edana told you, dragons will fly again in the sky over our land. Soon, we will rebuild our land to its former greatness under the leadership of our king, Raynhard, King of the Land of the Danu.

Raynhard held up a finger. "That's a short version. Sometimes he goes on and on. And at other times he answers questions. And sometimes, I answer questions. If I am to be their king, I have to be able to answer their questions.

"And before we leave, he makes sure I say: 'We are, once again, the People of the Danu, the People of the Dragon.'"

Nagora touched the side of her head. "After years of watching the horizon for the sail of the boat that would bring Da home to me, I had built an image of him. Now, since seeing him and hearing of him from you, I'm still trying to reconcile those images of him.

"Mum and Da both have a way with words. They can convince with their words and people listen when they speak. I saw that when Da brought Danuka out of the vent hole on the Isle of Smoke. Even though he and Danuka were chained and archers had them in their sights, they gave Da whatever he asked for and they carried out every suggestion he made. And I saw it in Godomor's court when Mum addressed Godomor and his vassals' counselors to plead for my safe return and to seek their support for The Cause, ours and yours."

Raynhard smiled at her. "They are definitely leaders, Nagora. And so are you, in your own right. Be proud of your parents. They are proud of you. I am proud of you. I came to get news of how you are doing. So let's talk about you now.

"From what I can see, you look as fit as ever. Though, I'm guessing you've lost weight."

He's looking at me in that way again. The desire is still there. Does it not matter to him I love another? Or does he realize it will be over, with time? Lars will become a lover in my past.

"I still do my daily ritual exercises. And Danuka has given me another ritual. I've had to make individual pouches for the eggs and, each day as soon as she leaves, I have to hide each egg in the cave in a different place. You know how extensive this cave's network is. They have to be spread out, never two together."

Raynhard's brow furrowed. "Every day you have to do this?"

"Yes, because as soon as she returns, she hunts each one down and brings them all back together to place in the original four-egg pouches Da had made for them. I have to hold each one for her and turn it over in my hands so she can examine it. She keeps them near her throughout the night."

"So that's sixteen eggs to hide each day." Raynhard had a smile on his face.

Nagora spread her arms wide. "I can tell you, I know every crack and recessed hole in here."

"And your food supply?"

"I'm glad you bring that up. I've just about depleted all the dried berries and meats you had stashed here. I should say 'we' because Danuka eats a heck of a lot of food. I know father feeds her during the day, but with all the flying around, she must work up an appetite."

"Have you been able to hunt?"

"That's the other thing. She wants me to guard the eggs. I can leave to go set snares at the earliest of dawn's twilight before she leaves. That doesn't give me much time. I can't go too far away either. As soon as she returns, if there's enough daylight left, I can go check the snares. I always have my bow with me in case I see something I can shoot. Based on what I've been catching in the snares, I think I've exhausted the supply of game around here. Berries and nuts are probably more plentiful further down in the valley, but I can't go there unless she spends a day here with her eggs. So far, that hasn't happened."

"Nagora, look, there's no way you can continue doing this on your own."

"But we've promised. No one else is to know about this cave."

"You're right. That's not what I mean." He held up a hand. "Listen. I'll arrange for a stock of supplies to be prepared for you."

"No, you won't. Who can we trust?"

"Nagora, give me a chance. I'll ask Geirador. You know we can trust him and Paruline. They'll prepare everything. I'll deliver it on a day Danuka is here. I'll bring the supplies by mule to the high meadow where you will meet me. We can lead the mules up from there, along the ridge and down to the valley stream entrance at the other end of the cave. We'll unload the supplies there as quickly as possible and then I'll lead the mules back down to the high meadow. I'll bring the mules back to Cairnmase. When you come back, you can take your time to sort and cache the supplies wherever you feel is best here in the cave areas."

Nagora bit on her lip. "Okay, we could do that. Raynhard, you've got me thinking. I have three tapers left, one at the other end and two here. And my supply of candles for the candle lanterns is running low. I would need at least three more lanterns to place at various spots in the cave, more if you can get them. And I'd need a good supply of candles for those lanterns.

"And before we know it winter will come. I'll need a good supply of firewood. Every time I go out to the snares I bring back pieces of dead branches I find. Once snow is on the ground, I won't dare venture out for fear of leaving tracks in the snow that could be followed. Snow will come earlier here in the mountains. Will Danuka fly in the cold weather? Probably not. She'll need to be fed."

Raynhard held out his arms and smiled at her. "Let me re-assure you. Yogari mentioned he was looking into that with Geirador at Danuka's request. He's resourceful and will have ideas on how we can set you up for the winter. I'll make this my priority. You and Danuka will have the best conditions possible here. I'll see to it. And the cave will remain our secret. I promise." Raynhard stepped closer to Nagora and opened his arms.

His words did reassure her and now she let herself slip into his embrace. It feels good to be held. It feels good to be encouraged. Lars, if only it were you holding me.

"I must take good care of my precious Edana," he said as he caressed Nagora's hair and then her cheek. He kissed the brand on her forehead and pulled her closer. His cheek rested against hers. "I've missed you all these days." The warm whisper of those words in her ear and on her neck made her hold him closer. It feels good to be wanted. It feels good to be supported.

"Is there anything else you need, Edana?"

Raynhard's words refocused her thoughts and her feelings.

What image does he hold in his mind when he calls me Edana? The naked, blood-spattered, vengeful Edana on the dungeon stairs of the prince's fortress or the fire-arrow-shooting Edana on the Isle of Smoke Bridge, protecting Danuka and Yogari from the deadly ballista?

I know what I want. "Remind Da I need a bridle and saddle of my own for Danuka. She always flies back here without the ones Da uses. Ask him to make them for me and send them with Danuka. They could help me protect her eggs. If he doesn't, I'll fashion them myself with her help."

Raynhard placed his hands on Nagora's shoulders. "I'm sure he'll do that for you. It's time I leave."

"You never answered my question. Is Da nearby?"

"He brought me to what was the prince's fortress at Yhorgal Cliffs this morning. He flew back with Danuka to help Tagnya. He'll be back to get me by mid-afternoon."

"Tell Da I miss him."

"Nagora, every day he tells me how much he misses you. We must arrange time for your family to get together soon, most likely when Tagnya and Sagora are close by. It'll be easier when they are. They too miss you."

The word "family" brought up mixed images for Nagora. Uncle Dangor's face still came up first, then Tagnyoriva's and Sagora's faces. When will Da's face and mine come up at the mention of "family"? Perhaps never because Uncle raised me since I was born. Though, I know Da and I are family too.

And when she said the word "Father," three faces appeared side by side. Uncle Dangor's was again the clearest.

Next came that of Godomor the Terrible, King of the Land of Skulls, a direct descendant of the *First People of The Land*. "*Ohtawimaw*," she called him in the *Language of The People*. It meant "Father." Until that meeting with Godomor I didn't know it was also the language the dragons spoke. Now I do and I learned it through my dragon tear amulet. It's been revealing its powers to me. It gifted me with the *Language of The People*. Godomor called her "*Mitanisimaw*." It meant "Daughter." And he also called her by another name, "*Ka Peyakot Mahihkan*," "Lone Wolf." When he used that name, he spoke directly to her heart from his own.

Finally, Yogari's face stood there in the background, her father, a man with such strength and self-assurance. From the moment he had first held her in his arms under Danuka's wing in the vent house at Queen Raganora's Fortress on the Isle of Smoke, she knew she trusted him. She knew she would follow him anywhere because he would protect her and know what to do, like Lars, the man she loved.

On that day too, for the first time, she felt the effect of Danuka's scent on her. It had spread through her body as a feeling of welcoming warmth, comforting her and, at the same time, giving her strength and an enhanced awareness of all within her reach.

And Da had also warned me. "Today, you felt your body being taken over by Danuka's scent. It might have worried you. It is how Danuka ensures you are receptive to me as my apprentice, and to her, to what she needs you to do to protect her and her eggs. But I want to warn you. When I am not with you, Mother's scent will have an even greater effect on you until she gains complete trust in you. Fear not.

"Also, at times Danuka will not have words to convey what she wants to tell you. She will use images. She'll convey them to you in dreams."

"But how will I know they are meant as messages for me? How will I know the difference from other dreams?"

"You'll remember them clearly. They'll seem so real you'll believe they truly happened. They'll be unlike any dream you've ever had. And you'll question why she showed you those images. The reason might not be apparent right away. Trust what she shows you. It will always be for a reason."

Her da reached for her hand. "You are strong, Nagora. Your will is your own to govern. Trust Danuka, and she will trust you. She knows so much more than we'll ever know."

"Raynhard, thank you for coming. If you can arrange all this for me, I'll be grateful, and so will Danuka. Please, though, next time, warn me. Send a message with Danuka."

"I will, Nagora." Raynhard gave her a final kiss on her cheek and made his way to the crack in the bowl-like entrance to climb down among the trees and bushes below. Nagora climbed the ladder up to the bowl's edge. I'm alone again. Uncle was always a presence. I miss that. I'm a loner, but just feeling another nearby is a comfort. I realize that now. It's not the same as being in Danuka's presence.

She lost sight of Raynhard.

Since Danuka's arrival, Nagora had dismantled the wooden platform that ran along the inner bowl. It had offered a variety of views below, but made Danuka's coming and going to and from the cave difficult. Removing it had been a necessity. At least she still had the ladder.

As she stepped back into the cave, thoughts of Lars filled her mind. You're so close. I wish I were with you. Knowing you're in Cairnmase will intrude on my days here. Time is going to drag. I'll end up spending my time trying to figure out a way to go to you. There must be a way.

Danuka, all I need is a day. No, I need two days. I'll leave at dawn on the first day and be back by nightfall the next. I need a horse. Storm could bring me back. He would return to Geirador's corral on command. Getting to Cairnmase, though, even if I ran. Tar piss! That would take the whole day, possibly more. Could he send Storm to me? No. My horse would have to be trained. He's trained to go back.

I know! Danuka, you could fly me to Cairnmase and come back. It wouldn't take long. Especially without me on your back, you can fly so fast. In no time you'd be back here. Your eggs would be fine. That's it. Now how do I convince you?

Oh! Lars! Just one more night of making love to you. You're so close. I want you so. I need you to satisfy me. In the meantime I'll have to do it, and once Danuka arrives my desire will only grow stronger. That's the way it is each day when I'm close to her scent.

Now the effect of Danuka's odor was greater, as her father had warned. But she hadn't expected it to be so intoxicating in this way. It was a presence that touched her, and that she could almost taste. A spice she had no name for. Its effect on her body was overpowering.

It also made her feel even stronger than the time with her father, when he showed her how to hold the eggs for

Danuka's inspection. All the muscles in her body tensed and relaxed and tensed again in a rhythmic ripple, like waves washing through her, making her want to dance wantonly.

It made her want Lars and to be taken by him.

That desire is so strong I wonder if I would be able to re-sist any man. I should be ashamed to have such feelings, but they're beyond my control.

Admitting to the effect of Danuka's scent brought her con-fused questions.

Is that how I become a receptive Dragon Talker? Danuka, are you teaching me something when my body feels like this? Are you doing this to control me? Is this a test to gain my trust? Did the same thing happen to Da's body? He said I was strong, that my will was mine to govern, and that I was to trust you to gain your trust.

I worry my mind won't be strong enough to hold my body back to keep it from doing what it wants to do. My body tells me it's inevitable, unpreventable. I no longer have control on what my body desires. Is it by putting all my trust in Danuka that I won't have to worry about what might happen?

It's as strong as my desire for Lars. How can Danuka's scent cause such desire? I wish I understood how it makes me a receptive apprentice. Maybe I don't have to explain it. Just acknowledge it exists. How would I even try to explain it to someone who has not experienced it? It would be like trying to explain a dragon's kiss. That's what I'll call it, "The Drag-on's Kiss." It'll just be another aspect of my secret life. I just have to accept it.

With that acceptance came a choice in the pleasure she could give herself in the moment of her desire. She could sat-isfy herself now and then again later on. Or she could wait, let it mount and build until it became a blaze she had no choice but to extinguish. And when she did, it would leave her body soaked and trembling and drained and exhausted to the point her satisfaction pressed down on her whole body as it spread its pleasurable weight out over her limbs, leaving her light-headed as she slipped into that dreamless place where she slept so soundly.

It was the awakening afterward that always intrigued her. She awoke with a hunger for more and a ravenous appetite. At first, she had tried to satisfy the craving for more before and after eating. Either way, the satisfaction was always incomplete. It confirmed the power of anticipation, the slow build of desire to the moment where she could lose herself in the sensations of the act.

Lars is nearby. I'll wait. She would keep herself busy until night, coax the flame instead until it became a smoldering fire, and then stoke the fire into a blaze and throw herself into it and let herself burn with pleasure.

Nagora found a stout spear among Raynhard's cache of weapons. A pickaxe was among the other tools available. She took both, along with two lanterns, one of which she lit, and headed for a spot in the cave that might yield an ideal hiding spot for Danuka's eggs. It was just past the small lake in the middle vault of the cavern. Because a few bats had made their home in the upper reaches of the vault at that end, she delayed exploring along that wall.

Eventually, I'll even have to make it to the island in the middle of the lake. From the path around the lake, the island appeared to be mostly stone with one pointed formation that looked like a big carrot set on its stout end. It must be at least six times as tall as I am. The lake, the island, and the wall where she was headed would be the last parts of the cave to get her attention.

Today she would attempt to pry a big rock aside to see if a recessed area lay behind it. She set down her tools and lit the other lantern. She set a lantern on the stone floor on each side of the stone. She poked the spear into the space behind the stone. There's more space behind it, I'm sure. How much?

If I move the big stone, I'll have the answer. She poked the point of the spear down behind the rock so her end of the spear was as close to the wall as possible. She moved one leg back and lifted the foot of her other leg up so it came to rest against the wall. She pushed away from the wall with one leg and pulled back with her body. The rock moved enough so she could place the spear behind it from one side. This time she got the rock to pivot away from the hole enough to work the point of the spear in behind it at its bottom. She moved one of the lanterns before prying on the stone. On this push the rock leaned over and fell on its side, exposing the space it hid.

Nagora set the spear down with the tip pointing into the space. She took a lantern and crawled forward. Wow! It was two spear lengths deep and almost as wide. It was not circular because of the cleft corner at the back that seemed to open onto another smaller space. She could stand but had to keep her head bent.

This space opens up possibilities. What's in the other area?

She went back to her knees and pushed the spear and the lantern ahead of her. Enough room to crawl inside on my belly on one side and then roll over onto my back on the other side. It was a dry crawl space with no sign of an animal having ever used it.

More possibilities here.

Once out of the crawl space, she sat with her legs crossed and the lantern before her. She gazed around the insides of the small cave. What'll I do with this place? Two words came to mind, "winter room." I could spend time here in the winter with Danuka's eggs.

Will she allow it? Perhaps if the eggs have to be kept from freezing. There might be a way to heat this space. I can't build a fire in here. Think on it, Edana. Oh! My! That's the first time I've called myself Edana or at least given an order to myself with that name.

It's like when I became Tars and would talk to myself. Maybe it's not so strange to call myself Edana. After all, I took on the role of Edana. And today Raynhard called me his Edana.

Nagora blew out the candle before crawling back out to the glow of the light from the other lantern.

I'll leave the rock where it is for now.

She left the pickaxe leaning against the rock and headed for the valley entrance with the spear in hand.

Danuka had squeezed out of that entrance, but coming in that way was out of the question. It was an alternate exit should the bowl entrance be blocked for some reason. The stream from the cave's lake exited here and flowed into the valley. How the water came into the lake was still a mystery to her and to Raynhard. His guess was it came from an underground spring.

Maybe when I explore the lake I'll find out.

Nagora pushed past the bushes that hid part of the entrance. The part visible from the mountain ridge above appeared as a fold in the rock formation. She had set a snare near the stream about thirty paces from the entrance. It only took a moment to check.

Nothing in the snare. Maybe tomorrow.

She headed back in. Oh! In winter this entrance will be blocked with snow.

Will that be something else I must do? Keep it cleared?

Raynhard's visit is making me look at things differently. I have to think long-term. That means planning and preparing. All the more reason for me to go to Cairnmase. Geirador will have so many ideas to help me out. I'll feel better if I can talk to him.

And then there's Lars. I have to see him before he leaves.

Keep your hands away, Edana. Let it build.

I must be blushing with desire.

Lars, I'm going to hurt you so bad when I see you, you'll beg to stay so you can recuperate.

Nagora smiled at the memory of their conversation about their passionate lovemaking and the pleasurable hurt he said she had inflicted on him. She became wet just thinking about it. She exhaled.

Move. Get busy. Wait until tonight, Edana.

Nagora retrieved the pickaxe on her way back, had a last peek into the small cave, and followed the longer path around the lake.

Will the water rise in here when the snow melts? What if there's an ice dam at the entrance? Will the cave fill with water? Will it spill out the crack in the bowl? Could ice freezing there have caused the crack?

I'll have to question Raynhard more about the cave since he spent time here.

But did he come in the winter? No! He only found it early last spring. Surely if there was a late snowfall he wouldn't have come. He wouldn't have risked leaving tracks.

Winter? Here? I better plan for it.

How many long days will I have to spend here? How many of those days will be with Danuka? What will we need? Where will we store everything that's coming?

Now she had more things to keep her busy.

I'll look at the grains, nuts, and dried meat in the food cache. There's not that much left from the little Raynhard had stockpiled. Still a few root vegetables and some flour. I'll try to figure how much food can be stored in there. I've picked all the fresh berries nearby and my snares will only catch less and less.

Danuka will be spending more time here in the cold of winter. Da won't be feeding her. I'll need food for her too.

Will the water in the cave freeze? What about the spring where I fill my waterskins outside? It'll freeze for sure. Danuka drinks the water from the lake. Can I drink that water? Will I have to melt snow and ice on the fire?

I'll need firewood to cook and to keep warm. I've kept the fires for the nighttime so the smoke won't be visible in the day. When the clouds are low and we're shrouded in mist, I can make a fire during the day. So how much wood will I need? How much do I use? I'll use more in the winter. To heat the space at the bowl end, I would need a curtain of hides to close off a part of it. What's Danuka's tolerance to the cold?

It'll be colder than in the cave in the vent shaft on the Isle of Smoke. The heat from the volcano below kept that cave warm, almost stifling.

All these questions kept her busy as she made the rounds of her cave that afternoon, imagining it ready for winter, where supplies would be kept, wood stacked, extra tools she might need, extra clothing, and things to occupy her time when not taking care of her basic needs.

And these questions made Nagora reflect on winters past. Winter days with Uncle had always been spent crafting new items or repairing older ones. A new bow was always on the list, and new arrows. She was always learning something new about bow making with Uncle. Together they prepared new strings from hemp. They always made more strings than they would need. They inspected their older bows and arrows and gave them the care they needed to keep them in service.

Nagora loved to work with leather. She always found satisfaction in making a new belt or bag. New leather leggings, shirts, and a vest were also on the list.

Paruline, Geirador's daughter, had taught her to knit, so a sweater or hat was always in the works ready to pick up and work on between chores or before going to bed while listening to Uncle tell a story.

Before last winter, on the coldest nights, they brought in the few sheep, goats, and hens they kept, and even their mule, Patches. They made a penned-off area for them with their table, chairs, and benches. Only the hens didn't respect the pen boundaries; so it was Nagora's job to check for and clean up their droppings. On those same cold nights, they both slept near the fireplace, taking turns to add a log to the coals before they died out.

In the daytime, when the weather was good, they would go set snares or check on snares. Being so close to the coast, snow often came in great abundance, but it also left quickly because of the warmer coastal air. The ground would often only be covered in patches of snow, but when the storms blew in, they did so with a vengeance.

During the coldest months, the ice in the bay would usually freeze thick enough to go out on. Uncle would hack holes in the ice with a big pickaxe and a chiseled-end spear. He had fashioned a big ladle to lift chips and chunks of ice out of the hole. He had woven it out of sapling branches that he tied together around a hoop of ash wood on a long pole. Sometimes, if the current was right, he could float a line under the ice from one hole to another and then pull a net in place.

The times he had done that, they would head back to the beach hut to make a fire and heat the soup they had brought. They would take turns going out to check the holes to make sure they weren't freezing over. Most times they were lucky when they hauled in their net to check their catch. It meant fresh fish meals for days to come, a welcome change in their diet of dried and smoked meat.

When they fished with a line in an ice hole, someone always had to be nearby to watch the jig, ready to haul in the catch before it slipped free of the baited hook. Often it did, and they had to bait the hook again.

Geirador and Paruline always tried to make at least one trip by mule and sleigh from Cairnmase to go ice fishing with them. They would spend three to five days with Nagora and her uncle. Those occasions were some of her happiest memories. Geirador would bring a cask of his mead and Dangor would pay him with a new hunting bow made for Geirador's frame. Only he and Uncle could draw its string.

Nagora and Paruline and would exchange handmade gifts, and would both start a new knitting project. They would spend time walking in the woods in the snow, talking about anything Nagora wanted to know. Paruline was seven years older than her, so she was like a big sister to her. She could never get enough of Paruline's attention on those visits.

Each evening after their meal, Uncle mixed goat's milk, honey, the juice from two handfuls of stone-ground oats he had let soak most of the day in cold water, and then he would add some of Geirador's mead. He would heat the mixture in a pot, but not let it boil. He would serve them each a bowl to drink before the fire. While they sipped the smooth drink, Geirador and Uncle took turns telling stories.

When Geirador got into one of his long stories, Uncle cooked biscuits made with the leftover oats, some honey, and butter on a skillet over the fire. When they were ready, Uncle served them hot.

Geirador called Uncle's biscuits "stones," and Uncle called his drink "the potion." If one did not eat the biscuits hot, they became hard as stone as soon as they cooled. As stones, they would have to soak them in hot tea to be able to eat them.

The potion, though, was her favorite winter drink. She tried her best to make it last. It always tasted best while it was hot. As it cooled, the bite of the mead took over.

I love to hold the glazed bowl in my hands and inhale the fragrance of the potion. I swear I can smell the scent of the summer meadows rise to greet my nose just as it does when I walk through them.

It went down so smoothly from her mouth to her stomach. Its rich flavor filled her mouth while the mead spirits traveled up to her ears and warmed them.

The potion was a sure giver of sleep. To resist its effect was futile. No matter how good Geirador's stories were, she always nodded off and would never remember going to bed. The next morning she and Paruline would wake up in each other's arms from what they always said was the soundest sleep.

If they were lucky, and the weather looked promising, she and Uncle would make at least one winter trip to Cairnmase. Patches would pull their sleigh, sometimes fighting through snow that was deeper than his knees. They would always leave at dawn's first light. There was a point on the trail where Uncle would decide whether they would continue on or turn around to head back home. In her memory it had happened only once. The snow had been just too deep and the crust too hard. Patches kept breaking through it and the ice cut into his legs.

How I looked forward to those trips.

It was like traveling to another land where the snow, instead of melting after a storm, accumulated from one storm to the next. Cairnmase looked like such a different place as we rode through on the sleigh. The mountains of snow heaped around all the huts, often obscuring their windows.

It surprised me on each visit, like I had forgotten about how much snow had fallen on previous winter visits.

Her privileged time with Paruline was what Nagora treasured most. She had even more of it on those visits as Uncle often spent time with Geirador at his smithy. In winter, it became a beehive of activity, with shifts of people making arrow heads, spear heads, swords, and knives. Part of the attached stable became a bow making area. All those weapons were stockpiled and hidden for the coming fight to put the rightful King of the Land of the Danu on his throne.

At the time, Nagora had no idea of the role she would be asked to play in all this. She only knew she was being trained as a warrior, like so many of the people her age in Cairnmase. So much had been kept secret from her. Even Paruline, who shared the most intimate of secrets with her, had never once mentioned a single thing of all she knew about Nagora and what was in store for her.

Well, that battle has passed. Raynhard has his throne. He's working to rebuild his kingdom. And I've lost Uncle. Winters will never be the same without him.

Nagora let the tears come as her sorrow returned.

Uncle would tell me to wipe away my tears and focus on my task. I'm an apprentice Dragon Talker. I still have much to learn about my dragon. Mother rarely shares anything with me. Only when it's necessary and mostly when I'm to be at her service. When I do prod her with questions, her reply is always the same—in time. It's like she knows things she can't tell me and doesn't want to take the chance that she'll let a detail slip out. Like she has a plan for me, but won't or can't share it. I don't think I'll have fifteen years of patience like Da.

I'm going to be alone for the whole winter. Alone with Danuka most of the time. Will she open up to me then? No shared activities to look forward to. No visitors to greet. No one to share my deepest thoughts with. No one to listen to my questions and try to give me answers. No one to braid my hair.

I'll truly be a lone wolf. A lone wolf alone with her dragon.

"*Ka Peyakot Mahihkan*, be ready. This is your story. You will tell it to me when you come to sit by my fire again. Remember, you are strong."

Am I imagining Godomor is speaking these words to me, or is he actually speaking to me? He is speaking to me.

"*Ohtawimaw*, I hear you. I am strong. I will survive and someday sit by your fire and talk to you as a daughter. And I will wait for you to ask me to tell my story. I will make you proud of Lone Wolf."

The tinkle of the small bell tied to the ribbon that hung from the ceiling of the cave entrance signaled the gentle flap of Danuka's giant wings as she approached to land on the lip of the bowl. She arrived in dusk's fading light, a shadow on the shadowed face of the mountain. She folded her wings to her sides. The claw of her left wing pricked the stone wall to the left of the entrance for support as she hopped down from the stone lip of the bowl and brought her long tail in behind her.

Even in this fading light of day and the feeble light of my fire, the edges of Mother's features and wings have the most beautiful, iridescent shimmer. Can I even count the number of colors I see? She truly is a beast of beauty to behold.

Oh! This is different. Mother is wearing a harness at her neck.

Straps ran from it and crossed in front of her to disappear at the back where her wings joined her body.

Danuka bowed her head close to Nagora's until the tip of her snout touched the scar of the Tiwaz brand on her forehead.

"Welcome home, Mother. You already know that Raynhard was here earlier today? He sends me food in the bags on your back? And other things? Thank you, Mother, for bringing them."

Danuka squatted so her front rested on the cave floor. She held out her folded left wing and let its big claw rest on the floor. The arrangement of three long leather bags tied together and attached to the harness on Danuka's back made for a balanced load. "Mother, I will climb onto your wing to remove the bags. I understand I am to leave the harness and reattach the bags in the morning."

Nagora unfastened the straps that held the bags.

Now I see why Raynhard came to visit me. He was also visiting Geirador with Da, and for good reason. Da must've asked Geirador to make the bags so Danuka can deliver goods to me. Raynhard could have said something. Geirador must've wanted it to be a surprise, I'm sure. That's just like him. They haven't forgotten me.

All the pieces of the leatherwork that formed the harness and the bags bore Geirador's brand, three rune symbols within a circle. Algiz appeared to hold Raidho on one of its arms and Jera on the other. The three together were open to many interpretations. But years ago, Geirador had told her what he meant them to signify. "*Courage* on the *journey* brings *reward*. The circle is a wheel, as on a wagon, one of the most essential items a good smithy builds and repairs throughout a lifetime. Make of it what you will. If it suits your fancy and you feel you can live by it, then do so, lass."

Geirador, more people should have your no-nonsense way of looking at things. The meaning you chose for your brand makes sense. Every time Uncle and I rode home in our cart I thought about it. The brand was on Patches' reins right where my hands held them. In a way, I can say my own life is like your brand. It describes how I've lived it up to now.

The three bags were heavy. She brought them down one at a time. What do they contain?

The first one contained lots of nuts and dried berries. Their smell was so recognizable. The second contained dried meats. Their smoky aroma gave them away. The last bag was a mystery. I'll look inside later. I have work to do.

"Mother, the egg pouches are here." She pointed to the four leather pouches on the floor to the right of the entrance where she had become used to putting them. Each pouch had four pockets inside, one pocket per egg. "While you hunt for your eggs, Mother, I will go check my snares and fill my waterskins."

Danuka, sounded her low moan of approval. It was almost the same sound a cow would make, though lower and longer and sweeter to the ear.

Nagora slipped through the crack in the bowl with her bow in hand and two waterskins slung across her back. It'll be dark when I get back, but my eyes will have time to adjust.

When Nagora returned, Danuka slipped the last single-egg pouch into the last empty space of one of the four-pocket pouches. The way Danuka held the strap of the pouch with her lips impressed Nagora as did the gentleness of her handling of the pouches. Mother does almost as well as I do with my thumbs and fingers.

"Nothing in the snares, Mother. I'll be with you in a moment." She slipped the waterskins from her shoulders and set them against the wall opposite the firepit. She added a few sticks to the fire and stirred the pot. After licking the spoon, she went over to sit cross-legged before Danuka.

Nagora pulled the first four-pocket pouch to her, removed a single-pocket pouch, opened it, and carefully took out the egg with both her hands. It's so heavy. It surprises me each time. She didn't remember them being that heavy on the day she had brought them up from the cave in the volcano vent shaft on the Isle of Smoke. Those were different circumstances. She had just fought for her own life against Hag, who wanted to destroy all the eggs.

Now she held up the blue egg with red and gold veins for Danuka to inspect. Slowly, she turned it in her hands. Danuka smelled its entire surface and examined it with one of her big red eyes. The eye was the size of Nagora's two fists held together, like a horse's eye, but bigger. When Danuka returned to the cave in the dark, a veil covered her eyeball, and that veil pulled back in one piece once Danuka was in the light of the cave. Does the veil somehow allow her to see better in the dark?

Fifteen more to go.

Nagora had learned to be patient with this nightly inspection. How would I describe what I'm doing to someone who's never seen a dragon? Right now Danuka crouched, resting on her hind legs and talons with her front almost touching the floor of the cave. Her long tail came around from the back on her right side and curled in front of her so its finned, bulbous tip rested next to her left hind leg. Her folded wings shielded Nagora on each side as each wing's big open claw dug into the cave floor behind Nagora. The first time Danuka had done that, Nagora feared she would fall forward on top of her. But no, Danuka controlled herself with such grace in the confined spaces of the cave. She always knew where Nagora was. She never tripped her or knocked her over. She was totally aware of all her body, even her tail.

As Danuka finished the inspection of her last egg, Nagora had that heady feeling once again, as if she had just bathed in the essence of The Dragon's Kiss. She couldn't help but breathe it in. Her clothes smelled of it and especially her hands. Even if she tried, she couldn't wash the scent away. It would leave on its own somehow.

Why does it make me feel taller and stronger when I stand? I feel every muscle on my body move as I move. Why does that happen?

And there's that sensation between my legs. It was a clutching feeling that almost bent her over, not in pain, but in desire. It made her squeeze her thighs together and jut her backside out in a momentary spasm that demanded relief. The only way she could stop the spasm was to spread her legs and straighten her back before walking on her toes so that all the muscles in her legs tensed.

Nagora would have to do this until Danuka curled up around her eggs, and then she would go to her bed. But tonight, she had boiled some meat to eat, and she had a last bag to look into.

She dipped her bowl into the pot, brought it out half full, and dropped a piece of dry bread into it, along with her spoon. She brought it over to the mystery bag and sat down on the floor next to it to eat. Now what might be in this bag?

Nagora released the buckle and pulled back the flap. She reached in. Ah! I know what this is. It was her sheepskin hat, the one Paruline had offered her that morning before she and Dangor left for the Land of Skulls. Now the moss green embroidered dragon had wings. When Paruline had given it to her the first time, she had not had time to add the wings. Oh! Pare! You kept your promise. You must've found it in my saddlebags.

Inside the hat was a folded piece of vellum. She unfolded it. The message was written in runes. She took her time to read each word.

‡

Our Nagora,

We hope this missive finds you well. We miss you, Nagora, all of us we do. You are in our thoughts each day. We wish you strength and courage to carry on your duty. We are proud of you, our Nagora.

Lars is here with us. He talks only of you. He lives each day in hope to see you again before he goes. He wants you to know he rides Storm each day. And to know that Aydan misses you too. Each time he hears someone say your name, his ears jump up. He looks for you everywhere.

May these gifts help make you feel like we are near. Think of us like we think of you. Look to our stars and know we do too, each night. We ask that they take good care of you.

Paruline
Geirador
Lars
‡

Nagora wiped at her tears with the sleeve of her shirt as she set the letter back inside her hat. She reached into the pouch and pulled out a heavy roll of hides. In the center of the roll she recognized the sheaths that held the narwhal tusks for transport when not in use.

They must want the unicorn to remain a mystery. I must hide these here somewhere. Perhaps in the crawl space of the new little cave.

How Godomor's Hundred Best Warriors had been amazed by the sight of the two unicorns in the morning mist of the meadow. Paruline had brought them so the twin Edanas could ride them for the first time. Sagora and I were a fascinating sight as we rode the white mares, each with a horn sticking out of its head. Geirador had made leather helms to hold the narwhal tusks in place to create the illusion of this new, memorable animal. All the warriors had wanted to touch the unicorns. They seemed to take pride in the fact they too would be spreading the myth of the unicorn's existence.

Nagora pulled out a bag that contained a set of leather punches and gouges, spools of hemp and linen thread, a block of beeswax, diamond-pointed needles to sew leather, an awl, a palm protector, a small hammer, and a great pile of leather lanyards of all sizes.

This'll keep me busy. How lucky I am.

Then she pulled out a new pair of knee-high, oiled leather boots. They were fur lined, with wrap-around lacing. There's a lump in this one. She reached in and pulled out a heavy pair of knit woolen socks. What's in the other boot? Oh! My! I can't believe it! She laughed as she placed it on the palm of her hand. Look at you! A miniature Aydan doll, made from Aydan's own curly red hair, poked into a felted body support. You look just like my big wolfhound that I love so much. She hugged the doll to her cheek. Now I miss you even more. She set it down.

I have to try on one of those boots.

Nagora pulled off her leather slipper, pulled on one of the socks, grabbed a boot, and slid her foot into it. This'll be a pleasure to wear this winter. What's that? Something under the arch of my foot. She pulled the boot off and reached in. She pulled out the tiny, silent, silver, whistle pendant Lars had given her to call Aydan to her. Her jaw dropped.

What could this mean? Am I to call Aydan? Could Aydan hear the whistle all the way from Cairnmase? No. That's too far. What did Lars say when he gave it to me? "Blow it anywhere within the walls of Skull Bay and Aydan will find you." I'm definitely farther away than that, by many times.

Wait. Could it be that Raynhard has asked that Aydan be brought to me so he can help me guard the eggs? He's a big dog. He needs to be fed and taken care of. He would be great company though. If that's Raynhard's intention, do I accept? That would mean a lot of food to be stockpiled. If it can be provided, I would love to have Aydan with me.

Or is it just a keepsake, to remind me of Aydan and Lars?

She slipped the fine leather lace over her head so the silent whistle pendant hung next to her dragon tear amulet.

That's more likely.

Still, I appreciate having this. Lars said Aydan chose me. Lars gave me this whistle. More importantly, he gave me hope and saved my life. And he gave me his love. I love that man.

Nagora found more in the bag when she tilted the bottom up to empty it. A leather pouch with draw strings fell out. The drawstrings were intricately tied around what Nagora recognized as the whistle attachment Uncle made for his whistle arrows. I know of no one else who even makes whistle arrows. And the bottom of the bag was branded with Uncle's stylized arrow head, close in its resemblance to the Othala rune symbol.

The bag's contents will tell me how to interpret the symbol. This pouch weighs at least as much as one of Danuka's eggs, and it's smaller.

Nagora committed the knot work to memory before untying it. She pulled the mouth of the pouch open. By my stars! I can't believe it! It was filled with gold coins struck with the dragon symbol on one side and King Bernhard's coat of arms on the other. The first one she had ever seen was a long time ago. Uncle showed her one in secret when she had asked him about gold, what it looked like. It was in the time when Queen Raganora had decreed the word "dragon" not be spoken and any and every object in the land bearing the image of a dragon be destroyed.

These coins must be from before that time when King Bernhard and Queen Julianna reigned. Now I have a bag full. How many are there? I'll count them tomorrow. "Othala" was well chosen. It means inheritance. Could this be my inheritance from Uncle? What else could it be? What will I ever do with this? What is its value? I have no idea. Another thing I have to hide.

Nagora stood and walked over to the cave entrance. She climbed several rungs of the ladder that rested against the bowl wall, near the crack. She looked up into the starry night sky and found their stars, *The Dragon Tamer*, *The Twins*, and *The Woman Waiting*, all of them from the star stories Uncle had told her as a child. Now they all made sense to her. They were stories about her and her sister, her father and mother, the only way Uncle could tell her without revealing her destiny.

Nagora searched and found *The Dogs*, as Lars had called them. Aydan the runt who'd grown to be as big as Lyam. And *The Bear*, with the frozen star the Moroes Island whalers guided their boats by at night. It truly did seem to be frozen in place like Lars had told her.

Thank you, all of you, for these gifts. They have touched my heart, and they make me feel close to you. May we be together again, soon.

She climbed down from the ladder and went to her bed to lose herself in the passion that had built the whole day.

Nagora awoke and rubbed sleep's grip from her eyes.

Danuka stirred in the last moments of morning's darkness.

I'll have to wash. My shirt's stuck to me. Where did all the strength in my arms and legs go? Come on. Move, legs. Get out of bed. As soon as she pulled aside her blankets, the cool air set her in motion.

Danuka had gone to drink at the lake. Nagora made ready the big bowl of shelled nuts, dried fruit, and chopped dried meat sprinkled with water and set it in place for Danuka. It would hold her until she joined up with Yogari. He would feed Danuka too, hunt with her, if necessary.

Then Nagora hurried to empty the food bags onto two spread out hides. She would sort everything later.

"Mother, your bowl is ready. When you are done, I'll tie the bags to your harness."

Danuka brought her snout to Nagora's forehead and touched her Tiwaz brand.

"Raynhard will return with you at the end of the day? And leave tomorrow?"

I might not have slept had I known last night. A second visit from Raynhard. I wonder what news he'll bring.

"Be safe, Mother. Tell Da I love him. Mum and Sagora too if you see them."

Danuka first gripped the edge of the cave bowl with the two huge claws on her wing joints and then brought one talon after the other onto the edge. With the aid of her tail, her balance never faltered as she spread her wings and pushed off with her powerful hind legs. She was gone, a silent shadow in morning's earliest twilight.

Nagora lifted the four pouches onto her shoulders and set off to hide the eggs. Today she made a quick job of it. She rushed back, grabbed her bow and two arrows, and slipped through the crack barefoot and dressed only in her shirt. The stream was not far away. She had two snares to check on her way back.

At the stream, Nagora set her bow and two arrows down on the bank. The deepest depression in the stream bed closest to the cave was here. The orange of the sky was turning to yellow. Soon the sun would breach the horizon. Nagora stepped into the cold mountain water up to her waist. She crouched down fast to submerge her upper body. She came up after the first shock and then went under again to shake her hair loose and run her fingers through it. When she came up, she pulled her long shirt over her head and dipped it into the stream repeatedly. She stopped several times to wring the water out of it before repeating the process several more times. After wringing the water from it a last time, she threw it onto a flat rock on shore.

Next her hands set about scrubbing the rest of her body. There. Can't get any cleaner than that. She stepped up onto the bank of the stream and let her hair drip some more as she looked skyward.

Sun's coming up.

She bent, picked up her bow and arrows with one hand and her shirt with the other and ran for the cave. She detoured to check the two snares.

Nothing in the first. A rabbit in the second. Its body was still warm. Fresh rabbit stew tonight. Raynhard will be happy.

Back in the cave, Nagora ran through the day's work that awaited her.

Gut and skin the rabbit. Cut it up, rub the pieces with salt, and pack them in the cold bucket. Stretch, frame, and scrape the hide.

Wash hands.

Dig out some potatoes, onions, and carrots from the wet sand cache. Wash, peel, and chop them. Throw them in the pot with some water.

Sort what's in the food bags, tally it all, store in appropriate caches.

But first, my daily exercises. Uncle had taught them to her many years ago: ward off, rollback, press, push, pull, elbow strike, shoulder strike, advance, retreat, look left, gaze right, center balance. She repeated them a hundred times. Today, she did them with her bow in hand. Each day she used a different weapon. Today she did them deliberately slow. She could have done them blindingly fast. Do them slow. My mind will work in the background on the coming day's events. Focus on the movements. My mind will take care of the rest and my thoughts will become clear.

It was mid-afternoon when Nagora returned to the small cave she had discovered the day before. Now she lay on her back to push herself into its smaller recessed space. She had brought a sheepskin and a long piece of cowhide with her. She pushed the sheepskin in first and then unrolled the cowhide over it. Then she lay on her back with her knees bent and her heels on the hide. She rested the pouch of gold coins on her belly. With her left hand at her side, she held the two sheaths that contained the narwhal tusks. With her right hand held above her head, she pushed the lantern ahead of her as her heels pushed her along into the recessed space.

Almost halfway in, she saw a break in the ceiling where two cracks met.

If there was a third crack to make a three-sided piece of stone, I might be able to pull it out. I can make that third crack.

Nagora wormed her way back out with the lantern, left the pouch of coins there, and went back to Raynhard's tool cache near the entrance to get a stone chisel and hammer.

If Raynhard can dig out holes and smooth out the edges around the holes to make their stone covers fit tight, I can surely whack out a small chunk of stone.

Back in position, Nagora held the chisel in place and struck with the hammer. Be careful, Edana. Position the chisel and close your eyes before striking. You don't want a stone chip to blind you. I've watched Uncle work with these tools. All I have to do is score a line in the stone where I want it to break into a new crack. It took over a dozen good whacks. Then she centered the chisel on the middle of the line and gave it her best hit. The dull impact sound told her she had broken the stone. A fine crack ran right along her line.

Now to get it out of there.

Nagora wiggled her way back out and reached over for her sheath of knives. The big blade wouldn't do, but two of the smaller blades would, based on what she had seen Uncle do.

Back inside with a knife in each hand, Nagora poked the tips of the blades along the bottom crack to find spots where she could slip them in just enough to pry the stone chunk up and back ever so slightly. Slowly but surely, she gained enough purchase on each pry and was able to pull the edge of the chunk out a little more. She did the same on the vertical crack of the chunk.

Finally, Nagora put the knives down and reached up with the tips of her fingers. She put as many as she could around the edges of the chunk and wiggled it out so the pads of her fingers could grab hold of it. Now she only had to pull it out straight and be careful not to drop it.

Nagora brought the piece down and set it on her stomach next to the pouch of coins. She lifted the pouch and slid it into place. There was plenty of room. She pushed the pouch back as far as it would go.

Place for two more.

Good work, Edana. She pulled the narwhal carry sheaths up alongside her and pushed the candle lantern further back until she came to the narrowest recess where she would hide the tusks. Well, Edana, the secret of your unicorns is safe here unless you tell someone else.

I could fill this space with dirt and stones. Maybe later. I might have other uses for it.

Time for me to clean up. Raynhard will come soon.

Everything for the rabbit stew was in the pot. Nagora just started the fire and was about to set the pot on the hook over the flame when the bell warned her of Danuka's arrival.

Raynhard is alone. How did he manage? Has Da taught him to ride?

"Welcome, Mother. You bring our king. A noble task for you today. To see a rider on your back is magical for me. Welcome, King Raynhard. We are honored to have you visit us."

"Thank you, Nagora, for your welcome and thank you, Danuka, for bringing me safely."

"How was your ride? How did you manage it?"

"I must say I had to put my complete trust in Danuka. Yogari gave her specific instructions. I climbed on to her back as a passenger, a terrified one at that. I'm in no way a rider. I never realized it would get so cold. The speed at which she flies is truly amazing."

Danuka had set herself down with her folded wings extended forward so the big claws rested on the cave floor. Raynhard could dismount on either side.

As he did, one hand reached back and rested on one of the three bags attached to Danuka's harness. Raynhard stepped down from the wing and went to Nagora.

Nagora held her arms open. "Raynhard, thank you so much for everything you sent yesterday. You knew that was coming, but you kept it as a surprise."

"That was what Paruline and Geirador wanted. And Yogari as well. They want you to be happy here." Raynhard still held her in his arms, but leaned back to look at her as he spoke to her. "And I too want you to be happy. You don't know how much you mean to me." Raynhard held her closer and brought his cheek next to hers as he pulled her even closer.

And then, he leaned back again. "There's more for you in the bags. They aren't as heavy as yesterday's, but what they contain should please you. And while I have you in my arms, I will make good on what they made me promise to deliver.

"From your big sister." He kissed both of her cheeks and then squeezed her tight. "From your mother." He repeated the kisses on the cheeks and added one on her Tiwaz. "From your father." The same three kisses as her mother had sent and one, ever so gently, on her lips.

It lingered. No, Edana. Don't kiss him back. You know what'll happen. Instead, when his lips left hers, she buried her face in his chest and held him tight. "Thank you, Raynhard. They mean so much to me. Return their kisses for me. Tell them I miss them." All the while she breathed in the essence of The Dragon's Kiss that enveloped him. Will you be able to resist, Edana?

Nagora released him. "Here. Wear your father's vest, it'll help warm you." She slipped it off her shoulders. He had given it to her, along with his father's hunting dagger. Now his eyes were on her, just like that time. Is that a look of desire or the effect of Danuka's scent on him? "I'll get mine. You tend the fire and stir the pot. It'll be awhile before it's ready to eat.

I'll remove the bags so Mother can tend to her eggs. I have a few snares to check before it gets too dark, and I have two waterskins to fill. I won't be gone long."

After removing the bags, and Danuka had set about on her search for her eggs, Nagora donned her own sheepskin vest, grabbed her bow, and disappeared through the crack.

As soon as Nagora set foot on the trail, her body staggered as it fought to control the tugging spasm between her legs. Her thighs squeezed together as her middle bent forward. She breathed deep, straightened her back, spread her legs, and moved along the trail on her toes.

This is a battle I'll win from one moment to the next.

On her return to the cave, Nagora found Raynhard still on his knees before the fire, stirring the pot. Danuka was nuzzling her eggs. "It will not be long, Mother. I will be with you soon." Nagora slipped the waterskins from her shoulders and leaned them against the wall behind Raynhard.

"Nothing in the snares, I take it."

"The rabbit in the pot was snared this morning. No luck since. Do you know how to prepare batter for skillet bread?"

"Oh! Yes! I made it many times on the Sea Wolf when I sailed with your father as a young man. Are the ingredients where I think they are?"

Nagora placed a hand on his shoulder. "In the cache you made. I'll be awhile with Mother to inspect her eggs."

Raynhard nodded. "I'll make the bread."

Nagora sat cross-legged before Danuka. She spread her vest on the cave floor before her. Danuka bent and brought her snout to Nagora's forehead. "Change of plans, King Raynhard. Mother requests your presence to inspect her eggs."

"I am honored. What Yogari told me is true. You help Danuka inspect her eggs each day." Danuka held a folded wing up to let Raynhard into the shelter she always formed with her wings for the inspection.

Nagora nodded. "It's one of the Dragon Talker's duties. Mother wants you to sit behind me with your legs at my sides."

Raynhard complied.

"Sit closer. We'll take turns holding an egg for her. Watch how I do it. I don't have to tell you not to drop one."

"I won't. This is the first time I've seen her eggs. I'm truly honored."

Nagora leaned forward and over to her left to reach for the strap of one of four big pouches to pull it to her. The side of her breast brushed against Raynhard's hand. From one of the four pockets of that pouch, Nagora pulled a single pouch and brought it to her lap. She lifted the flap and reached in with both hands to bring out the big blue egg with red and gold veins. On occasion she had witnessed Danuka use her tongue and lips to remove the first egg from its pouch, but not today. Raynhard would be impressed to see Mother's dexterity. Nagora lifted a finger from the egg, pointed to the empty single pouch, and whispered. "While I was out, did you see Mother place the individual pouches in the four-pocket pouch?"

"Remarkable." Raynhard's single-word reply was barely audible to Nagora as she turned the egg in her hands.

Raynhard whispered his next words in her ear with reverence and awe as Danuka smelled and then eyed the entire surface of the egg. "So it's true. The veins are of gold."

Nagora returned the egg to its single pouch and then brought another to her lap. "Take it."

As Raynhard reached for the egg, she lifted her arms. She rested her hands on his forearms as he handled the egg. His voice was a warm whisper in her ear. "I never imagined it to be so heavy. It's beautiful. The red and gold veins are embossed in the blue surface, just enough to give it texture. This blue is unlike any other I've ever seen."

Within the confines of Danuka's wings, the essence of The Dragon's Kiss had surrounded them. My head feels so light. I can't get away and Raynhard is so close. Is he feeling its effects also? She leaned back against Raynhard as he deposited the egg in the lone pouch in her lap. Her cheek rested against his, their lips only a breath away from kissing. She moved to return the pouch and retrieve another. This time, his hand touched the side of her breast and a finger the curve beneath her breast. Do it, Edana. Rest your breast in his hand. Let him caress it. No. I won't dare. If I do, I won't be acting of my own will.

Mother, why do you do this to me?

She won't answer me. But in her mind Danuka's answer was clear as if spoken out loud. "He is our king. We will not deny our king." I can't believe I'm hearing this.

The remaining inspection of the eggs was sheer torture for Nagora. From one egg to another she fought for control of what her body wanted. She became wet with desire, and Raynhard pressed his into her lower back. Her breasts ached for the full touch of his hands, not the lingering caresses. Her mouth had become dry. Let me quench my thirst in yours. The only thread of control she had left was her will to resist. I must be strong, but that means the want in my body will only build and grow so strong it will win. I won't be able to hold onto that thread. What do I do? Abandon resistance and embrace what my body wants without question? Is that what's expected of me? Is that my duty?

Why? Why do I have no control of the events in my life? Why can I not choose my own path? Is it because I have been chosen?

The last egg had passed inspection and Danuka raised her wings to release Nagora and Raynhard from their roles in her ritual.

Nagora stood on her toes with her legs spread and her vest in her hands.

Do I flee into the night? I could go to my small cave, spend the night there.

"I'll check on the stew."

Raynhard was quick to add, "And I'll prepare the batter for the bread. You'll want to look into those bags."

"Yes. For sure." She fought for control. Go on. Get busy. Focus on each little task. One battle at a time.

Nagora made her way to the fire and added pieces of wood to the coals. She stirred the stew and then spooned out a leg. The meat was still tight on the bone. The piece of carrot was still hard so she added two more pieces of wood to the fire. She looked over at Raynhard. He had just finished rubbing the skillet with a piece of fat and was about to add water to the bowl of ingredients.

She looked past him to the leather bags and walked over to them.

...

Nagora chose the heaviest one and brought it next to her low stool near the fire. She unbuckled the strap that held the flap closed and peered inside. Not much was visible to her in the cave's firelight and candle light, so she reached in and pulled out a linen sack. It was heavy. She held it in both hands. These are candles. A good quantity of them.

Next, she pulled out six lanterns wrapped in pieces of linen tied around each one. She untied the first one. Oh. This piece of linen is big enough to make a shirt. Three of the pieces had been dyed forest green; the other three were the linen's natural color.

At the bottom of the bag she found another bundle of items to unwrap. It contained scissors, needles, thread, embroidery threads, and a hoop. I'll have to make a sewing bag to hold all these.

"Nagora, are you happy with what you've seen so far?"

"You've listened to what I wanted. There are plenty of candles, and now with all these lanterns, my life in here will be easier. Mum and Sagora must have wrapped the lanterns. Now I have plenty of cloth to work with."

"You still have two bags to look into."

Nagora unbuckled the flap on the second bag. She pulled out a small medical scrip with items she could use in case she injured herself. There were various salves and a flask of disinfectant, linen bandages in a variety of sizes, tweezers, and a tiny knife.

Then she found three leather-bound books of blank vellum pages which had been sewn in place. In the first one, she found a letter.

‡

Twenty-nine days after Edana's victory

Our dear Nagora,

We miss you. The news our king gave us of you has made us miss you even more. We will do our best to be of help to you and send you goods that will be of use.

I know you do not write well. Now would be a good time to practice a new skill. It will help you occupy your time and provide you with a way to record what you do. You can also keep track of the days, the weather, and your supplies. In one of the books, I wrote examples of how you could use the books. I know you can learn from those examples. Your uncle Dangor would be proud of you if you learned to write well. You can read, so learning to write the symbols only requires practice. Practice each day and soon you will find it is easy.

Your father is so proud that you too are a Dragon Talker. He says if you listen and are patient with Danuka, she will reward you. He trusts you will continue to take good care of her. He looks forward to seeing you again. We all do.

The king will tell you how busy we are. You have your duty, and we have ours. Soon we will all meet as a family. We know you want that also, and we will arrange it as soon as we can.

Until we are with you again, we wish you strength and courage in your duty.

Tagnya, Sagora, Yogari

‡

I will learn this skill, Mum. I promise I will practice writing.

The last package from the bag would help her do just that. It contained a wooden box. The box had a hinged cover that closed with a tiny latch. Inside, it held two bottles of ink in separate compartments, a neat stack of vellum pages in their own section, quills, and three fine-pointed brushes in the longest section. Tagnyoriva wrote with a quill and Dangor had always written with a brush. Paruline had written yesterday's letter with a brush. It was a matter of preference. I have the opportunity to try both. Which will I prefer?

The last bag waited its turn as Nagora made temporary space on one of the stone ledges for most of the items from the two other bags. She took her time to group the items that belonged together. Best I occupy my time and keep my thoughts focused on all these objects. Now if I start to sew or practice writing, I'll need a table and a chair. They'll make sewing and writing and even eating more pleasurable.

"Well, Nagora, the contents of these bags seem to be brightening your day."

"I didn't realize that reading a letter from Mum would be so precious to me. It was the same yesterday when reading the news Pare sent me. When I read them, I can hear their voices. It is like they are right here, next to me. Words on a page can be so powerful. Mum has suggested I practice the skill. I will. Now I see its value. If I had a table and a chair, it would be easier."

"I'll see what I can do about that, Nagora."

...

In the last bag, Nagora found two dozen skeins of natural sheep's wool. All were three strands of twisted yarn. Most were natural color. Six had been vegetable died green, almost the exact color of moss. I love this color. A sweater knit with this yarn will shed rainwater for a good while before it becomes soaked.

Someone had wrapped linen cloth around several sets of knitting needles. She spread it out. Oh! It's a sack with a drawstring closure. I can stuff all the wool in this bag.

She did so and stuck the needles inside as well. She found a place for it on the shelf right away.

"Nagora, I think the rabbit is cooked. I'm ready to cook the bread."

"Just a moment." Nagora brought Raynhard a bowl, a spoon, and a ladle. "Here. Two ladles of broth in the bowl. Add a small handful of flour. Stir away the lumps. Pour into the pot and stir. Then you can pour your batter into the skillet and put it on the coals, your Majesty."

Raynhard laughed. "Oh! Nagora! Those last two words sound so funny coming from you. I'll never get used to anyone calling me that."

"I didn't want to sound like I was giving you orders."

"You didn't. You were just being helpful. Besides, when I'm not wearing my crown, you can order me around all you like." Raynhard stirred away, stopping now and then to mash the lumps against the side of the bowl.

"Did you find your crown?"

"Oh! Yes! At the castle in Windhaven. I was afraid the mercenaries had left with it. But no, it was still where

Raganora had hidden it away for her son. Your father insists I wear it whenever we fly to an appearance. I don't wear it on Danuka's back, of course. I put it on when we set down."

"How does it feel to wear it?"

"I don't think I'll ever get used to it." He showed her the bowl, stirring it for her to see the texture. "How's this?"

"Looks smooth. Pour it in and stir."

"Is that bag empty?"

"No, but it will be in a moment."

Nagora's heart almost stopped for an instant as she retrieved the last bundle. At once she recognized Umma's scarf. The fingers of her hands identified the objects wrapped in the scarf. Their familiarity was unmistakable. She had an identical set. But the set she held belonged to Uncle. Through teary eyes, she pulled the scarf from around the set of blades and ran her fingers over the oiled leather of the sheaths. Four small sheathes on the shoulder straps held the throwing knives tight halfway up their cherry-wood handles.

She pulled on the big blade's walrus hide handle and held it up. Uncle had given her the first one Geirador had ever made. She had wet a finger on her tongue and touched the side of the blade. Uncle had answered her puzzled look, "Blue steel. Made from skystone. Geirador traded with the Little People for it. For what? You know Geirador. He just smiles. We'll never know. Do I believe him? Can't prove otherwise." She held that picture of Uncle in her mind. How I miss you.

Why had Uncle's blades been sent to her? As part of her inheritance? If someone should have gotten them, it should have been Da. They were wrapped in Umma's scarf. Are they destined to be given to Umma, in the Land of Skulls? Uncle had fallen in love with Umma at just about the same time as she had with Lars. Ever since, he had worn her scarf around his neck.

"Raynhard, does Da have a set of blades like we do?"

"Yes. I gave him mine. Why do you ask?"

"This set belonged to Uncle. The big sheath bares his brand. I wonder why it was sent to me."

"As part of your inheritance. He was like a father to you, Nagora. I know your da kept Dangor's bow and quiver."

Something else for me to hide in my small cave's nook. For now at least.

She folded the scarf and placed it with the blades on the ledge next to the bag of wool skeins.

Raynhard was filling two bowls with hot rabbit stew when Nagora returned to her low stool. He handed her a bowl. "Careful. It's hot."

She set it on the floor next to her and took the piece of hot bread he offered her. She placed it on her knees and reached for the spoon in her bowl to stir the stew.

"Where have my parents been staying?"

"So far, with me at Windhaven Castle. That's about to end, with your mother and sister heading out to villages along the coast. They'll be traveling with a team of people they've trained to make sure the wells are properly decontaminated. Your father will join them when he can to spend the night with them. My appearances are coming to an end soon. We've been tallying grain stores in all the communities we've been to so far and have asked local councils to plan for next year's crops so we can arrange to set aside surpluses. This coming winter could be harsh as far as food supplies go in some areas.

We want to arrange it so the villagers suffer as little as possible."

"Are my parents happy?"

Raynhard looked at her for a moment before his eyes returned to the bowl of stew he held. He gave it a stir and looked back at her. "Well, yes, they are. Mind you, after such a long separation, reuniting has not been easy. I feel responsible in great part because they've sworn to help bring the Land of the Danu back to life. Your mother and sister are doing their best to cleanse its wells of poison. Your father is helping me spread the word of my return and the coming of more dragons. You've taken on the care and protection of Danuka's eggs. What they are hoping for is that Danuka will soon hatch her eggs. Plans have to be made to create the ideal conditions for that to happen. That could mean finding a better location for Danuka to be with her eggs. It could even mean training a new Dragon Talker."

Nagora frowned. "What do you mean?"

"Nagora, I won't try to hide anything from you. I've discussed with your parents and Sagora about many possible scenarios. Let's face it; the members of your family are all adults now. Sagora has ties to the Land of Skulls. Gabe is waiting for her. You have Lars. He'll return there. Will he wait for you there or will he come back if you are still here? Though, that's not certain. Is it?"

Should I even try to answer that question? She shook her head and shrugged.

"Your father's been talking of returning to the sea. Who can blame him after all those years of confinement in a cave? He wants your mother to go with him. This might seem strange to you, but she's not certain to follow. I don't know more about it than that because they've not spoken openly about that aspect in front of me. To readjust to each other has not been easy. Your mother realizes Yogari is not the same man now as the one she knew before, and she feels she may never be able to bring back that man. So in a way, she's dealing, to a certain extent, with a complete stranger. That's why I say it's not been easy."

Nagora had been staring at the flames on the edge of the fire while he spoke. Now she looked up at him. "Thank you, Raynhard, for your honesty. I think I can understand the situation. You are right. It mustn't be easy, and now I doubt my presence among them would change things for the better. Though, I must say I dearly want to see them and be with them, as a family, even if only for a few days.

"And your words give cause to reflect on what I want for my life. What'll I do later on? I'm a trained warrior. I've been gifted as a Dragon Talker. Does my future lay with the dragons? With building the future of this land? What say do I have in all of this? To be honest, right now I feel at a loss. Given a choice of paths, I don't know which I would choose. But I want to make my own way, find my own path. When will I be able to do that? I don't know. These past two days, I've received gifts and encouragement from people who care about me. And I care about them too. Yet I feel so far away from them. And then, I try to imagine myself with them, and when I do, I wonder what I would do. It makes me feel so lonely."

Perhaps that is my destiny. Perhaps that is why Godomor calls me Lone Wolf.

Raynhard reached over and took her hand in his. He looked at her for a long moment before he spoke. "Nagora, I've known you for a long time. In the past you knew me from a distance and rightfully gave me the name, The Watcher. I kept my promise to your father and watched over you. I watched you become a warrior. I watched you accept all that had been kept from you, for your safety for and for that of The Cause. I watched you accept the role of Edana. Believe me that was most difficult for me.

"I feared for your safety and for the outcome of our quest. When you returned with Godomor's Hundred Best Warriors from the Land of Skulls and I saw the brand on your forehead and learned of all you had lived through, I was shaken. I was frightened about continuing on with our plan to free Yogari and Danuka.

"At one point, I was almost ready to give up for fear of losing you. But know this, Nagora. It was your mother who told me to take strength in the example you set with your actions, to trust in you so I could find trust in myself again. Nagora, you can never know what you mean to me and how much I care for you."

She lowered her gaze and let her fingers slip from Raynhard's. She was humbled by this man's admission, her king's admission. "We should eat before it gets cold. The bread tastes best when it's warm." *I should respond to his words, but I feel he's left something unsaid.*

Danuka had curled up with her eggs. Her breathing had slowed. *She's asleep now. Is she truly, though? I wonder because she can open a single eye in an instant and watch me with it.*

Nagora stood at the entrance bowl, looking up at the stars while waiting for Raynhard to return from the latrine outside the cave. *Keep your mind on your story stars, Edana. It's not* easy when your eyes are looking for another star story, the one you fear will be written this night. Where will it take its place among the others?

Raynhard, climbed back in through the crack. Without a word, he stood behind Nagora, put his arms around her, and brought his cheek next to hers. "Where are you looking?"

"*The Woman Waiting.*"

He repeated her words in a whisper and his lips brushed her ear as he spoke them. The spasm pressed her into him as her back arched. She waited no longer. She grabbed his wrists, pulled one hand to her breasts, and pushed the other between her legs. Her mouth found his and bit at his lip as her body abandoned itself to him. She did not deny her king.

The tinkle of the entrance bell woke Nagora. The shadowed silhouette of Danuka's wing, barely visible in the twilight's early purple gleam, disappeared, and the silence of the cave surrounded her. She struggled to set her body in motion. Climbing out of the deep well of sleep was impossible. Layer upon layer of blankets, great heavy winter wool ones, weighed her arms and legs down. Sleep pulled her back into her bed, not wanting to lose her company. But the purple haze of early morning was turning to orange. I should have been up long ago.

Nagora cast aside her covers and swung her feet out of bed. The cool morning air asked where her naked body had been. As she rubbed the sleep from her eyes and the coolness of the stone floor worked its way up her legs, her memories of the night flashed before her in static images of two bodies writhing, twisting, and turning and joining in every manner possible. Lips and tongues tasting, exploring, and feasting. Hands holding, slapping, restraining, and caressing. Mouths moaning, screaming, pleading, and begging. And then answering.

Nagora stood. In the moment it took to assure her balance, she felt the seep. She reached between her legs. Her fingers confirmed it before her eyes did. I can't deny it. The king's seed. Will it take?

And then the words of the past night echoed.

"Please, be my queen."

"No."

"I beg you. Be my queen."

"No."

"I need your strength. My queen must be strong. Say you will be my queen."

"No! I can't!"

"Nagora, I order you to be my queen."

"Raynhard," she inhaled and closed her eyes, "for this night alone, I will be your queen."

He made me his queen. Let it be for that night only.

Thief
Kimotisk

Even though it was now daylight, Nagora went to her spot in the stream to bathe. She spent more time there than usual. *Perhaps if I lay facing the stream's current, any possibility of an heir will be washed from me. Though, if it's to be my star story, I won't be able to change that.*

It won't mean I'll be queen. That, I can control.

Nagora used Uncle's big blade for her morning exercise ritual. She did each exercise in a slow, measured pace, matching her breathing to the repertoire of the twelve moves as she counted through the cycle of a hundred repetitions. When she finished, she was energized with her memories of Uncle who'd initiated her to these exercises. And she was hungry. She took time to eat before getting on with her tasks and a new intention.

After hiding Danuka's eggs, Nagora brought Uncle's blades, wrapped in Umma's scarf, to her small cave. She had also brought along a small sheepskin hide and two lengths of leather lanyards. Inside her small cave, she set the wrapped blades on the fur side of the hide, folded the sides over the ends, and tightly rolled up the hide to form a secure bundle. She kept her knee on it until she had finished wrapping the lanyards around the package and tied it.

She crawled into the small recess of her cave and wedged the precious bundle in next to the narwhal tusks.

Today, I'm going to get away from this cave. It'll be only for a little while, but it'll do me good. The sun is shining, and the sky is clear. I need to see something else besides the insides of this cave and the view from the bowl entrance.

Nagora pushed out past the bushes at the cave's valley entrance and followed the stream to check her snares along the way.

Nothing, no sign of passing game.

She took an arrow from her quiver and placed it in the hand that held her bow. She scanned the area around for any movement and listened. It's clear. She climbed the valley to the mountain ridgeline and followed the trail until it met the adjoining ridge. She paused. If I could peer straight down through the rock, I would be close to looking at the spot where my little cave is. Nagora crouched, looked back the way she had come down into the valley. She moved on a hundred paces and paused to scan and listen again. The left side of the ridge she was on would take her to where she could climb down to the high meadow. She had ridden there with Raynhard the first time he had brought her to his secret cave, months before.

...

Before continuing down the slope to the high meadow, Nagora sat on a rock to take in the view. Rocks and boulders were strewn across the brush of the slope as if they had fallen there out of a drunken giant's scrip. The brush met pine trees growing tall and a canopy of leafy maples that spread out. Just beyond lay the meadow. I'll go to the spot where we had tied our horses that first time. I'll drink from the stream near there.

Deer tracks crisscrossed the slope, but no deer were to be seen.

If I see one, I'll take a shot. If I don't, I won't follow their tracks. I'll go where I'm headed.

Into the maples, she kept an eye out for wild garlic. If I find some, it won't be as good as in spring after the snow melts and the plants bloom. Just the same, a few big bulbs will add flavor to a stew, especially if made from dried meat.

After her drink at the stream, Nagora walked to the edge of the meadow. Wildflowers dotted the tall grass. She scanned the edge of the meadow all the way around. The chances of someone being up here were slim.

She set off into the middle of the meadow. She put her arrow in her quiver and picked a bouquet of daisies. This is what freedom feels like—alone, at peace, in the sunshine in a field of flowers, doing something of my own choosing.

Storm, if you were here we would ride like the wind as we did when we came here. Raynhard rode Yhoura, and we overtook them. Then you and I brought Yhoura back to

Cairnmase. Lars was not in my life yet. Would I give away this freedom to be queen? No.

Back then, I didn't see myself as queen even if my amulet showed me Raynhard had spoken as much. 'Soup fit for a king, and his queen. Let's go see if my queen is awake.' Would I be among the stars if he hadn't saved me? What would the situation be now? Would Da and Danuka have been freed?

At the time I thought I might be imagining things, that perhaps I had even died, or was living in a strange dream. Not anymore. My amulet has power, and I trust it.

Back among the maples, Nagora took an arrow from her quiver and stuck it in the ground next to her foot. She slipped the quiver off and stuffed her bouquet into it so just the flowers stuck out. She put her quiver back on. If someone saw me now, would I get strange looks? The grin on her face almost hurt. I need to smile more often, don't I, Edana? If I were free, I would.

Nagora headed back up the slope by a different way, further downwind. Maybe I'll spot a partridge or a hare.

She had no luck by the time she reached the ridge. Time to go back.

Inside her small cave, Nagora tied her bouquet together and placed it so it touched the leather package holding Uncle's blades.

Before Danuka returned, Nagora gathered a hammer, a stone chisel, branches to be used as pegs, the ladder, and the six candle lanterns. She hauled them to the spots in the cave where she wanted to hang the lanterns. The ladder made it easier for her to carve out peg holes in the stone walls, allowing her to hang the lanterns high enough, yet within reach. By her tally, it had taken her almost seven counts. In the cave, without the help of the sun, it seemed she was always counting time, though it had become an almost effortless habit. A day's work was twenty-four counts, and a day was three times that.

Next, she swept a section of the floor near her bed. *I could even rinse it with water to make it clean enough to spread out the hides I'll be working with. I'll start with a new shirt and leggings.*

The entrance bell signaled Danuka's return.

It's been a long day. I'll do that tomorrow.

"Welcome home, Mother." *What do the bags hold today?* As soon as Danuka left to hunt for her eggs, Nagora opened the first bag. She pulled out a bridle.

Da didn't waste time. Now I'll be able to fly with Danuka properly.

The two other bags each contained dowel chairs which had been disassembled. She had such chairs at home and would help Uncle repair them during the winter. It was usually the woven leather straps of the seats that needed attention. The legs, back, and seat frame of the chair were made of branches big enough to have holes drilled in them to connect the pieces. The pieces were then lashed together with brine-soaked leather lanyards that would dry and shrink tight, holding the chair together.

An easy enough job for a curragh maker like me. Assemble, lash, let dry, weave in the seats, and done. I'll be able to sit. The table might be a little more tricky to fit into the bags. I bet Da asked Geirador to figure that one out. Nagora started a fire to reheat the leftover stew. When Danuka returned with the last egg, Nagora sat in her usual place on Danuka's side of the cave, ready for the ritual inspection.

What is different this evening? The essence of The Dragon's Kiss hasn't taken over me as much as usual. Is that because of the intensity of my coupling last night? Images from her night with Raynhard crept into her mind and aroused her. It was the moments of pain that excited her. Why those images? Because I had begged for them? Was it pleasure I craved or punishment I deserved for succumbing? Is there a line that separates the two? Now how do I get these images out of my mind?

Think of something else—the meadow with all its flowers. I'll go back there in my mind when I go to bed. Or plan a different exploration for tomorrow. Those are my choices. Perhaps tonight I'll be able to resist. The choice will be mine. I'll be in control.

And then it struck—the clutching where Raynhard had penetrated her over and over again last night. Perhaps I have no choice in this.

The next morning in the dark, Nagora opened an eye. In that same instant, Danuka, across the glow of the lone candle lantern, also opened an eye. Nagora stared and Danuka stared back. The lethargy and weight of sleep were not present this morning. Why don't I actually remember going to bed? But I'm in my bed. And I don't remember a single dream whatsoever. I'm not tired. I'm not weak. I'm awake and ready to move.

As Danuka ate her small morning meal, Nagora fastened the bags to her harness. "Mother, I have a bridle now. Soon, I will ride you. Your eggs will be fine here. Only three of us know they are here, unless King Raynhard has told Da or someone else of the location. I doubt he would do that. That means as soon as Da has finished his rounds with the king, it will be my turn to ride you for a day."

Danuka moaned, but did not touch Nagora's forehead with her big snout. I wonder why. She rarely answers a question and she only speaks when she decides to for her own benefit. I've learned to live with that.

Nagora completed her count of the hundredth repetition of her ritual exercise routine. Today she had done it, as fast as she could, with a small knife in each hand. Once, Sagora had witnessed her do it and said: "You did each set so fast, with only a brief pause between sets." It meant she had to maintain total control of her body's balance at all times, and to do that she had to control her breathing. It had taken her years of daily practice to attain the level of speed and control she now possessed.

And as strange as it seemed to her at the time when Uncle had initiated her to the practice of those exercises, time had proven him right. The exercises were a benefit if practiced in opposite sets. A slow set had to be balanced by a fast set the following day. Only the slow and deliberate would lead to the fast and effortless, for, as Uncle would say: "In the slow practice, one learns to breathe, and in the breathing one controls effort and gains speed."

It had taken her three years to absorb that lesson to the point of experiencing its benefits. Sagora had wanted to learn the exercises, so Nagora initiated her not even two months previous. Does Sagora still practice?

"For most skills, time is the only teacher. Once you accept that, progress will come. It is the way." How often she had wrestled with those simple words Uncle would repeat when she became discouraged. "Once you accept the way, then you will begin to see." That one was still a mystery to her. How often had he held her back with the words: "Look again. What do you truly see?" It meant looking for the unexpected, and answers could be found in small details. It meant cultivating the ability to pick out those details. "I can't teach you to see. I can only ask you to look again. Being able to see can save your life."

Well, I know sometimes the unexpected is unpredictable and unseeable. That was how a giant bolt shot from an un-manned ballista they had set on fire had hit Uncle. It was the fire that had set off the release mechanism. The bolt struck the stone bed of the bridge, bounced, and hit one bridge wall, to be deflected across toward the other wall along where Uncle was running. Somehow he saw it at the last moment. He jumped, but the bolt caught his leg just above the knee and smashed him against the stone wall, almost tearing off his leg. Uncle died of his wounds the next day.

With the eggs hidden, Nagora strung her bow and climbed out of the bowl entrance. She took a quick look at her snares and then set off down the mountainside among the trees, stopping now and then to scan the way ahead and listen. It was her first time down this way. *I'll get a sense of the terrain.* To help her do that, she headed to a big rock she had spotted earlier. The small clump of spruce trees that grew on its top drew her there. *If I climb it, I'll be covered and have a good view of the area below.* Nagora circled the rock to decide which face she would climb. But before climbing, she went back three hundred paces and circled the area around searching for tracks, movement, and any signs of a two-legged presence, recent or past. The most dangerous of animals, Uncle called them.

Okay, I'm alone. She climbed and found a comfortable moss-covered spot among the small spruce that grew there. Lying on her belly, she surveyed the area below. She looked to the right and let her gaze travel left among the trees and other big rocks on the slope. *Good. Now try to take in as much of the whole scene ahead.* She let her eyes search at will, making a slow sweep from right to left.

Now eyes, mark the trail we'll take to go down to the limit of where you see. Good, now follow the trail back. This time choose an alternate trail down.

That's when she saw it. Movement. A shadow. Not of a tree, or a rock, or a bush. A shadow in movement. A tall shadow.

Watch and wait. Look. Look again. Nagora waited for a full count. The shadow did not move again. *I'm sure I saw it.* She waited for another count. No movement.

Was I spotted? Could be. Who could it be?

Too many questions to even consider. *A good scout would stay and watch, not make a move until certain. A good scout could die if no one had their back.*

Time to retreat.

Fall back. Stop and watch. Leave no tracks. Repeat.

Back at the cave, just in case, Nagora set up another ladder at the bowl. She tied a quiver of arrows to each ladder and hooked a strung bow on each quiver. Then she leaned a spear next to one of the ladders.

She stood watch on one of the ladders, keeping below the lip of bowl and away from the crack. Ears, you'd better pick up any sound that could warn me.

Darkness approached and not a sound raised an alarm in Nagora's mind. She removed the bows and quivers and the extra ladder and waited for Danuka's return.

The beauty of Danuka's iridescent features appeared and settled on the lip of the stone outcrop of the cave's bowl-shaped entrance. "Welcome home, Mother."

Each of the bags contained a plank to which either legs or the tabletop frame parts had been tied. The flaps of the bags had been left open and their contents lashed to the harness. In the middle bag, Nagora found a hemp sack which contained tapered wooden dowels and a leather bag of wet, brine-soaked leather lanyards. If I lay out all the pieces, I'll be able to fig-ure out how to assemble the table.

I'll start on that tonight. Complete the assembly tomorrow. I'll do the chairs too.

She started her cooking fire. She was hungrier than usual. The water was on the boil and she was cutting up dry salted meat when Danuka returned. The sound started as a moan, but became an extended shriek that frightened Nagora as Danuka directed it at her, a handspan away. Nagora fell to the floor and raised her arms to protect herself as she tried to back away. But Danuka's head, with eyes that now bulged, followed her.

Nagora swallowed. "Mother, what's wrong?"

Danuka opened her mouth and came at Nagora. *Tar piss! I'm about to die!* Danuka pulled Nagora's vest and shirt into her mouth with her big red scaly lips and picked Nagora up. Danuka's mouth pressed close against Nagora's chest. The tightness of Danuka's pull on her clothes squeezed the breath out of Nagora.

Danuka swung Nagora around and set her down on the floor next to the four-pocket pouches. There were sixteen pockets in all. Two of them were empty.

"Mother, how can that be?" *Tar piss! I shouldn't have asked. Danuka always finds her eggs.*

Danuka swung her head, bringing it right into Nagora's face. "Mother, I can guess what you're saying: 'You tell me.'" Her words came out in a stammer.

Danuka turned to an unlit lantern, touched it, and waited.

Nagora went to get a stick from her fire. She was trembling when she lit the candle.

Danuka headed into the cave.

Nagora followed.

At the side of the lake, about three hundred paces from where Nagora's small cave was located, Danuka stopped and lowered her snout to the water's edge.

Nagora approached and shone the lantern over the spot. In the mud at the edge of the water was a handprint to the right of a boot print. *Pug!* His name popped into her mind.

"Pug! You fucking bastard! That is your hand as sure as there are stars in the sky. I will find you and keep the fucking promise I made to you. You'll pay for this." Her voice echoed off the cave walls.

"Danuka, I know who did this. See there, the middle finger is missing two joints. Pug tried to rape me. He thought he would get away with it. In a way he did, but I cut his finger off. Let me ride you and we will find him by tomorrow at the latest. I can get your eggs back for you."

Nagora shone the light on the trail. The ground was still wet with the tracks headed toward the valley entrance.

Of course, I hid two eggs over there. Not well enough. But why did he go to the island in the middle of the lake? What did he expect to find there?

Nagora followed along the stream until she found a taper on the ground near the exit to the valley.

Did he spot me yesterday and follow me? Tar piss! Now I'll pay for this. I have to find Danuka's eggs.

Dreams
Pawâtamowin

Danuka had already returned to her eggs. I'll go to her.

"Mother, you can see in the dark. Let me ride you. We will find him. He can't be that far away."

Danuka brought her snout to Nagora's forehead. "Mother, you will bring Da here tomorrow. But Mother. Okay. Okay. You are right. Someone else knows. Da will know what to do. You will not risk leaving your eggs tonight. Yes, Mother. Okay. I will guard your eggs with my life. I will not leave them out of my sight tomorrow. Yes, Mother. I will hide with them in my small cave and you will roll the stone over its entrance. I'll only come out when you return with Da. I understand."

Danuka took her position to inspect her eggs. Nagora did not keep her waiting.

Could it be someone else? Who?

Nagora had seen people with a missing thumb and some with the opposing finger missing and others missing both.

Uncle had told her that often they had lost them working as punch holders for the strikers who struck the coins in Queen Raganora's mint.

Those who held the punches with their bare hands were quicker and helped strike more coins than those who held the punch with pliers. They were paid more, not much more, but the risk was great. Even so, hopefuls ready to take that risk always filled the holder's bench outside the door of the mint.

No, she had never seen someone else with only their middle finger missing.

Where had Pug gone to after she had been banished from the trainees of Cairnmase for a hundred days? She hadn't ever seen Pug again since the day Randsord had pronounced her banishment for taking his finger. She never told her side of the story, except that he had cut her braid.

Instead of cutting off his finger, I should have kept my promise to him. I wouldn't have this problem today.

Nagora did not sleep that night. Had Danuka slept? She kept going over possible actions she could take. I could leave Danuka's eggs to go track Pug, but now that was out of the question. I don't dare imagine what Danuka might do if I took that risk.

She got up earlier than usual to prepare a waterskin, rations, a spear, and her bow. When Danuka was ready, Nagora slipped the carry straps of the egg pouches over her shoulders and headed for her small cave. It was going to be a long day in the dark. Perhaps I'll catch up on the sleep I missed.

Nagora was sitting cross-legged in the dark, waiting, and listening. Now it was quiet. Only a distant hint of the gurgle of the stream carrying water away from the lake made its way to her. If I had to I could push the big stone away from the entrance. And I would only do that if Pug returned. If he did, he would come with a torch, and there was enough space above the top of the stone blocking the entrance for her to see the light.

Will he come back? What brought him here in the first place? Did he know of the gold on the eggshells of dragons? Where would he have learned of that? Who would have told him about that? Nagora strung her bow and prepared an arrow.

Or had he come for me and found the eggs by venturing into the cave? He must know by now those veins are truly gold. Will he come back? Will he come alone or bring others with him? Was he alone yesterday?

I'll forget about sleep. If he comes back, I'll be ready for him. Did he see this cave? Is anything missing? She reached for the opening of her recessed area. When she found it, she pushed herself in with her heels. Her fingers found the chink where she had stashed the pouch of gold coins. The pouch was there. Further back she found the flowers, Uncle's blades, and the narwhal tusks.

Nothing missing.

She wiggled out and moved Danuka's eggs into that space.

Now I need a plan in case he comes. I need him alive. An arrow would risk killing him. He would hear the stone roll away. He would run. I need to distract him. Nagora reached for her quiver and found two arrows, one with the big, blunt end, used to sting a horse's backside so it might throw its rider, and a whistle arrow. She removed the heavy whistle end from the latter, which Uncle had designed to flip over into its whistling position once the arrow, shot skyward, reached the end of its run. I need the blunt-end arrow to whistle as soon as I shoot. Now I have to tie the whistle on in the dark.

With what? Nagora took the spare bow string from her scrip and cut it in two. She tied a double hitch around the blunt arrow's shaft. Then she alternated a hitch on the whistle with another on the shaft to lock them tight together. She did this until there was no more space on the whistle for another hitch, ending with a double hitch on the shaft.

This'll do. Nagora nocked her arrow and rested her bow on the ground before her. Then she held another arrow in her hands as she began her watch, eyes peering into the dark across the top of the stone, ears listening. She was ready.

But Pug didn't come.

Danuka and Yogari did. As her father made his way along the lake's edge, followed by Danuka, Nagora set aside her bow and arrows, put her feet on the stone, and pushed it away from her small cave entrance. Then she reached over to find her lantern and crawled out of the cave to greet them.

"Mother, welcome back. Da." Nagora was in his arms. "I'm sorry, Da. I left my post. If I hadn't, this wouldn't have happened."

He held her arms. "Perhaps, perhaps not. This cave network is big, and you are here by yourself. You can't be everywhere at once. At least you have an idea of who did it. Now we have to find him."

"Da, let me find him. I know him. I can take him. I can get the eggs back if he hasn't harmed them yet. I could search for him with Danuka."

Yogari shook his head. "No, Nagora. You can't search with Danuka. Mother has already submitted to us as Dragon Talkers. Because of that, she's bound by an oath not to harm our kind. But if she discovers the person who has harmed her eggs, she will break her oath. She'll kill him. If she did, that could become a big mistake."

"Da, I don't understand."

"It's important we find this thief to find out why he took the eggs. There might be motives greater than the gold he could reap from them. We need him alive. We have to find out how he found this place and how he knew there were dragon eggs here."

Nagora lowered her gaze. "He might have followed me here two days ago. I left the cave during daylight. I took the valley exit, walked the ridgeline, and climbed down to the high meadow. I thought the eggs would be safe. They were all here that night. He had to have come yesterday while I was away again. I went down from the bowl entrance about half-way to the valley to explore. I shouldn't have left the eggs."

Yogari put an arm around her shoulders. "But you did. He came here and found them. He must have followed you here two days ago. Why was he in the area? What brought him to the area? Those are some of the questions we need answers to."

Her eyes were on his. "Da, I did everything to cover my tracks and make sure I was not seen."

"You went into the meadow? In the open?"

Nagora hung her head. "Yes, to pick wildflowers."

He lifted her chin. "Look. It's done. We have to focus on finding him. For all we know, he might have known about this place before and he came back again to discover that it was occupied."

I didn't think of that.

"Did Danuka tell you what I told her about him?"

Yogari nodded.

"Da, he's a lazy lout. I just can't see him make the effort to come and explore this area on his own unless there was something in it for him, or someone pushed him to it."

"If he did see you, do you think he recognized you?"

Nagora held up a fist. "I cut off part of his middle finger because he tried to rape me. He would recognize me all right. He was a trainee in Cairnmase and was always on the receiving end of my training weapon whenever paired with me."

"He tried to rape you?"

"Not only that, he cut off my braid. It was longer than it is today.

"And yes, I cut his finger off. I tried to make him swallow it, but he couldn't."

Yogari's eyes widened.

"So I had his friend shove it up his ass. When I catch him, I swear, he'll swallow whatever I find hanging between his legs. He knows I'll do it because I promised him I would. I should've done it the first time."

Her father shook his head. "Would he know you as Edana?"

Nagora shrugged. "I don't know, perhaps. Is it common knowledge you were freed by Edana, who is your daughter, Nagora? Do they know Nagora has a twin sister? Is it known to people in the land that two unicorns and two Edanas were used to create the illusion of Edana appearing in two different places at the same time?" Then the mirror image of herself as

Edana, the Dragon Warrior Princess, made her think of a possibility.

She pointed to her face. "He might've connected me to Edana by the warrior makeup I chose to wear as Edana."

"The four red stripes across your face?"

"Yes. When his four accomplices pinned me to the ground after they ambushed me, Pug stuck his hand inside my pants. His fingers found blood. That pissed him off. He wiped them across my face and then had his friends roll me over so he could try to take me in the ass. He spent before he could penetrate. Then he cut my braid and kept it. He threatened to kill me if I told. I didn't. I got even. But he told about that, and I got a hundred days of exile. I'm sure Mum told you the story."

"She did, Nagora, but not with all those details." He was shaking his head. "I understand why you want to find him. If you do find him, will you promise me to get the information we need?"

"Da, you can be sure I will."

"So how do you plan to find him?"

Her legs barely allowed her to keep in place. "If it's not too late, if Lars hasn't left yet, I'll find Pug with Aydan's help."

Yogari frowned. "I heard he was supposed to be leaving any day now. The recovering wounded warriors are anxious to return home. If they haven't left, Lars might be able to help you."

"Tar piss! I hope he's still here. With his two wolfhounds, we would be able to track down Pug for sure. I could even do it with Aydan alone. Get me to Cairnmase as soon as possible. I'll start the hunt."

Yogari held up a hand and waved a finger. "Danuka will not leave her eggs at night. Here's what you'll do: Tomorrow, just before first light, have her set down in the meadow near Geirador's place. Send her back. I'll spend the day here with her. I warn you, don't use the valley entrance. Warn Lars too, if he is with you, and keep the dogs away from it. I'm going to turn it into a trap for this Pug, should he come back that way."

"Will the trap kill him?"

"It could. Let's say, if he walks into it, he won't be going anywhere soon."

"Da, do you think he'll come back?"

"From what I've seen some do for dragon gold, I would not be surprised. Prepare what you need for tomorrow."

"I'll surely be gone for more than the day. Who'll guard Danuka's eggs?"

Her father bit his lower lip in thought. "In three days from now, I'm supposed to take Raynhard to a meeting with Stone Stander elders." He waved his hand as if to dismiss the thought. "Let me figure that out, Nagora. Find Pug. That's your job, now."

Nagora crawled back into her cave to retrieve Danuka's eggs. Yogari helped her carry them back to the front entrance area.

There, Nagora paused next to Danuka. "Mother, let me start the fire to cook our meal, then I will be with you so you can examine your eggs."

"Da, I wish I had something more for you in the way of a meal. Boiled meat with carrots and onions from my supplies and skillet bread are what I have to offer."

"That's fine, my daughter."

...

Danuka took her position and Nagora took hers. Her father joined her as Raynhard had on his stay. How will this go with Da? I'm his apprentice. If what he told me is so, it should be like the first time. Or will the essence of The Dragon's Kiss overwhelm us too? Would that be Danuka's wish? If it were would I dare resist? Please, Mother, do not do that to us.

Nagora hadn't slept in two days and now, as she leaned back in her father's arms, a sense of well being overcame her. Yogari rested his cheek next to her ear. His breath was calm on her neck and when he was not holding an egg, he rested his hands on her shoulders. Now and then he kissed her cheek ever so gently.

After their meal, they sat by the fire watching the flames die until the embers glowed. Yogari held her in his arms. It was a longtime wish come true for Nagora. All those times I sat on the cliff above my beach, watching for a sail that would bring Da home, I wished for such a moment. Despite the task that awaited her, she was at peace in his arms and savored the attention he gave her. He kissed the top of her head and the brand on her forehead. He caressed her cheek and her hair. Now and then he would kiss her lips and whisper. "My Nagora, my Nagora."

It was early when Nagora awoke. I must've fallen asleep in Da's arms as the fire burned itself out. I don't remember getting into bed.

But in her dream she awoke under her blankets, naked, as a clutching spasm made her arch her back. Her buttocks pressed into hardness. A hand caressed her neck, another her stomach. Her neck twisted to find lips. Not enough, and she reached back, took hold, and pulled, bringing a leg up over a hip—Raynhard's hip. They moved in natural rhythm, pleasing each other, without awkwardness, without hurry.

Then Yogari appeared. He was small, and she became a tree that grew before him, welcoming him among her branches—strange branches, huge, long, curved bones. He placed an amulet around her neck and pointed to another that hung from a higher branch.

To reach for it, she shrunk and he grew. She climbed on him. The branch receded in the distance. He became Storm, and she rode him. He responded to the pace she set until she was no longer in control and she became Storm. Now he was riding her. He took hold of the amulet's leather lace and kept control of her until she lost sight of the branch.

Then Pug turned her over on her stomach, tried to mount her, couldn't, and lost control. He found her face and kissed her with trembling lips and tears on his face. His voice was hoarse with the words, "My queen. My queen."

Then sleep took her again into another dream. I can't remember that one, but this one is so vivid, so strange. Danuka, what message are you giving me?

Yogari had made a small fire to boil water. Nagora wasted no time getting out of bed. She prepared Danuka's small breakfast then headed out the crack in the bowl to her spot in the stream to wash away the evidence of last night's dream, even though she had found none.

"Nothing in the snares. I'm hungry."

What! Tar piss! Beyond the firepit, near the wall with the supply shelves stood an assembled table with two chairs. Why didn't I notice this before leaving? What a surprise! "When did you put that together?" Nagora point to the table first. "And the chairs?"

Yogari smiled at her as he placed four bowls on the table. Two with oats, dried fruit, and honey. "Our meal. When you sit, sit carefully. Twine is holding them together until the leather lanyards dry tight. Eat it all. I'll pour you a bowl of forest tea to wash it down.

"I couldn't sleep last night; so, since you were sleeping soundly, I put you in bed and got to work. Are you happy?"

So it was a dream. Just a strange dream. Oh! Thank the stars! "Of course, I'm happy. Thank you, Da." She went to him and hugged him. He hugged her back and pulled a chair for her.

Her father poured the tea and sat in the chair opposite her. "It'll be cool out there. Put on another shirt and tie your vest. You have a hat, wear it. Make sure your bow is tied to your quiver. I won't help you with the bridle. I want to see how well you handle Danuka."

Nagora crushed the honeycomb and dribbled it over her oats. It would taste so much better with milk, a hunk of cheese, and a piece of bread. "Don't worry. I can handle her. It won't be long, Mother. We'll be leaving soon."

Danuka moaned.

"Da, I had a strange dream last night. One I've never dreamt before. Something about it has me wondering."

He put his spoon down and looked at her. "Are you sure you want to tell me about it? If it's a message from Danuka, it might not be destined for my ears."

She bit her upper lip. "I'll just tell you the part I'm wondering about."

He laid a finger next to his bowl. His eyes didn't leave hers. "Okay. Go ahead."

"In my dream, you placed an amulet around my neck and you pointed to another one hanging from a tree branch. Where did you get the amulet I wear?"

Yogari leaned back in his chair. "It's a long story, Nagora. I'll make it short for now. We had wintered on the Ice Islands. I had been sick for many days. Spring was coming. The ice was leaving the inlet. Soon we would be putting our boat in the water to leave. My crew and the locals were worried about me. Everything your mother tried had no effect.

"So the locals said I was to go see Old Mother. She would cure me of whatever ailed me. But I had to go to her alone. It was a day's walk inland for a healthy man. In my condition I arrived on the third day.

"Old Mother greeted me at the door of her stone hut. Inside, it was framed with whale bones that seemed to be older than she was. She sat me on furs and brewed a terrible tasting tea. I had to drink it all. I lost consciousness; I don't know for how long. When I awoke, I was awfully hungry. She fed me a stew she had made with mice she'd trapped. I felt so much better after eating it.

"She had me stand and do a dance with her around her fire. When we stopped, she reached up to a branch that was stuck among the whale ribs. The amulet you now wear hung from it. She took it, placed it around my neck, and, for the first time, I understood what she said when she spoke to me. She said I was to leave and set sail for the Land of the Danu. She said the amulet would guide me.

"That's where it comes from!"

He raised his eyebrows and pointed at her. "You have plenty to do, so finish what's in your bowl so you can be on your way."

Wow! That's something to think about. I wonder what message Danuka is sending. Back to what you have to do.

"Da, I'm going to get Pug's handprint in the mud. Even if it gets messed up, Aydan should be able to pick up Pug's scent."

Yogari got up to get the shovel and brought it to the fire. He held it over the flames. "What are you going to put the mud in?"

"An empty pouch, I guess."

"I think I have a better idea." Yogari stepped over to the wood pile and picked out an old, dry spruce log. He held the axe over the fire for a few moments, and then he split the log in two. Next, he hacked out the center core on each half of the log. "Just pour the mud in here, slap the two pieces back together, and tie them tight. That way there shouldn't be much odor of spruce to throw the dogs off Pug's scent."

"Da, if I didn't know you were Uncle's brother, I sure would guess you are. He was always teaching me things like that."

"And I learned a lot of things from him too. Here," Yogari handed her the shovel and the log halves, "go get the mud. It's almost time to go."

When Nagora came back, Danuka was waiting to be saddled and bridled.

Nagora held out the log halves she had tied together to hold the mud. "This much is done."

Then she went to get the saddle and bridle.

"Good job, Nagora. Next time, I suggest you put the bridle on last. She's used to that routine. When she has it on, she's itching to go."

Nagora hugged her father. Yogari kissed her forehead and the tip of her nose. "Good luck to you, my Nagora. Be careful."

"I will." Nagora climbed onto the saddle and took hold of the reins. Patting Danuka's neck, she leaned closer and said, "Mother, I'm ready when you are. Let's go."

Feeling the strength of Danuka push off of the lip of the bowl was like taking a jump with Storm, but many times stronger. Nagora's heart jumped in her chest and raced with excitement. Skimming over the treetops in the first light of morning filled her with strength. I can take on the world, do anything! I've got a job to do. I'm going to do it well.

Lars, I can't believe it. I'm going to see you again! You better be there. I need you.

And Pare and Geirador. Your gifts made me so happy. And your letter, Pare. I never thought I would see you again so soon. Here I am, flying to you on Dragon Mother, Danuka.

Nagora blew the silent silver whistle as soon as Danuka left the pasture near Geirador's corral. Aydan and Lyam came running to join her.

Lars is still here!

"Aydan! Lyam! Look at you two! You big, bad boys!"

It was a happy reunion with the two big hounds vying for her attention. There was no way for her to avoid a face washing from both of them. She fought to stay standing as the two jostled her in their excitement. She smacked their hindquarters, pulled on their paws, and scratched behind their ears and down their necks.

"Nagora!" It was Geirador.

Ever the early riser, he must've heard the dogs bark. "Geirador! It's so good to see you again." She walked into this big man's gentle embrace, with the dogs nipping at her sides.

"You must've come on Danuka."

"Yes, she set me down over there." Nagora pointed to the field behind from where she had walked.

"This is a surprise! There was talk of organizing a time for you to come to be here with your parents, but nothing was finalized to my knowledge."

"True enough, but something has come up. Da decided only last night I was to come. I take it Lars is still here?"

"Still asleep, if the dogs haven't woken him. So was everyone else. They'll be stirring now though. Curious like I was. Your business seems urgent."

"It is. I'll be needing Lars if he can be spared, and the dogs. And Storm too. We've some tracking to do."

"Well, lass, you've come in time. The warriors are on the mend. Should be ready to travel in two days or so. No problem in them staying on longer should you still need Lars."

He patted her back. "I want to know more about this tracking. Save it for inside. We'll go rouse Lars if he's not up yet. Have you eaten yet?"

"I have."

"Paruline baked bread last night. I bet you'll have a piece with some cheese and tea."

"I won't say no to Pare's bread."

Geirador put a hand on her shoulder and walked her to the door of his home. "You know, Lars has been taking good care of your Storm, riding him every day."

"That's good to hear."

"Paruline's going to be happy to see you."

"And I her. Though I won't have much time to spend with her. I have to take care of this business as soon as possible."

"If there's anything I can do, say so."

"I know. I can always count on you. Are you the one who sent the chairs and table?"

"How'd you guess?"

"No one else works like you do. Da assembled them during the night. He said he couldn't sleep."

Geirador tilted his head to one side and nodded slightly, as if what Nagora had said confirmed something. "So he'll be spending the day with Danuka? Perhaps he'll catch up on that missed sleep."

Nagora smile. "Maybe."

Geirador pushed the door open for her.

"Nagora!"

"Pare! I'm so happy to see you." She rushed into Paruline's open arms.

"What a pleasant surprise! Let me look at you. You need to get out in the sun more often. You're as pale as in winter." Paruline's smiling face and eyes stared into Nagora's.

"That's something else I could use, a mirror. You know, I haven't been out in the sun for such a long time. I must look like a ghost." She held her open hands to the sides of her face and opened her eyes wide.

"It's true. You look like a ghost, but I'm happy to see you just the same."

Lars! She looked up to the loft from where Lars had spoken. His big smile had her heart racing.

"I knew those were happy barks. That's why I didn't rush down. If I knew it was you … " He paused as he stepped onto the loft ladder.

"You would've stayed in bed, right?" Yes! I beat him to a tease. He always teased her. She loved it and loved teasing him back, especially if she could best him, like she had.

On the ladder, Lars turned to point his finger at her, wagging it. "You are a fast one this morning. A true early bird." In two big stretches of his legs he was on the floor, heading her way.

Hold me in your arms. How I miss their strength. She nuzzled the warmth of his chest. I wish I was under the blankets with you at this very moment.

"You didn't come here just to drag me out of bed, did you?"

"No, I didn't, and I'm glad you were able to drag yourself out of bed." She stepped back and poked him in the stomach. "Makes my job so much easier."

"How about coming over to the table so we can all learn what brings you here?" asked Paruline.

"Good idea, Pare. We'll have to feed this big lug because I have a lot of work for him, today and maybe another day or two more." Nagora looked back up at Lars. "I hear you planned to head back to the Land of Skulls soon. Can you convince the warriors to put off their departure for a day or two? Or can they go on ahead on their own?"

Lars's eyes focused on hers. "This sounds urgent. Give me the details and I'm sure I can get them to agree to a delay. My orders are to accompany them, so they won't be going back on their own."

Nagora glanced around. "Say, where are the warriors?"

"They're in the big room adjoining the smithy, in the stable where we used to make bows and arrows in the winter. They'll come at their own speed later for their morning meal," said Paruline.

"We set them up there to give them more things to do to pass the time. They can make arrows, help out in the forge, make axe handles, and other useful things. And care for the horses. It keeps them busy and gets them moving. Now they're all in travelling condition if they take it easy on the trail," said Geirador.

Lars put an arm around her waist, "Nagora, you should look in on them. They'll be happy to see Edana, and more receptive to a request if it's to help you."

"That's my intention. After all, they volunteered to fight for The Cause. They risked their lives."

Nagora had explained about the theft of the eggs and her plans to find them and Pug. "So that's the situation that has brought me here today. Geirador, Pare, have you ever heard anything about what became of Pug after my being banished?"

Paruline looked to her father.

He was holding his chin. He's collecting his thoughts and searching his memory for details he can remember.

Geirador took a breath. "He had been living with his mother and sister here. After your sentence, they moved to

Yhorgal. If I'm not mistaken, his mother moved in with her brother at his place on the edge of town. From what I remember hearing from those that run rumors and such, Pug wasn't much help on the uncle's farm, and he bullied his mother and sister. His uncle kicked him out. He took to hanging out with those that only work for an easy coin and then go drink it at the ale house. Other than that, I haven't heard a thing. I'll ask around, though, and let you know if I learn something."

"Thanks, Geirador, anything that can help us."

"Do we bring a mule with supplies to set up a base camp, and then search from there?" asked Lars.

"That's a good idea," said Nagora. "Let's get moving."

After Nagora visited the warriors with Lars and he had informed them of what he would be doing and why, they all agreed to delay their departure for the time Edana needed Lars.

Then Nagora and Lars packed a mule with a tent and food for themselves and feed for the animals. Once they had tied their bed rolls, wrapped in their rain capes, to their saddles, they were ready to go.

"Be careful. We want you to bring back good news," said Geirador as he and Paruline hugged Nagora.

"I will." Those were Nagora's words to her friends, but inside she felt her stomach tighten into the beginning of a knot of worry. What will be the outcome be this time? I made a promise to you, Pug. I intend to keep it this time.

Chase
Nawaswâtêw

Nagora called for a stop as they were about to make their way to the high meadow. "If Pug came the long way from Yhorgal to go to the high meadow, he would most likely have come this way. I think we should let the dogs smell the mud for his scent and see if they can pick up his tracks."

Lars dismounted and untied the log from the mule's pack saddle. He untied the lanyard that held the halves together and set them on the ground. The dogs were curious. He didn't have to call them over. He petted them as they smelled the mud. Then he sent them on the search. He retied the log halves and set them back in place.

Once Lars had remounted, Nagora had a question for him. "How will we know when they've picked up the scent?"

"They'll tell us as soon as they find it and wait for us to come to them. We might find a track or something that could show us how he traveled. Then I'll send them off to follow his tracks. We'll follow them."

"And if the dogs find him?"

"I've given them the command that tells them who they are looking for could be dangerous. When they are sure he's nearby, they'll double back to us. From there, it'll be up to us to make our approach."

Nagora looked up to the sky.

Lars did too. "Let's hope they find tracks before it rains. If it rains and rains hard, we risk losing the scent, and our search will take longer."

"So do we wait or move on?"

"We move on. Don't worry. We'll find him. It's just a matter of time," said Lars.

They were getting close to the high meadow, and the dogs had yet to pick up Pug's scent. Rain was threatening. "We're almost there. We'll set up camp before the rain sets in."

"Do you have a spot in mind, Nagora?"

"Yes, there'll be a stream nearby. It's on the other side of the meadow. We can take shelter among the trees. Rig a tarp or two to be comfortable."

"When we get to the meadow, tell me. If the dogs haven't picked up his tracks, we'll take the long way around the meadow instead of crossing in the open. We might get close to him and not know it. We'll lead the horses on foot through the trees. I'll scout ahead. You wait. Give me a full count before you move ahead for another count. Wait again. Same drill."

"Got it." I like how you work. You remind me of Uncle, yet you're so much younger. Still, I feel secure with you. I always have.

...

The dogs still hadn't picked up Pug's scent. Nagora was on her third count waiting with the horses and mule to move on. Aydan appeared and then Lars with Lyam. "Nothing. No sign or trace of him. He must've spotted you up higher on the slope or perhaps even on the ridgeline or perhaps not at all, like your father thought. We'll set up camp. If the rain hasn't started, we'll widen our search from there to eliminate the possibility he's nearby. Tomorrow, we'll work our way up the slope."

"Makes sense."

A light rain fell, but their tent was up under a tarp and their firepit and dry wood were beneath a second tarp. Lars and Nagora had unsaddled and tied their horses and continued to search on foot within the immediate area. The dogs were out ahead of them. By the time they circled back to where they had entered the meadow, the rain poured. For their return sweep, they hugged the forested area at the base of the slope leading up to the ridge until they crossed back, well past the other end of the meadow.

I'm glad we have our rain capes. They both had their hoods up. The dogs' curly, shaggy coats were soaked and covered in burrs and other debris they had picked up on their hunt. Only one thing we can do to remove most of it—cut out the hair it's stuck to.

Lars started a small, hot fire to limit the smoke it produced. Nagora had chosen their spot well. The slope they would climb tomorrow was on the other side of the big rock. Our tent won't be visible from the slope. Anyway, we have two dogs to be on watch for us. If someone with a good eye is out there, they'll have spotted us by now. Our night should be peaceful.

"Hot tea with rations good enough for you, Nagora?"

"Fine with me. Early to bed, early to rise. I want to find that creep as soon as possible."

"We'll get him even if we have to cross the kingdom. He doesn't seem to be the type to make himself scarce. He'll surface for a drink sooner or later. Unless someone else makes him disappear. But we won't think about that possibility for now," said Lars.

"No, we won't. I want to be the one to make him disappear," said Nagora.

Their lovemaking had matched the rhythmic pattern of the rainfall. His climax on her stomach came at the same time as the first violent clap of thunder overhead. As Nagora lay with her head on Lars's chest, the sky flashed with lightning and the rain came and left in spurts and starts. Thunder rumbled and groaned down the valley and echoed off the mountainside. Their tent was on a high spot, and they had a tarp to deflect the showers. And she had Lars without the essence of The Dragon's Kiss. Simple and pure, without any pressure. Completely of her own will. What I desire. What I control.

The storm blew past and the wind came. Possible clear skies for our hunt tomorrow. Nagora fell asleep in the arms of the man she loved.

...

After a good breakfast, they set off on foot with hopes their climb up the slope would not be too muddy. It was damp and misty in the valley beneath the trees. The patches of blue in the overcast sky above the leaves promised sunny skies. We'll be climbing toward the sunshine and be able to look back down on the mist-covered valley.

The going was wet and slippery. They waited for the dogs to show them the best route. It made for a slow slog uphill. Momentarily, they broke through the mist to sunny skies. Are we in a race with the mist rising from the valley?

Aydan and Lyam waited for them at the top of the ridge. "That's just like you lads. You take a breather while we fight our way up. Stay. Go no further. Wait for us."

Nagora smiled at how Lars talked to those dogs. They had surely fought by his side like they were his brothers when he had chased Vorpinger's brother to bring him back for questioning by Godomor. I still can't believe it. Not only did he bring Rhysonnger back, but the counselor and the candlestick maker.

Are any of those three still alive? They must all be rotting in their holes with the ravens still pecking at their brains through their eye sockets.

"We've earned a break, haven't we?" Lars wrapped an arm around her shoulder.

"We have, and we better take it because from what I can see, the going will be slippery. There's a lot of wet and loose stone ahead."

"At least we won't be climbing up any further," said Lars as he grabbed one of her ankles to pull it up so it rested on his knee. He slapped a piece of slate on his other knee to break a piece off and scraped the bottom of her boot, tossing the clumps of mud aside. "Next."

Nagora lifted her other foot. Tar piss! I've been carrying that much weight in mud on my climb.

Lars handed her the piece of slate when he was done. "My sweet lady, Nagora, if ye could ever find the kindness in yer wee gentle heart to clean the soles of me boots, I'd be forever grateful to ya." She had to laugh at the voice Lars took on along with the manner in which he feigned to be a bashful boy, requesting her help.

"Only if you promise to continue being polite to all the young lasses you meet, young Master Lars. With such a promise, I'll render the service you ask."

"I promise. I promise. Sweet lady. Sweet lady." Lars replied in jest.

Nagora answered likewise. "Your boot. Your boot. Young Lars. Young Lars." Thank you, Lars. It lasted but a moment, but in that moment I forgot about our hunt. When she finished cleaning his boots, she stood up and rubbed her boot soles on the rocks until no more mud residue came off. He did the same and followed her along the ridge path.

Aydan and Lyam waited for them where the ridge divided. Lars scanned ahead. "This is where the valley forms, and I'm guessing the valley entrance to the cave is down there somewhere. Is that right?"

"That's right."

"Okay, take me to the spot where you head down to the valley entrance."

Nagora took the ridge to the right and walked the distance Raynhard had showed her the first time he brought her there. She stopped, turned back, and pointed. "See where the two slopes meet? Follow along and down it. Tell me what you see."

"I see a small stream. If it's not coming down the side of the mountain, it has to come from inside it. So that's where your cave entrance is. Okay, let's move along the ridge further. I want to see more of the shape of this valley."

Another thousand paces further, Lars stopped at a spot on the ridge where they had a clear view with no bushes to block it. He sat cross-legged on a big rock there. Nagora sat next to him and scratched Aydan's head as she looked across to the other ridge that now ran parallel to the one they were on. Her eyes crisscrossed it as they made their way down to the valley floor.

Lars pointed. "From what you've told me, the cave network where Danuka's eggs are would be under that part of the ridge that heads off in that direction, but it's not under the part of the ridge where it turns and runs parallel to the one we're on."

"That's right."

"And the other entrance to the cave is on the other side of that slope."

"It is."

"And you've told me it's shaped like a bowl or part of a big bowl sticking out of the side of the mountain slope there."

"Yes, and there's a crack in that bowl I can climb through."

He pulled her to him so her cheek rested on his shoulder. "Sight along my arm and follow where my finger points as I make it travel along the ridge on the other side."

Nagora did until Lars stopped moving his arm. "Right there. Look. Tell me what you see."

"Okay, there's a stand of tall spruce with some of their tops well above the ridge."

"Good. What else?"

Nagora looked to his face. "Is there someone over there I should be seeing?"

He didn't lower his arm. "No, no. Let your eyes go from one side of the stand of spruce to the other, then back to the other side. Repeat that a few times and tell me what you see."

She did. "There's a notch in the ridge there. I see it now among the tree trunks. So?" Her eyes searched his.

"Think about it. A long, long time ago water filled this valley."

Nagora nodded. "I get it. And water spilled out of the notch there, down the mountain side. Where the cave entrance is, there once was a ledge with stones on it. The force of the falling water spun the stones. Over time, they ate into the ledge to carve out the bowl shape.

"Uncle showed me a place on a river's rapids once when the water was low in summer. There must've been a dozen or so 'buckets,' he called them. Some of them still had the stones the current swirled around, causing them to dig the bucket holes."

Lars's smile broadened. "Very good. Now we have a valley that once contained a lake out of which water fell, carving the bowl entrance to the cave. I won't even guess how the cave came to be. It contains water, and the water runs out into the valley on this side. Did it always run this way, or did it long ago spill out of the bowl entrance?"

Nagora placed a hand on his arm. "Lars, what are you getting at?"

He leaned his head to one side as his eyes found hers. "You've been in that cave for over thirty days. Has the water level in the lake ever gone down so the stream stopped flowing into the valley while you were there?"

"No. What does this have to do with finding Pug?"

Lars held up two fingers. "It could have everything and nothing to do with that. I want to eliminate the 'everything,' or have it as a possible trail for us to explore."

"Now I'm lost." She shook his arm.

"Let me explain. Before the rain yesterday, the dogs did not pick up Pug's scent. I don't doubt the ability of my dogs to track. We came the long way around, as if Pug had come that way from Yhorgal. We were on horseback. From what I know about him, he can't afford a horse, let alone a mule. So I'm betting he traveled on foot. Would he have come the long way? Or would he have climbed up and over and down a series of hills and mountains to get to this valley, an even longer way?" Lars held up his finger. "You know, and I know, the answer is no."

"Because he's too fucking lazy." Nagora bared her teeth.

"Exactly. So he came from Yhorgal roughly by the same route Raynhard used when he was Chive."

Nagora held out her hand. "Raynhard came from Yhorgal on foot the first time he came to visit me a few days ago. He promised me he had been careful and had not been followed."

"Yes, Nagora, a promise made to the best of his knowledge. But there's another possibility. Perhaps Pug was already in the area of the cave entrance and spotted Raynhard go by. Perhaps he had a vantage point that allowed him to see where Raynhard went."

"But what would Pug be doing so high on the mountain-side?"

"Perhaps Pug has a hideout of his own. A cave of his own, like Raynhard had when he took on the role of Chive. Perhaps he hides stolen goods there. His kind often resorts to thievery rather than do an honest day's work to earn their living."

Nagora was nodding. "Okay, so his hideout could be near-by. I told you about the shadow I had seen. That was much lower down. Could there be a cave down there?"

"There could be, for sure. The mountains are riddled with caves." His hand moved to his chin. "I keep thinking about your cave. The water level in the lake is constant. The stream flows continuously. Where does the lake get its water?"

Lars didn't let her answer. "Probably not from runoff rain on the mountain. There'd be a change in the water level. The stream would stop flowing now and then."

The hand on his chin shot up. "That suggests an under-ground source, a spring of some kind. This high in the mountains, it would need pressure to make its way to the lake."

His eyes narrowed and moved from side to side. "Water veins run in mysterious ways. The spring could originate in the mountains over there." He pointed.

Nagora pointed too. "Well, there is a lake high in those mountains. I remember Uncle telling me about it because of its name. It's called Lake Tear of the Clouds."

Lars nodded. "The spring could originate from there. But there's something else you've said that puzzles me."

"What?"

"You said you found Pug's handprint and boot print in the mud coming out of the lake. Did you find any boot prints going into the lake?"

Tar piss! Did I? No. "Now that you mention it, I didn't look for any. I assumed he had gone over to the island to have a look and then came back. I didn't check all along the lake's edge. I should have."

"When you found those prints, they were pretty obvious?"

"Yes, they stood out in the candle light and the path at that spot was still wet. What are you thinking, Lars?"

"What if Pug came into the cave from the lake?"

Her mouth hung open for a moment. "What? How could that be?"

Lars put a hand on hers. "Think about it. When you were a prisoner in the dungeon sea cave and the tide was rising, you knew the water was coming in from the sea, but the sea level in the cave hid the entrance below where the seawater came in."

She nodded. "I get it. So the level of the lake water could be hiding an entrance to an adjoining cave. But how would he know my cave was on the other side?"

"Someone or something told him, and I'm guessing it was something—the light from your lantern reflecting in the water caught his eye. He took a chance and swam under to find the source of the flickering light in the water."

Nagora held up a finger. "That could be it. The extra lanterns I hung on the pegs I had set in the cave wall. I lit them that morning before hiding the eggs and left them lit to know how long they would stay lit. Some of them were near the lake."

Lars gripped an imaginary object. "And when you moved from one part of the cave to another, you always had a lantern with you, right?"

She nodded.

"Steady flicker, no more moving flicker, time to go take a look."

Nagora brought her hands to her face. "That means Danuka's eggs could still be in danger."

He touched her shoulder. "Only if there is light near the lake. I don't see how he could bring something that wouldn't get wet to light his way. Or, if he knows of the exit where the stream flows. But your father set a trap there yesterday."

Nagora balled her fingers into her fist. "If that's the case, whoever watches the eggs should have their eyes on them at all times."

Lars nodded. "And not leave candles lit near the lake. But we don't know for certain if there's another point of entry by the lake."

She took hold of his arm. "I like your thinking. It gives us an area to search. We go back to where the ridge forks and then explore that slope all the way to my cave's entrance."

Lars nodded. "Lead the way, Nagora."

When they stopped at the junction with the other ridge, Nagora asked, "How shall we do this?"

"We'll each take a dog. They'll keep just ahead of us. If they spot something or someone move, they'll lay down with their paws together, pointing to where they spotted it. We always keep within sight of each other as we move across the slope. You keep above me on the slope.

"If you see Pug, point to me then to your right eye. One finger across your lips, he's within a hundred paces. Two fingers, two hundred paces. Remember, we want him alive. If I see you draw your bow, it's because you have a clear shot that will stop him, but not kill him."

"Got it." She strung her bow and pulled an arrow from her quiver.

Lars called the dogs to him. He gave them two commands. Aydan joined Nagora and the two of them set off along the slope, above Lars and Lyam.

Nagora and Lars took their time as they picked their way through the trees and past boulders, always checking they had each other within sight.

The going had been slow and just when she found the terrain underfoot had become steeper, Lars signaled. He pointed ahead and below Nagora and then to his left eye. He held his thumb and first finger together to make a hole. With his other hand he made two fingers walk toward it.

She nodded. You see a cave entrance.

Nagora moved on, taking her time and keeping Lars in sight.

He bent and picked up something. He held it up.

Small bones?

He pointed to the ground all around him, bent, and picked up a few more to show her.

Aye, those are bones. Must be refuse from the cave.

He signaled for Nagora to stop and wait.

He picked his way up to her, following Lyam as he did.

...

"The cave entrance is just ahead and down. I'll go up, over, and down to its other side. I have a feeling that's where the access trail is. Wait here until I signal you to come forward. In the meantime, clean off the soles of your boots. We'll not want to leave tracks if we go in."

Nagora did as Lars had asked. The wait seemed endless, but then she caught his quick wave before he ducked out of sight. She crept toward his position, being extra careful on the steep terrain. She took Aydan's lead. Whenever she paused, she tried to spot Lars.

When she did, he had his big sword in hand. He signaled he was going in. As soon as he disappeared, she moved on with her bow and an arrow nocked. Part of the entrance came into view. Lars had been right about the approach trail being on the other side. I can make it from this side. Once in the entrance, I'll be on solid ground.

Lyam was laying in the entrance with his paws together, pointing inside. That's a good sign. Either Pug is there, or he was there.

Just as Nagora pulled herself past the side of the entrance, she came face to face with Lars as he came out, bent over. Her heart stopped for a moment.

"Sorry about that. You'll have to stoop when you go in. No sign of him. Come." He took her hand and led her into the cave and pointed. "I found that taper, so I lit it. We'll have light to look around. Maybe there'll be another." He took the taper so they could have a closer look. They approached the firepit. He pointed. "There. He's built a wall of stone. See why?"

"Not exactly a lake. More like a pond on the other side. He must've realized his fire could be visible like my candles were," said Nagora.

Nagora's eyes took in the space around her. "Not a big cave compared to mine."

Lars pointed. "A pile of rags over there. And some dirty sheepskins."

"His bed?" Nagora asked.

"Unless he carries a sleeping roll."

"Not Pug. Only if he had someone else carry it for him. Did you check for the eggs?"

"No eggs. Oh!" He pointed. "There's a lantern I didn't see earlier." He brought the taper closer to shine the light of its flame in the crook in the rock where the lantern had been wedged. "Nothing else in there."

Nagora held out her hand. "Can I have the taper?"

Lars handed it to her.

Slowly, she walked the perimeter of the cave, careful to avoid stepping into the water. When she had completed her circuit, she stopped near the firepit. "If this is a hideout, he mustn't use it for long stays. He doesn't have any supplies stashed here. No firewood to speak of, and only rags to sleep on. If he's a thief, he truly has no honor. He has nothing to hide. Why would he come all this way for only a short stay?"

Why? Why? She looked up. Hmmm? She slowly lifted the taper. "What do you make of that? It just seems to be hanging there. What is it?"

Lars took the taper and held it up. He stepped from one side to another, obviously trying to get a better view. "We'll soon find out." He gave the taper back to Nagora. "I think you'll want to come wait outside until I get back. I won't be long."

Nagora placed the taper back in its hole and followed him out.

Lars climbed the slope. He angled over above the cave entrance out of sight. What noise is that? It sounds familiar?

Then Lars came back down the slope, sporting his big grin. He closed one eye and made to reach for his sword. "Let's go see what treasures hide in this here cave, lass."

"Are you trying to sound like a pirate?"

"Actually, I'm a pirate doing a bad imitation of a pirate."

"I thought you said you were a whaler."

"And so I did, lass. Whalers and pirates be of the same family. Pirates take what's floats on the salty sea. Whalers take what's swims under the same salty sea. We be just as bad, but not as scarrrrry." He crossed his eyes and tilted his head as he bared his teeth.

"Aye, well get your sorry bag of pirate whale bones in that cave before I break your harpoon."

"Oh! Sweet lass, you give me cause to surrender to yer threats."

"To the treasure!" Nagora smiled as she pointed. I love this man.

"He's got a system of pulleys rigged in the trees above. The stout rope that runs through them had a heavy load on it," said Lars, as he pointed to the rope, which hung down from the hole in the cave ceiling.

Nagora scratched her head. "How come rainwater doesn't come down that hole?"

"A hide's been rigged above to deflect it, but still let the smoke out." Lars held the taper closer to the floor.

"Tar piss! That's complicated lashing job. All those branches lashed with leather lanyards and ropes. The bottom and sides covered in hide. It's a huge basket. It was made in here for sure. No way to pull that through the entrance. So someone's spent considerable time here. I just can't picture it being Pug. I can't imagine him making something this elaborate. I doubt he would have the patience."

Lars bit into his lower lip and nodded. "He might've learned of this place from someone else. They could've given him loan of it, so to speak. Or he could have a resourceful partner."

"Lars, I can't wait to get my hands on him. I have so many questions I want answers to."

They untied two of the basket's four sides and pulled them down onto the cave floor.

"Hemp bags, leather pouches, lanterns, an axe, a shovel, a quiver with arrows. Do we go through all of these bags? Do you think the eggs are in one of them?" asked Nagora.

"I'm not going to overlook that possibility. We'll check them all. Let's light a few lanterns so we can see what we're doing. It shouldn't take that long."

After rummaging through all the bags, Nagora and Lars sat outside the cave entrance eating trail rations, sharing them with the dogs. "No eggs. Obviously too valuable to leave here and he feared by now someone would've noticed they were missing. And someone would be looking for him," said Lars.

Nagora made her hand into a fist. "We have to find him as soon as possible. He won't keep it a secret for himself."

"He might if he wants all the gold from the eggs for himself."

She shook her head. "I keep imagining hordes of people climbing up here set on killing a dragon to get to her eggs. It's a possibility."

"Okay, so if you were him, Nagora, where would you go with the eggs?"

She put her face in her hands. "I don't know. Somewhere he can get the gold from the eggs. They would have to be heated in a fire of some kind. He would need to know how to catch the gold once it melted. What good would it do him if it were not in the form of coins? Is there a way to sell it or trade it otherwise?"

Lars's eyebrows shot up for a moment. "Those that mine it sell it by weight, but what is mined surely does not look like what he'll end up with. That'll raise suspicions. My guess is that he's holed up somewhere thinking of his options, trying to figure out what to do with the gold once he gets it. He must've hidden the eggs in the meantime. I figure we're headed for Yhorgal tomorrow."

"Do we put his supplies back in the basket?"

"No. We want him to know we're onto him. But he won't come back here soon unless he has a plan to deal with the gold," said Lars.

"Do we head back to camp or spend the night here?"

"Neither—we head to your cave. It can't be far from here. Just around the bend in the slope. We spend the night there."

Tar piss! No. I need an excuse.

"Or we could stop by the cave. If Da's still there, we'll inform him of what we've found. And then, we'll get a head start down the slope toward Yhorgal before dark. We could sleep under the stars."

"It'll be cold."

"There are blankets and hides in the cave we could bring."

Lars nodded. "Okay, we could do that. You want to find him as soon as possible. Maybe we can check out that spot where you saw the shadow move the other day."

If it comes to spending the night in the cave, I'll bring Lars with me to my small cave, away from Danuka's essence.

Lars pointed to the trail on the slope. "Let's follow the trail Pug most likely uses to come up here. It'll bring us further down, but from the look of the terrain, the slope gets steeper as we move along it at this level. We might even gain some time."

"It'll be easier on our ankles too." The last stretch of her approach to Pug's cave entrance had been painful. "I wouldn't want to continue on to my cave on such steep terrain."

The trail took them down and across the slope. Ahead, bushes and trees grew denser. "Up till now, this path seems to be well worn from use. There's no obvious path like this up to the bowl entrance of my cave," said Nagora.

"Must be because there's no direct view of the crack in the bowl to attract someone to it. Plenty of trees and bushes blocking the view to it," said Lars.

Nagora pointed. "That's true. More trees and bushes ahead on this trail."

Lars nodded. "The trail will not be as obvious when we get in there."

Lars was right. They relied on the dogs to take them through the brush. As they came out of the worst of it, the lookout rock she had used days previous appeared to her right further down the slope. "Lars, we've gone far enough. My cave is straight up from here. See that big rock with the clump of spruce trees on top?"

"Yes. Is that the one you were on when you spotted the shadow?"

"It is."

"Okay, we've got plenty of daylight left. Do we go to the spot where the shadow moved? Or do we go up to your cave? How far away are we?" asked Lars.

"From here, we're about mid-way from either one."

"It's your call, Nagora."

"Down to the shadow spot."

"Do you want to go up on the rock to take your bearings?" asked Lars.

"Yes. Come up with me."

After she had shown Lars where she had seen the shadow move, they climbed down from the rock.

Lars took a rag from his belt. "It's from Pug's cave." He had the dogs smell it, and then they made their way down.

They came to a knoll near their destination. "I'll go around and down. Watch for me from behind this tree. I'll signal for you to come down," said Lars.

Nagora watched and listened. Lars signaled. He had his sword drawn. She strung her bow and nocked an arrow before moving to join him.

On the other side of the knoll, Lars pointed with his sword. Lyam was laying at his feet, paws together, pointing in the same direction Lars had indicated. She moved quietly until she was next to Lars. They were looking at a hole in the ground. One would have to crawl in. The hole's timber frame entrance was overgrown with grass. It's like the entrance to a root cellar, like the ones most people in Cairnmase use to store vegetables for the winter.

Lars whispered, "Whoever or whatever caused the shadow could've gone in there. Do we call him or it out? Or do I send Lyam in?"

In a whisper, Nagora asked, "Is he there?"

"Could be. Something with the scent is. Perhaps just more rags."

"Will Lyam be in danger?"

"He can defend himself."

"Let's call him out," whispered Nagora

Lars bent down and picked up a few small stones. He approached the entrance, stood to the side of it, and tossed the stones in. "You in there. Come out. No harm will come to you. We want to talk."

Coughing and then muffled swearing came from within. Then someone's backside backed out of the entrance on hands and knees. The man had a staff with him and used it to help him stand. When he faced them, the old man squinted in the daylight as he looked at them. He spoke through his grizzled beard. "For shit's sake, a man can't even find a quiet place to rest out here! What do you want with me?"

Nagora stepped forward. "We're looking for someone. Perhaps you know him? He goes by the name of Pug. Do you know him?"

"What if I do? What business do you have with him?" Snares hung from the man's wide leather belt.

"I want to buy his services. I've been told he'll do just about anything if the price is right," said Nagora.

"You're not wanting to get your hands dirty, is that it?" The old man spat.

"You could take it that way. So you know him?"

"Aye. He would be your man if you've got the coin." He rubbed his thumb and finger together.

"When's the last time you saw him?"

The old man scratched at his beard. "Six, maybe eight days ago."

"Where was that?"

"Right here. He was passing by."

"Headed to his cave on the mountainside?" asked Nagora.

The old man poked a thumb at his own chest. "My cave. I don't have the legs I once had. I let him have the run of it."

"Does he go there alone?"

"As far as I know."

"We were there earlier. Do you know where he would be now?" asked Lars.

"Can't rightly say. Could be anywhere, now."

"What do you mean?" asked Nagora.

"Last time we talked, he said his fortunes were about to change. Said an old mother read the runes and told him so. He must've believed her. I hadn't ever seen him in such good spirits, other than when he took a drink. And that never lasted long."

"Does he live with his mother?"

"Oh! No. Not that one. She has nothing to do with him."

"Where can I find him, in Yhorgal?"

The old man scratched his beard and shook his head. "No idea. You'll have to ask around. He did say he'd be off to better things. Never said where though, or when."

Lars stepped forward and pointed to the trapper's hole in the hill. "Has he ever slept in there?"

"Aye, twice in the past. You're welcome to have a look. Candle lantern's on the floor, just to the left as you go in. It's my home away from home until the snow takes me home to my dear woman. I swear, every winter with her is like a year taken from my life."

Lars moved toward the entrance and went on his knees to get the lantern.

"So you trap for a living?" asked Nagora.

"Always have. Mostly around here. Mostly for rabbit now. Foxes are a young man's job. You have to live like one to catch one. Caught a few in my younger days."

The old man watched Lars back out. "I know it's not much. It keeps me dry when it rains and warm until the snow comes. A space for my supplies. When I cook on a fire, I go down yonder near the brook there." He pointed a dirty finger. "I put a hook in the water while I'm there. Sometimes I'm lucky. Catching a fish makes my day."

"Thank you, old man," said Lars.

"Name's Phersen. Who should I say asked about him if I see him again?"

Nagora raised her bow. "Tell him Edana's looking for him."

...

They left in the direction of Yhorgal. Once out of sight, they had doubled back and made their way up to her cave. Is Da still there?

"Nagora, if we can get by the trap your father set at the valley entrance to the cave, we could be back in camp well before dark. We'll be better off with our horses if we go to Yhorgal. Our search for Pug might bring us elsewhere."

Nagora nodded. "Since we know it's there, we can surely figure out how to get by it. We won't be caught by surprise. If Da is still there, then it won't be a problem at all." That's a relief. I'm glad we won't be spending the night in the cave.

"Lead the way," said Lars.

They made sure no one followed. Something Phersen said about Pug having his fortune told to him—that bothers me. Was his discovering the adjoining cave and the dragon's eggs simply good fortune? I doubt that.

Is Old Man Phersen an accomplice to the theft of the eggs? Is he aware of the bigger cave? He's trapped in the area long enough. Does Raynhard know him? Does Phersen know Chive, the scrounger of herbs and mushrooms who used to come through this area on his way to the cave? Where can Pug be? How far has he gone with the eggs?

Tar piss! So many questions and no answers.

After climbing through the crack of the bowl into the cave entrance, two ladders tied together end to end greeted Nagora and Lars. They were set up as one ladder near the back wall of the cave's entrance chamber. Holes had been chiseled high along the ceiling from the side of the entrance over to the wall. Wooden pegs had been hammered into the holes.

"Looks like Da's been doing some work. What for, I can't rightly say. Let's find out if he's in another part of the cave." Nagora took a lantern and lit it. "Follow me."

Just as they were making their way from the entrance area of the cave to the passageway leading to the lake area, she paused. "Do you hear that?"

"Voices," said Lars.

"Yes, and not just my da's." Nagora drew her big skystone blade and gave the lantern to Lars, who pulled his own sword from its scabbard on his back. She moved ahead in the dark, with only the dim light from the lantern Lars held above her shoulder to light her way. Faint light appeared ahead.

Da must have lit the lanterns along the lake path.

The voices grew louder. Nagora heard the sound of a slap, and then her father spoke. "Think about it. You'll be better off telling me than having to face the dragon when she returns. I'll be back in a little while to find out if you've changed your mind."

I can't believe it! "He's got Pug!"

"Da!" She ran toward the light. Lars was right behind her.

Yogari came toward her and the smile on his face and his words confirmed it.

"Nagora, guess who I've captured."

On his knees with his hands tied behind his back and to his ankles, Pug looked up at her. The closer she came to him, the more fear showed itself on his face.

"Well, who do we have here? I was right. It's my old friend, Pug." She waved her blade before his face and then pointed it down between his legs. "Pug, I have so many questions you have answers to. I want you to take some time to think about how you're going to answer them because, Pug, you know me, don't you? You know that I keep my promises."

Pug swallowed and then hung his head on his chest.

"Caught him just as he was coming ashore here. He's not told me a thing. Says he never will. Says he'll die before he does. I don't see us beating it out of him. On the other hand, Danuka might get him to talk, but that's risky. If she gets a hold of him, he'll die a terrible death. Maybe we should just deliver him to Raynhard."

Nagora glanced at Yogari for a moment then returned her gaze to Pug, waving the tip of her blade back and forth above Pug's head. "I'm not so sure about that," Nagora said as she glanced back at her father and winked. "I know someone who can make him talk. It might take her longer than a day or so, but she has plenty of time. But that means I have to keep Danuka from him. Da, I have an idea. Can we leave him here for a count so he won't hear?"

Yogari nodded. "He'll only get out of those knots if someone cuts him free."

Nagora headed back to the cave entrance. Yogari and Lars followed.

Yogari listened intently as Nagora and Lars described how they had found Pug's adjoining cave and their encounter with the old trapper Phersen.

Then Yogari spoke. "I think he heard your approach and decided to escape detection by swimming to this side. The lanterns on the lake path were lit. I hadn't passed by since early morning. Since then, I had been working here. I had just finished hammering in the last peg," her father pointed to the one high on the wall, "and I was on my way to check on the trap at the valley entrance when splashing got my attention. That's when I caught the two-legged fish. I don't think he's a good swimmer."

"We're lucky you were here to catch him," said Lars.

"True enough. He could've hidden in a shadow unseen and even found more eggs before chancing a return to his cave," said Yogari.

"With you working here at this end and the trap at the other end, if eggs had gone missing, that would've caused you to suspect an access by the lake somehow," said Nagora.

"Surely. So, Nagora, what do you have in mind for our captive?" asked her father.

"I want him in my little cave to keep Danuka from him." She went over to the shelf of the weapons cache. Next to it stood six spears. She took hold of them and set them on the cave floor before Yogari and Lars. She put two together, crossed them over two others to form an X, and laid one across the top of the X as a brace.

When she stood up, she pointed with the spear she held. "I want them lashed together like this and I want Pug's arms and legs spread and tied to those ends of the spears. Remove his boots."

Nagora rested the last spear on the others. "I want this spear down the middle, on top, like it is. I want his neck to be tied to it with enough slack so he can lift his head."

"We can do that for you," said Lars.

...

Nagora went to the pile of firewood and found seven logs all about the same size, which she set on the floor next to the spears. "And I want each end of the spears to rest on one of these. I want this one to be placed so it's under the spears at the level of the middle of his back."

Yogari nodded. "Well, you know what you want. I trust you'll get the information you need from him. Are you sure you don't want one of us to stay here to help you?"

"Da, trust me. I'll get the information." Nagora turned to Lars and took his hand. "You've already delayed your return to the Land of Skulls. Those men are anxious to get back to their families. And Gabe surely has work waiting for you. Thank them for me. You've been a great help."

Nagora reached for her father's hand. "And Da, the Stone Stander elders are expecting Raynhard. He would never fly Danuka that distance on his own. They want to meet you too. Help Raynhard attend to his affairs. I can deal with Pug."

Yogari placed a hand on her shoulder. "You're sure?"

"I'm sure, Da." She did her best to give her father a reassuring smile. I don't want to live through another night of strange dreams about you, Raynhard, and Pug. Not in this cave. That night of dreams when you were here scared me.

Yogari looked to Lars. "If your intention is still to return to your camp near the high meadow, I'll accompany you. We'll go on to Cairnmase together tomorrow. Geirador has tool samples and forged metal recipes destined for the Stone Standers. I'll be delivering those along with Raynhard the following day."

Lars smiled at Yogari. "Glad to have your company, sir."

"Call me Yogari."

"You'll not go with Danuka, Da?"

"She's with Raynhard now and will return here before nightfall. Tell Danuka she's to meet me at Geirador's tomorrow as planned before we go to Raynhard, and then on to the Stone Standers. That will give me a chance to meet with Geirador and discuss possibilities to make your cave comfortable this winter. I already have some plans."

Yogari pointed to the pegs he had set in the ceiling and along the cave wall. "These are temporary, to mark where I'll set iron rings on pintles to hang a curtain made of hides which will help keep the heat from your cooking fire on that side of the cave. I'll hang another for the side where Danuka sleeps. When coming in, the curtains will give way to her wings as she folds them in to step down from the bowl's lip. She'll be able to get past such a curtain to her side of the cave.

"And knowing Geirador, he'll have many other suggestions worth considering."

Yogari hugged Nagora to him. "And I want to plan a few days when we can be together as a family. I know it's something you want and, believe me, so do Tagnya and Sagora."

"Da, you know I can't wait for that. A few days would be great. All of us together as a family." Nagora looked to Lars. "It's too bad you're leaving. It would be great to have you with us too."

He held out his hands. "If it were happening in a day or two, I might be able to squeeze another delay out of the warriors." He shrugged his shoulders. "But they, too, are anxious to return home to their loved ones. It's my duty to bring them back. Like you said, Gabe is waiting for me to return. I'm sure he'll have work for me to do. I'm betting that bridge won't yet be complete. I'm not indispensable, but he is my commander."

Nagora squeezed his hands. "I understand. Promise me that as soon as you can get leave, you'll come back to visit me here, now that you're among the privileged few who know of the existence of this cave."

"I promise, Nagora." Lars pulled her to him.

She gave him a hug and a kiss and mouthed the words "I love you."

Yogari cleared his throat. "Lars, we have our work cut out for us. We better get to it if we want to make it to camp before dark. Disabling the trap when it's time to leave by the valley entrance won't be a problem."

Yogari picked up the firewood logs and Lars took the spears. Nagora brought along another lantern, coils of rope, and leather lanyards.

Yogari crawled out of the small cave last. Pug was still yelling, "What are you going to do to me? What are you going to do to me?"

"He's tied as you asked. He's all yours now," said her father. "He keeps asking the same question over and over. I told him to be patient."

"He'll find out soon enough. Thank you, both of you. I'll get answers to my questions."

They stepped away from the small cave. "Come with us, Nagora. I'll show you how the trap works. You can decide if you want it armed or not," said Yogari.

Lars held the dogs back as Yogari showed Nagora how to disarm the trap. "There are two trip lines. One triggers the other. Tie off the second one here like this." He undid the knot. "Now you do it."

Nagora tied off the second trip line as her father had shown her.

"Good, now you can release the first. It falls to the floor."
She did it.

"Good. Now that big log won't come flying down to strike someone in the knees."

"Da, that would be painful." She gave him a big hug. "I love you, Da. I hope we meet soon as a family."

"So do I." Yogari held up a finger. "As soon as I can, I'll have Danuka bring a net to block off that underwater access from Pug's cave. In the meantime, always be armed and ready in case he has an accomplice who knows about it."

"I will, Da."

Nagora held Lars in her arms, not wanting to let him go. "You don't know how much I'll miss you."

"I, too, will miss you. Are you sure you won't keep Aydan?" asked Lars.

"As much as I would love to have his company, I fear I wouldn't be able to feed him properly. Getting supplies here just for Danuka and me is already a problem. Living in a cave would not be good for his health. Lars, I'm hoping by next spring I'll be free of this cave. Until then, our eyes to the night sky. We'll meet at our star." They kissed for a last time.

Her two men disappeared through the valley exit.

Questions
Kakwecikemowin

Nagora crawled into her small cave to look in on Pug. Da and Lars did a good job tying you.

He watched her stare at him. He struggled against the ropes that held him spread-eagled over the spears. "What are you going to do to me?"

"I'm not going to do a thing to you, Pug. Don't worry." Edana will. She left him.

Back in her part of the entrance chamber of the cave, Nagora found the jar of leftover, brine-soaked, leather lanyards. Geirador had sent them to bind her chair and table parts together. She set it on the table along with a big bowl, washcloths, a piece of soap, and extra candles.

She also set on the table the small medical scrip Tagnyoriva had sent.

In her own scrip, Nagora found the pot of red war paint her mother had made for her, the paint she wore when she took on Edana's identity.

She opened the pot to apply the blood red paint. The first time she'd applied it, she had hesitated for a moment because of her reason for choosing how to apply it. Today she painted her face for the same reason.

After dipping a finger into the red paste, Nagora drew a line from the side of one eye, over her eyelid, over her nose bridge, and over her other eyelid. The next line crossed from one cheek bone, over the tip of her nose, and on to the other cheek bone. The third line went from one ear to the other, across her lips. The last line crossed from one side of her jaw to the other, across her chin.

Nagora put the little pot of paint in the bowl, along with the other items she had set on the table.

She slipped her blades back onto her shoulders, adjusted the side straps tighter, then pulled her big blade from its sheath on her back and held it before her. Her eyes stared back from the burnished blade. Pug, you bastard, you painted my face once like this with my own blood, the blood from between my legs. If you only knew the fire that memory lights in Edana.

She returned the blade to its sheath, slipped the strap of the small medical scrip over her shoulder, picked up the big bowl, and the lit lantern.

Pug, Edana is coming.

Edana paused to listen as she looked at the glow coming from the cave entrance.

It's quiet. Not for long.

She placed the items from the bowl at the side of the entrance next to the small scrip. Then she went to the lake to fill the bowl with water. She brought it back and set it at the entrance to the cave.

As Edana crawled through the small cave entrance, she took her time, being careful of where she set the big bowl so as not to spill the water. She brought the other items in and set them aside, all the while not saying a word to Pug who was staring at her, his eyes wide open in terror.

"Whhaa whhaaa what are you going to do to me?"

Edana did not answer. She smiled at Pug from between his legs where she knelt. She reached over to her left side and withdrew a small blade from its holster on the shoulder strap that held her blades.

Pug swallowed and screamed his question once again.

"Watch me and you will see," she said.

Edana cut along the stitches of his left legging from the ankle up to the hip where it was tied to his underpants. She peeled it from his leg, folded it, and placed it on the floor beneath his bottom before doing the same with his other legging.

She pulled up his shirt and straddled his midsection. As she placed her left hand on his stomach and pressed down, she watched his reaction. Go ahead. Hold your breath. Her hand slid up to his chest and found his right nipple. The tips of two fingers caressed it as she moved her right hand to the top of his breast bone. The tip of her small blade touched his neck just above his throat apple. When he stared back into her eyes, she pinched his nipple with all her strength and pulled it until it slipped free. She did it again and again. And each time, Pug screamed.

Then she cut the right side seam of his shirt all the way to the sleeve, cutting its seam as well. She repeated the process on the left side of his shirt. With that done, she slit from the neck hole to the sleeves, pulled the shirt from his body, and threw it aside.

Edana crouched again between his legs to cut the knots at his hips that held his undergarment. She pulled the front piece down and let it hang between his legs. After she replaced the small blade in its holster, she reached for her big blade. Pug's eyes widened with despair as she brought it before her and laid it flat on his stomach, where it trembled.

She reached for the bowl of water and placed it at his left side. Then she set a washcloth, a piece of tallow soap, and a length of twine next to the bowl. She moved over to his left hand with the twine. "Open your hand. Make the back of your middle finger touch the spear."

Pug swallowed hard as he watched her tie his finger to the spear with two double hitches.

Edana took the washcloth, soaked it in the water, and rubbed the piece of soap on it until she had a good lather. "Your hands must be clean, Pug." She took her time to wash each finger. Then she loosened the hitches that held his middle finger, slipped them off, and then slipped them onto its neighbor. She made sure the middle finger was clean also before untying the other.

She moved over to his right side, pointed to his middle finger, and said, "Poor Pug, what happened to this one?"

He didn't answer, but his eyes spoke hatred.

She tied the finger next to it to the spear and washed his hand, making sure the stub of his middle finger received more attention than all the others.

When finished, she moved to his right foot and said, "Your feet must be clean too," before proceeding to wash it.

After finishing with his left foot, she moved between his legs. "Pug, are you getting hungry?"

Panic flooded his face. "No! Not that! No! You can't do that to me!"

"Pug, I'm surprised. You don't want me to wash you down there?"

"You know what I mean." He gritted his teeth.

"Do I? Tell me. I don't understand." She washed him. She rinsed and lathered him up again, this time using her bare hand. "You know, Pug, I think you're enjoying this." I don't remember him being that big. She reached her other hand to one of her holsters for a small blade. "It's important you don't move. You wouldn't want me to nick you, would you? Not only does this have to be clean," she gave a tug, holding it up and letting it slip from her fist, "but these as well," and she grasped them, squeezed them, and pulled them up as far as she could.

"Noooo!" He grimaced as he yelled. "Please! No!"

"And not only clean, but free of hair."

His whole body shook.

"Calm down, Pug. Your squirming is going to cause me to nick you." She scraped and shaved him with her small blade, pausing now and then to wipe the suds and cut hair onto his thigh. "Don't worry, I got most of the hair. I'll singe off the few stray ones that got away."

She gave him a final rinse and sat back on her heels. "How does that feel, Pug? Did you enjoy the attention? Your extremities are all clean, now. Almost good enough to eat. Isn't that right?"

He squeezed his eyes shut and shook his head from side to side.

Edana stood, stepped over Pug, placing a leg on each side of him so she could lower herself to straddle his stomach. "One thing left to do for you, Pug. Do you like my war paint? I bet you do. I bet it brings back memories."

He stared up at her. His eyes wide with fear.

She picked up the small blade. "I want to warn you. This will hardly hurt, if you stay completely still, because the tip of my knife will barely scratch the surface of your skin. Just enough to draw blood. You saw how sharp my blades are when I shaved you down there. Let my sharp blade do its work and it won't hurt. Struggle against the work it does and it will hurt you more than you can imagine.

"Here's your chance to be a true warrior and show how strong and brave you can be. Who knows, someday someone will ask you how you got those scars on your face and you'll be able to tell them about your great act of bravery."

Edana leaned her left forearm on Pug's chest and grasped his chin. She leaned her face closer to his and rested the tip of her knife on the side of his right eye. "Close your eyes," she whispered.

He did and swallowed hard.

She cut and pulled the tip across his eyelid, nose bridge, and other eyelid. "Don't open your eyes." He didn't, but bared his clenched teeth.

The next cut crossed from one cheek bone, over the tip of his nose, and on to the other cheek bone. The third cut went from one ear to the other, across the first half of his top lip and on across the bottom half of his lower lip. The last cut crossed from one side of his jaw to the other, across his chin.

She sat back. The droplets of blood trickled and oozed from the cuts to give them completeness. They look good. "Pug, can you taste your blood?"

As he worked his mouth to swallow, the blood on his tongue and teeth mixed with his spittle, which spilled from the corner of his mouth.

"You have a choice. You can let the blood clot on its own, or I can put something on the cuts to help stop the bleeding. Just tell me what you'd like me to do for you."

Pug strained against the rope at his neck as he blinked his eyes and licked his lips.

"Keep that up and the bleeding will only get worse. Lips bleed for a long time, you know. I know that from experience, Pug. So what'll it be? Spider webs and salve? Or do I let you bleed?"

"Salve," Pug growled.

"It doesn't make you less a warrior, Pug. You'll still have your scars to show."

After dressing Pug's cuts with spider silk and an overcoating of salve, Edana knelt again between his legs. She placed the lantern between Pug's left leg and the spear that ran along his back. He sucked air in between his teeth.

"Did you feel the heat from the lantern?" She opened the jar of brine-soaked lanyards and fished one out. "Pug, can you see what I have in my hand?"

He could.

"You have a choice again. I can use this right out of the brine or rinse the salt from it. Which would you like?"

"What are you going to do?" He blinked blood tears from the corners of his eyes.

"You'll see, just tell me your choice."

He shook his head.

"Okay then, since you don't want to choose and you are anxious to find out what I'm going to do, I'll use it straight out of the brine." She reached for and held his testicles. "Oh! I almost forgot. I have some singeing to do." She slipped the lanyard back into the jar and opened the lantern window to retrieve its candle. "You can yell if you want." He did, a good dozen times, as Edana burnt off the stray hairs from the underside of his scrotum. The short one at the side of the base of his penis brought out a wild whoop from Pug. Edana laughed. "Let me check. There might be another one like that." There was, right on the underside of his prick. "All done." She put the candle back in the lantern.

"Now, where were we? Oh! Yes. The lanyard." Again, she fished it out and took hold of his balls. "Another choice, Pug. Left or right? The one that hangs low or the one that hangs high? I truly like this one. So this one," she pulled it with all her might, "is going to be the one."

Pug screamed as Edana hauled on her choice, his right testicle.

Edana tied a double hitch above the testicle so the skin tightened around it. She tugged on the end of the lanyard. "I know you know what happens to this when it dries." She tied the other end to the spear pulling the nut just enough so it almost touched the spear. Then she moved the lantern closer to the wet lanyard. "What happens to the leather as it dries, Pug?"

"You bitch! You can't do this to me!"

"My name is Edana, Pug. And yes, I have done this to you. It's part of a promise I am keeping. I know you will be getting hungry. This," she struck his testicle with a flick of her middle finger off her thumb, "is only the first of many morsels I'll feed you, if you don't tell me what I want to know. Think about it. I'll be back later with my dragon. I promise I will do my best to keep her from you."

Later that evening after Danuka's return, Edana was back in the small cave with Pug. "No! Mother! Stop! No! You must not harm him. Please, Mother, if you harm him, I will not be able to find out what happened to your eggs." She stood inside the small cave, her back against the wall, her hands braced against the ceiling, and her legs spread wide between Pug's outstretched arms. Danuka's huge head squeezed through the cave entrance.

Her mouth snapped, and she grasped at the spear ends to which Pug's right leg was tied. She shook the cross frame and pulled it closer to the entrance. "No, Mother! Stop! Do not harm him!" Danuka's snout ran up Pug's leg to his crotch.

Pug screamed.

Danuka's lips sucked up his genitals, picking him and the spear frame off the ground.

Pug kept wailing and lost control of his bowels, spewing diarrhea down the back of his legs and onto the floor.

Edana swung out with one hand and hit Danuka on the head. "Stop! Your promise! Mother! Do not break your promise."

Danuka dropped Pug and backed her neck and head out of the cave.

Edana reached down to touch Pug's heaving chest.

His heart thumped beneath her hand. He was swinging his head from side to side with eyes closed and his mouth open in a silent scream.

"You'll be fine, Pug. She's leaving. I'm going with her. I'll be back later. You're in one piece, Pug. Try to calm down."

Trying not to breathe in the stench of his excrement, she stepped over him, crouched, and crawled out of the cave. I think he'll talk.

Danuka made her way along the lake where she paused to pick up the pouches that contained her eggs. Nagora followed and joined her at the cave entrance. "Mother, that was great. You did better than I expected. I am sure I will be able to find out what he did to your eggs. Just give me some time with him."

Danuka assumed her egg inspection position. Nagora didn't hesitate to sit on the floor between Danuka's folded wings. She sat before Danuka, turning an egg in her hands. Danuka, I wish there were a way you could display emotion other than through your actions, though I'm happy with your display of anger. You did as I asked. I'm sure it had the desired effect on Pug.

Another egg, and then another. Am I absorbing more of the essence of The Dragon's Kiss? Danuka has not finished, and already I feel the clutching between my legs. Could it be because of my single night's absence from the cave?

Her night with Lars was one of controlled passion. The essence of The Dragon's Kiss that controlled her body's desires here in the cave had not enveloped her. Instead, she was in control of her yearning for Lars. It had been a more tender and peaceful coupling.

How will I deal with my body's lust tonight? Had Raynhard too succumbed to The Dragon's Kiss? Or was it his true desire for me?

Now, what of Pug? What will happen this night? Will it be to my advantage?

Stop your questioning, Edana. You've no choice but to let it play out when and if it does.

After her meal, she left for her small cave with a blanket, a waterskin, and a bowl of the stew. Tar piss! I have to clean up his mess.

"Pug, I never thought I would have to clean up your shit for you. You're clean as a baby again. I understand how frightened you must have been. I lived through worse. I know saying that doesn't help you. To tell you the truth, I didn't think that I would be able to stop my dragon, but I did. It was the first time I ever hit her.

"You must be thirsty and hungry. I think you're cold. I brought you a blanket. Do you want me to cover you?" She threw the blanket over him. "Here, I'll give you water to wash out your mouth. Then you can drink as much as you want. After that, you'll probably feel like talking. If you prefer to eat before you talk, I'll feed you."

She brought the waterskin's spout close to Pug's mouth and poured water. When he had finished rinsing the inside of his mouth and spitting out the bloody slurry, she poured more and he swished it around before spitting again. He wanted more. She gave him more. He drank and drank again.

"Feel better?"

Pug nodded.

Edana brought a spoonful of stew to his mouth. He accepted it.

Her knees were on the blanket at his side. She waited.

"Will you untie my nut if I talk?"

"It depends on what you tell me. Tell me the truth and I'll untie it."

"You'll not believe what I tell you."

"That'll be for me to decide. I'll listen and I'll have questions. Answer them truthfully. Let me decide if I believe you. I'm the one who'll have to convince my dragon you've told the truth."

Pug swallowed. "I no longer have the eggs."

Edana waited.

Pug swallowed again, this time twisting his head in an odd way with his eyes rolling, almost as if he were listening for a sound from far away. Then he spoke. "I gave them to the one who read my fortune. She paid me in gold coins. Coins with dragons on them. I hid the coins in my cave. If you didn't find them, I'll tell you where to look. I don't know what more to tell you. Ask me what you will. If I can answer you, I will."

"Tell me about the one who read your fortune."

Again, his head cocked in the same odd way. "An old woman. Had a bag of runes in her cloak pocket."

"She didn't read the runes for free. What did you give her?"

Pug turned his face away, closed his eyes, and shook his head.

"Pug, I told you I would listen. Let me decide."

His eyeballs bulged from their sockets as he spoke. "If I tell, you'll surely want to finish what you've started on me down there. You might as well get it done with."

"There's no reason for me to do that if you tell the truth."

"It is the truth, but it's a truth that'll be my end."

"Speak it, Pug."

He took a deep breath and kept his wide-open eyes on her. "I was in the back lane behind the ale house. They sell the dregs of the mugs served inside for the smallest coin in your scrip. This old bag of bones comes along the bench asking each of us if we want our fortunes read. Why, I couldn't fathom. Shit, we barely had two coins left among us. Anyway, she says to me: 'You must have something of value in your scrip that's worth a peek into your future.'

"'Well,' I said, 'I've got this. I reached in and pulled out ... '" Pug paused and looked away.

"Go on. Tell me, Pug."

"Your braid of hair." He closed his eyes and turned his face away.

Rage grew inside her, but she fought to control it. Her ears burned. She forced her fists to unclench. She spread her fingers on her thighs and took a deep breath. There's more to come. Don't lose it now.

"She accepted my braid?"

"I swear." He looked up at Edana, his eyes almost pleading. "It was like I had taken out a handful of gold coins. Her eyes came alive. She took me by the hand and led me inside the ale house to a lone, back-corner table. She had the maid bring me the biggest mug of the best ale in the house."

"How did you feel about that, Pug?"

"I was mighty happy to get the ale. When she insisted on sitting with her back in the corner, I had a hint of something not being right. Like maybe she had a confederate who was going to come behind me to take my purse. But I didn't have a coin to my name so that passed."

"So she had you pick some runes?"

"Oh! No! Not right away. She asked me to take out the braid again. I'd tied off the cut end with a leather lace. The same knot you used on the tip. I laid it out on the table, kept hold of the cut end. She picked up the other end and said: 'First, tell me all about this braid. Tell me everything. Only the truth. If you lie, I'll know, and your future will suffer for your lies.'"

Pug licked at the cuts on his lip. "More water, please."

Edana poured from the skin. His lips bled a tiny bit in a few places. "So, did you tell her the truth?"

Pug closed his eyes. "Yes, I told her everything."

"You'll have to be more specific, Pug."

"Everything. The ambush. Pinning you to the ground. Everything. Cutting your braid."

"Did you tell her how you lost your finger?"

"Yes, that too."

"Did she want to know everything about me?"

His head craned in the same direction again, seemingly out of his control. "Yes, everything. I told her everything I know about you. Where you lived, who you lived with, your uncle, the work you did, the training we had in Cairnmase, how I lied about what you'd done to me, your banishment, the last time I ever saw you. Everything."

"Everything you know about anyone who knows me?"

"Yes, all of that."

"All of that for a mug of ale?"

"More ale and promises." His neck twisted again, cocking his ear as if to listen.

"Did she keep her promises?"

"Yes, most of them."

"Okay, let's back up. She's holding onto one end of my braid, and you're holding the other. You tell her everything you know about me and anyone who knows me. When you are finished telling her everything, does she have you pick runes?"

His bulging eyes focused on Edana as he spoke. "Yes. She pulls a leather pouch from inside her black cloak, lays it open on the table, and asks for the braid. I hand it over. She places it in a pocket inside her cloak. 'Reach in with both hands,' she says, 'and take ten runes, not one more or one less.' I does so. I keep them in my hands, waiting for her to blow on them. My hands start to burn. I can barely hold on. Finally, she blows and it's like a cold wind in winter. I let the runes slip through my fingers onto the table."

My mind is logging all this information, matching it to my past, and setting it all in a drawer I'll open later. For now I must register Pug's every word.

"Pug, describe the runes, the tile pieces. What are they made of?"

"Bone, I'd say. White, almost like cloudy ice. The rune symbols are blood red, like they were scratched deep into the bone, and the cracks were filled with blood or something the same color." Pug paused. He blinked, yet kept his focus on Edana.

Is he thinking about another detail? She waited.

"The same color as the scarf she wore in a strange way. A few turns around her neck and then down her sleeves I guess, because her hands were wrapped in it too."

Another confirming item went into Edana's drawer. She would put the pieces together later.

"What did she read?"

"You'll not believe me."

"Let me decide, Pug."

"She said it in a whisper." Pug paused and seemed to fight to control his blinking and when he did, he took a great breath. Then he added, "'Edana awaits you,' is what she said."

She stared at Pug. He held her gaze. *He's telling the truth.*

"How did you react to what she said?"

"It all came together clear as spring water. I knew at that moment you were Edana, the Dragon-Warrior Princess. I don't know why I didn't make the connection until then. And then I became terrified. Your promise. I knew you'd keep it. That's why I never returned to Cairnmase after you were banished for those hundred days. Now, look at me." A solitary tear spilled from the corner of his eye.

"Pug, why did you cut my braid and keep it?"

"You truly want to know that?"

Nagora waited.

"I'm good as dead anyway." He paused before going on. "Look, you were always so good in all the warrior skills. Always besting us. Always beating us, even two and three against you in training. We always came away bruised and hurting. You were unbeatable and a mystery to us. So alone and so different and so strong and so beautiful. It made us want you. We all wanted you. I wanted you so badly that I tried to take you. I was furious when I couldn't have you as I'd planned. I cut your braid and kept it. It was part of you, part of what made you so beautiful. If I couldn't have you, at least I felt I could have that and for once hurt you."

"And after I got even, Pug, how did you feel?"

"I felt worthless. I lied. I still wanted to hurt you because I couldn't have you."

"You had my braid."

"That's the worst part. It made me think of you constantly. I pleasured myself with it daily. It had been a part of you, and I took pleasure in possessing that part. Now I don't even have that. I'm in your hands. My life is in your hands."

Pug had an erection. It was a tent pole under the blanket. How can that be? Was it him thinking of what he did with my braid? Him being in this predicament? Or is it the essence of The Dragon's Kiss doing its work? He wants me so much. Now that I have him, perhaps he feels in some way he has me. Could that be?

"Promises. You said that she made promises to you, and she had kept most of them. What did she promise you?"

Once more, his neck contorted to point his ear and his eyes rolled before he answered. "Gold coins for each egg I bring her. The amount doubles each time I bring her an egg. And for each egg, a night of pleasure like no other I've ever known."

"Do you mean in bed with her, sexual pleasure?"

"With her, but not with her in the body she wears, but in her true body, the body it will become one day."

"I don't understand what you're telling me."

His eyes seemed to thrust at Edana from their sockets. It's as if someone else inside him is looking at me. He licked the corner of his mouth. "She transforms, changes into another, her true self. She becomes a black-haired beauty with black eyes and a body with skin white as snow. Her lips glow red. She wears only a scarf of fine, red silk that barely covers her. You wouldn't believe what she does to me and what I do to her in that state. Look what happens to me when I think of her like that."

Edana had another piece to her puzzle. She dropped it in the drawer with the others.

The blanket moved. His erection had grown bigger and was twitching. She pulled the blanket from him and stared.

"Another promise she kept. Have you ever seen anything like it?"

She hadn't. When she looked to Pug's eyes, they entranced her.

"Touch it. It's me. Can you believe it? I still can't, but it's there, connected to me."

I don't want to, but I can't resist. She reached out and put her hand around his thick pulsing shaft.

Pug's back arched as he struggled to move it back and forth in her hand.

She tried to pull her hand away but couldn't.

His eyes closed and he groaned as he came in great spurts that landed on his stomach and chest. His groans of pleasure turned to loud laughter.

Only then was she able to pull her hand away in disgust. "What's so funny?" she demanded.

Pug was slow to catch his breath and when he did, he said, "Erin! She promised you would pleasure me. Ha! Ha! You just did! Another promise she's kept!"

Hag! It has to be Hag. Tar piss! She's back! She's controlling him somehow. She's using him to get to me.

Edana slapped his tied testicle.

"Owww!"

"What does she do with the eggs, Pug?"

"That hurt!"

She raised her hand to slap again.

"I don't know! I don't know! She puts them away somewhere. Before she does, she cradles them like they were babies."

"Where is she, Pug?"

"I don't know!"

"Where do you bring the eggs?" She raised her hand to strike.

"To her place at the fortress at Yhorgal Cliffs."

"I thought there was no one at the fortress. It's locked down."

"It is. But she has a way in to her rooms."

"She brought you there? To her rooms?"

"Yes, that first time she met me and read the runes. After that, she said I was to only go on a specific day. Always a count of seven days after meeting her. And only if I had an egg or more."

"So you've only been to her place twice. If you had found another egg today and not been caught, when would you go to meet her?"

"In five days."

"So you wasted no time in getting the eggs to her."

Pug smiled. "She kept her promise."

"Is she expecting more eggs?"

"As many as I can find."

"Where did you hide the coins in your cave?"

"In the firepit. Move the ashes aside. There's a stone that covers a hole in the floor beneath. They're in a leather pouch in that hole."

"How did you learn about the cave, Pug?"

"From an old trapper, a year ago."

"Tell me about him."

"He used to trap from the valley down below up along the mountainside and in the valley below his cave."

"How did you meet him?"

"By chance. I'd come in this direction from Yhorgal hoping to hunt something big enough to butcher and smoke to have as food for the coming winter. I saw smoke and went to investigate. It was the trapper. He'd broken his ankle and hoped to attract someone to come help him. It had been three days since his accident. He'd been hobbling along on a crutch he'd cut from a branch. He'd run out of food, but still had water and he was too weak to continue on. He had me hobble together a pallet to drag him back home.

"In payment, he told me about his cave on the mountain he used as a base camp for his trapping in the fair-weather seasons. He hadn't used it in a few years because his legs weren't good for the steep climb anymore. He said it was mine, if I could get him home. I got him home. He died that winter. His woman fed me that winter. Even offered I move in with her after he died."

A flag went up in Edana's mind.

"What was his name, Pug?"

"Phersen. He told me to call him Old Man Phersen. I did. He was good to me. Gave me lots of tips about what to trap, when, and how."

This doesn't make sense! Wait! Maybe it does.

"Did he tell you the water in his cave was connected to the water in this one?"

"No. I was about to make a fire one day in the fire pit when I saw light in the water. I didn't think too much about it. I thought maybe there was a hole above letting light hit the water somehow, like the one the rope goes through for the supply basket. But when I saw light at night after my fire had died out, I knew it had to come from another source. All I needed was the courage to go in to investigate."

"Did you know you were going to find the dragon's eggs over here?"

"Only a clue that I might be led to gold."

"Explain that, Pug."

"Erin had promised that I would find gold, dragon's gold, the purist of gold, and that I'd be led to it by the light. The light in the water was the clue. If it hadn't been for her promise, I don't think I would've tried to cross underwater."

"So you were frightened."

"I was."

"When did you decide to explore?"

"There had to be light. I couldn't go in the dark. The first time, I waded in with a stick. I stuck it under the water in the direction of the light and pushed it. I let it go. When it didn't come back, I figured it had floated up to the surface on the other side. It couldn't be that far. So I went."

"But Pug, did you know you'd be looking for the dragon's eggs?"

"She'd shown me an egg. A blue egg with red veins on its surface. She told me it was a dragon's egg. That she'd give me gold for any I found."

"So when you brought her the eggs you had found, what was her reaction?"

"Erin was in awe. It was as if I had brought something unexpected, yet something she desired above all else. She pointed to the gold veins on the egg and said, 'Dragon's gold.

The purist.' And she doubled the amount she'd promised for the eggs."

"And you were pleased with your reward?"

"I never dreamed to be so rich, to be paid in gold for so little work. And then, that night of pleasure. Undreamed of. Unforgettable. She equipped me to pleasure her. You see it." Pug was erect again. "You saw it before. This is not something I can lie about. You touched it. You know it's real. Touch it again." He arched his back and thrust his cock at her.

Nagora resisted the urge, the need to satisfy the clutching, even though the essence of The Dragon's Kiss seemed to rise from her own skin and fill the confines of her small cave. She would not give Pug what he most desired of her. In her mind, she held up Edana's shield.

She reached over her shoulder and pulled her big blade from its sheath. "What if I do as promised, Pug, and remove your piece of equipment and make you swallow it? How would you feel?"

His erection died.

Edana put her blade back. "What more can you tell me about this old woman, Pug? You've called her Erin. Does she have another name?"

Pug's neck twisted as he leaned his head as if to better hear a voice. "Erin. She told me to call her that."

"Did Erin walk with a staff?"

"I'd call it a stick. Came up to her elbow in length. No more than that."

"If I were to follow you to her rooms in the fortress, where would you lead me?"

Pug's eyes were bulging once more. "Down the road to the fortress, turn right at the gate, follow the wall all the way to the cliff at the back. You'll come to a big rock at the wall, not far from the cliff. You have to go around it. When you do, you see two others, smaller. Between those two, there's a bush. The entrance is just behind the bush."

"That would be through the stone wall of the old Yhorgal Castle, not the newer timber wall?"

"Yes."

"Do her chambers have a view to the sea?"

"One does."

"Is that the chamber where she keeps the eggs?"

Pug's eyes seemed to blink out of his control for a moment until he spoke. "I gave them to her in the other room. I can't say if she keeps them there all the time. It's the last place I saw them."

"On the two times you were with her, when did you leave her?"

"At morning's first light."

"Did she ever feed you anything while you were with her?"

"No."

"Drink anything?"

"Fine mead, both times. And water. No food. We fed on each other's body."

"If I were to let you go free, would you find her to tell her about what you've been through?"

His eyes widened and he licked his lips. "I'll not lie to you. I'd go to her as soon as I could and tell her all."

Edana pulled a small knife from its holster. "You've earned the freedom of your nut. Don't move while I cut the knot. It shrunk. I might not have the choice but to nick you down there."

Pug grinned. "I might not be able to control how my piece reacts to you playing with me down there. That's the way it is since Erin gifted me with it."

"If I were you Pug, I wouldn't think of it as playing. Try to imagine the worst I could do to you. It might give you control."

Once she had cut it free, she threw the blanket over Pug. "Do you want something to drink?"

He nodded. "More water would be good." She poured from the skin and let him drink until he had his fill. All the while he kept his eyes on hers.

"Are you hungry?"

"Not for food. That kind of appetite is part of Erin's gift too." He leered at her.

Ever the pig. "Sleep well, Pug. Do I leave you with a lantern?"

His expression became remorseful. "I'd like that. Before you go, can you promise me you'll keep the mother dragon away from me?"

"I'll do my best. I'll tell her I know where to start looking for her eggs."

Edana crawled from the small cave.

Danuka placed the tip of her snout on Nagora's brand. Nagora told her where she would start looking for the eggs. Danuka replied that she would take Nagora there before sunrise. There was no more time to waste. They would go in darkness to Lars at the camp near the high meadow to get Aydan and inform Yogari. Nagora was to prepare what she needed before going to bed. She was to dress warm. It would be cold in the dark, and Danuka would fly fast.

"Your eggs, Mother! What about them? There will be no one to guard them while we are gone.

"While Pug sleeps and I sleep, you will hide them where we cannot find them. I'm to sleep in my bed? Are you sure, Mother? You do not want me to watch over Pug?" Tar piss! Is Mother going to kill him? If she is, she'll not tell me, and there's no way I can stop her. Da did say she would kill him and break her oath, even though years ago she swore not to harm any of our kind. If she does, it'll be a terrifying execution. I'll not worry about that. If it happens, it happens. I'll only be a witness to it after the fact.

Nagora prepared her scrip and clothes and weapons. She found the whistle to call Aydan and put it around her neck, next to her amulet. Mustn't forget my sheepskin hat. She placed it on top of the two sweaters and vests she would wear. She would bring a bag of leather straps to rig a harness for Aydan so she or Lars could attach him to Danuka's harness.

In bed, Nagora opened the drawer in her mind to take out and put together all the pieces of information she had gathered. Everything pointed to Hag, except for the name, Erin, she had given Pug to call her. It also pointed to Alizarine. Nagora had witnessed Hag transform into that raven-haired beauty in the vent shaft cave on the Isle of Smoke when Hag drank from what she thought was the last of the dragon eggs.

I thought Hag had died in that cave. But now that doesn't seem to be so.

So how did Hag know the eggs would be here? Who did I see at the shadow place today with Lars? If it wasn't Phersen, could it have been Hag in disguise or in another form? Hag fears me. She fears my dragon powers. If she knows of this cave, would she come here, even if she knew there was no one guarding the place? Could she free Pug? He's brought her eggs. He could bring her more. He's given her pleasure with her "true body," as Pug called it. He's an asset to her.

But not if Edana or Danuka kills him. Would that be a mistake? He could be of use. We could bring back Da or Lars to guard the cave and Pug while we go to search for the eggs.

Hag wants the death of the dragon and all her offspring. With their demise, she gains eternal life in her true youthful body. She came close to getting her wish on the Isle of Smoke. How will she even dare to attack Danuka?

Who could Hag get as an ally to help her do that? She had Queen Raganora and her mercenaries at one time. Pug? What could Pug do to help her? Is she grooming him for such a role? She needs someone more powerful than Pug to help her. Who?

Pug's words came back to her. The old woman, Erin, had read the tiles he had held in his hands: "Edana awaits you." How could I help Pug kill Danuka? This doesn't make sense. I'm missing something. It's like trying to find my way out of a maze. The maze took her back in time.

Nagora too had a teller of good adventures tell her what the future held for her. She too had held the translucent rune tiles in her hands. She too had waited for the old woman with the red silk scarf around her neck and hands to blow air, cold as winter's wind, on her burning hands before letting the tiles slip through her fingers. She too had the old woman whisper a prediction: "Child, a dragon awaits you."

My first encounter with Hag. That was after my banishment from Cairnmase. I was carrying out my sentence because of what I had done to Pug. And now he's been put on my path once again.

Why? Because I'm a Dragon Talker? Because of my powers?

Why would I ever want to harm Mother or her eggs?

If Hag fears me and can't harm me, as long as I wear my amulet, how could she plan to use me against Danuka?

The pieces clearly pointed to Hag, but not to the plan she was designing. I know what Hag wants. The question is: What will she do to get it? What had Hag done in the past?

She had promised a jealous Raganora the kingdom in exchange for the death of all the dragons in the land. She had poisoned Queen Julianna and King Bernhard, and most of the people in the land too by contaminating their well water. Hag had almost gotten what she wanted. Had it not been for Raganora holding on to the last dragon, she surely would have. She tried to get the sea to drown me. Had it not been for Raynhard, it would have.

What is Hag's plan? How will she attack? Who will she use to get to her ends? What does she have to offer?

What if she has already attacked? What if everything is going as planned for her? Has Pug told the truth or only part of the truth? Have I fallen into a trap? Am I being led into a deadly trap?

Who had caused the mysterious death of the last Dragon Talker of the Land of the Danu? What would have happened if Da hadn't come to the shores of this land and become their new Dragon Talker? Would the dragons have all been hunted?

If the Dragon Talkers are killed, what becomes of Danuka? What will she do? Danuka will be on her own to fend for herself and defend herself. No one will have the power to control her, to speak to her on behalf of the people. Raynhard's plans to rebuild his kingdom would fall apart. The people are only starting to regain hope thanks to Danuka and her promise of more dragons to come. They would lose hope again. The future of their country would look bleak again. Greed would take hold of their hearts. Danuka would be hunted for the gold in her eggs. Where would she go?

Fog has settled on this battlefield. The enemy is in motion, but I can't discern from which quarter. I can't see their weapons. And I see no issue but to stand and fight. Do I strike the first blow? At whom? At what cost? Or do I wait?

All these questions kept her awake. Danuka will wait until I sleep before moving to hide her eggs. Will sleep even come this night? She took a deep breath. What would Uncle do in this situation? What would he tell me? What advice would he give me?

What am I doing? What is my task? I'm a Dragon Talker and a warrior. My job is to protect Danuka's eggs. Am I doing that? I've failed in that duty. If Uncle were here, he would scold me.

I'm trying to think like a commander, to see the big picture. It just gets more confusing to me with all the possibilities it brings. I have no control over those events. Even if I did, it would be little. So what should I be doing? The stars know I've caused this turn of events. Or is there a greater force involved that I can't see?

"Focus on those things you can control. Prepare yourself to carry out your task to the best of your abilities. Prepare your weapons. Be ready to follow orders. If you have information you think will influence the task you are assigned to complete, speak." How many times had Uncle told her that? Many times.

Tomorrow, I will tell Danuka that I will stay here until she brings Da or Lars to replace me. Even if she has hidden her eggs, I'll not leave them or Pug unguarded. If she forces me to go, Edana will kill Pug before she leaves. That much I can control.

In the early morning darkness of the next day and by the light of a candle, after Nagora had dressed, she repainted the stripes on her face, put on her blades, and hurried off to go kill Pug. Danuka was saddled and wanted to be on her way as soon as possible.

I should have killed him after questioning him.

No light came from her small cave. Nagora pushed the lantern in ahead of her. "Tar piss!" He was gone. The spears had been broken. He had been able to untie himself. She searched the space. He had taken his belt with his knife. Only the rags of his clothes remained.

Wait! Did Mother kill him and eat him? No! There'd be blood everywhere. She could have drowned him in the lake. I didn't notice any tracks into the lake.

A chill ran through her. Could Mother have freed him? No! Why? Why would I even think she would do that?

Nagora swallowed. Her eye caught sight of part of the now-wilted bouquet of flowers she had set with her uncle's blades. She bent and held the lantern into the recessed space. "Shit! Tar piss!" Uncle's blades are gone! Why did I even leave them here? And Pug's knife? If Uncle were here, he would have my hide. I've piled on mistake after mistake. Did I not learn anything from him?

She pushed the lantern further in, rolled onto her back, and reached for the notch in the ceiling. Her pouch of gold coins was still behind the chunk of stone.

No more questions next time, Pug! You're going to die! I'll live without answers to any questions I might have. I'll cut you to pieces!

She crawled out of her cave.

On an off chance Pug might have been caught in the trap Yogari made, Nagora ran to check the valley exit. Nothing there. Her next impulse was to swim to Pug's cave. In the dark? That would be another stupid mistake. I'm such an idiot!

If he's still there, he would be waiting for me. No. He's probably on his way to Hag. He doesn't have an egg to show, but he has something else. Is Hag even where he said she was? I bet it was a lie. Tar piss! Pug! I should have killed you! Would he run to Hag in the dark? The moon's still in the sky. How far did you get, Pug? Can we track you? Maybe.

Mystery
Mâmaskâc kîkway

"But Mother, are you sure your eggs are safe? Perhaps Pug saw where you hid them. I can stay here until you bring Da back. He's not far away. Okay. You say Pug was asleep when you hid them? Good, then we will leave."

Nagora held tight on the reins as Danuka pushed off from the lip of the cave bowl. She glided down and forward on her huge spread of wings and climbed. With enough room over the trees, she pumped her wings, once, twice, and a third time, climbing and turning left up into the valley past Pug's cave. If Pug had been there, Danuka would have landed, I'm sure. Danuka continued on and upward over the ridge, then down into the high meadow valley below. Nagora guided her over the trees until she spotted the campfire. Danuka circled, and Nagora brought her down on top of the big rock behind which sat their firepit.

Nagora slid down on the back of Danuka's folded wing.

Yogari looked up at her as she clambered down the rock's side. "Nagora, what's wrong?"

Lars watched and listened as Yogari held Nagora's shoulders while she rushed through the events with Pug, the information she had gathered, and the doubts and questions she had about what she had learned.

Yogari's face filled with concern. "Hag is a powerful witch. She may fear you and me, but she's putting together ingredients to make a powerful charm to protect herself. She has your braid of hair and Dangor's blades. We can't even guess what she'll concoct to use against us to attain her ends.

"For all you know, that might not have been Pug we dealt with. What are we to believe? Did that Old Man Phersen truly exist, or did he die that winter? If that wasn't him, then who is the old man you saw yesterday?"

"Could it be Hag?" asked Lars.

Yogari shrugged.

"So what do we do, Da? Do we track Pug? Do we go to the fortress to see if her rooms truly exist there? If he's on foot, can we make it there before he does?" asked Nagora.

"Or is this a plan to lure you away from the cave?" asked Lars.

Nagora looked from Lars to her father. "If it is, we should waste no time in returning to guard the cave, even if Danuka says she hid her eggs while Pug slept. They could be found. Perhaps he was hiding and watching our cave entrance, waiting for us to leave. Da, we have to protect Mother's eggs. No matter what, we can't leave them alone. We can't take that chance. Leaving them this morning, we've already taken too big a chance."

Yogari touched her arm. "Do you think Danuka can put down at the mouth of Pug's cave?"

"It'll be a tight fit, but she'll be able to hold on with the talons of her wings."

"This is what we'll do." Yogari pointed at her. "You'll go with Lars and a dog. Lars will track Pug from there. Danuka will bring you back to our cave. Then she'll come back here for me. I'll go with her to the fortress. If we find nothing, we'll circle back in the direction Lars should come from. We'll try to spot Pug. If I meet up with Hag, I'll deal with her."

Nagora looked to Lars. "Are you good with this? I brought leather straps to make a harness for Aydan."

Lars nodded. "Both dogs will want to come. If you can get Danuka to the meadow, it'll be easier for us to get on. I'll tie them to Danuka's harness with rope."

"Let's do this, Da."

Yogari beckoned to Danuka. She sank onto the big rock and lowered her head until it was level with Yogari's. A few moments later, Danuka raised herself on the rock and spread her wings. With a push from her legs and a single pump of her wings, she soared above the trees and glided over to the meadow.

Before Nagora got on, she helped the dogs climb up onto Danuka on each side of Lars. He tied them to Danuka's harness and held on by putting an arm around each dog.

Getting the dogs off at Pug's cave was trickier. Nagora slipped off first and coaxed Danuka to reach up with a wing talon and grab onto a tree. This gave Nagora some footing so she could help the dogs down, one at a time.

Before leaving with Danuka, Nagora followed Lars into the cave. He lit the taper and led her to the firepit. The ashes had been pushed aside, as was the rock Pug had said was there. The hole was empty.

"Lars, I want to know where the cave connects to the lake on the other side."

"We'll take a good length of rope, tie a piece of firewood to each end, and push one of them under the water and over in that direction. If it doesn't come back up here, it'll have surfaced on the other side," said Lars.

Nagora went to the supply basket for the rope. Lars found a pole to which he tied a piece of kindling at one end, making a fork to push the piece of wood. He stepped into the water. Nagora handed him a piece of firewood tied to the end of the rope. Lars had it in place on the end of the pole. He pushed it under, letting the rope slide with even tension through one hand on the pole while the other continued to push. "I think I've found the hole. It's gone. It should be on the surface on the other side."

"Great. Thanks, Lars." She gave him a hug and a quick kiss.

Lars had the dogs smell around the cave and then sent them on Pug's track. Lars disappeared down the trail behind Aydan and Lyam.

"Mother, I trust you can do this. You fly so well. Whatever you do, I will hold on. I'm ready." Nagora held on with all her might. Thank the stars! Danuka had pushed away from the mountainside and shot back with such force that for a moment Nagora was upside down until Danuka spun, glided, and pumped her wings to rise above the trees, rushing through the air. Within moments, Danuka had alighted on the lip of the bowl of their cave. Once inside, Nagora climbed down.

"Mother, please go check on your eggs. I'll wait here."

When Danuka reappeared, she wasted no time leaving the cave. Good. That means the eggs are still here.

Nagora lit a lantern and headed for the cave's lake. She followed the path to where the stream emptied from the lake. From there, as she made her way back along that path, she lit all the lanterns she had hung days before.

Can I spot that floating piece of firewood? She took the long path around the other side of the lake. I thought it would be here. Tar piss! Where is it? Of course! I should search the water where light from the lanterns reflects. There it was, opposite where the first hanging lantern she had lit shone its light.

Now, to mark the spot along the path. I'll get stones from that pile near the lantern across the way. Nagora set the lantern she carried on the path and went to get three stones.

Can I see my lantern from this side of the lake? Two strides from the pile of stones, her lantern lined up with the tip of the island in the middle of the lake. Good. The spot will be easy to find.

Nagora set the stones one on top of each other on the edge of the path.

Now where would I hide the eggs if I was Danuka? She said I wouldn't find them. Let me see if I can. It'll keep me busy while I wait for someone to return.

Nagora had been around the lake three times. She had looked up to the ceiling and all along the walls. She searched along the way to the valley exit. Nothing there either. She was getting hungry so she headed to the main entrance, taking her time as she scanned along the walls and ceiling. Still nothing.

As Nagora was washing down her last mouthful of dried fruits and nuts, a shadow approached and the bell tinkled. She rose from her chair. "Mother, welcome back. Da! Lars!" The looks on their faces already told part of their story.

"Nothing, Nagora. There is no opening in the wall where he told you. Nowhere along the whole fortress wall. If there is, I'm a blind man and a cripple. I felt my way all around, poking and prodding with a staff." Yogari looked disappointed as he leaned onto the table with two clenched fists. "I think we've been played."

"And you, Lars, anything? The dogs seemed to have been on a scent," said Nagora.

He had been standing next to Yogari, nodding. "I thought so too. If it was there, it disappeared." He looked from Nagora to her father. "And guess what?"

"What?" asked Nagora.

"The small knoll where we met Old Man Phersen? The knoll is there, but there is no hole. I stuck my sword into the sod all along that side. Walked around it. Stood on it. Nothing. We can't have imagined that encounter, Nagora. By the stars! Yesterday, I even crawled into that hole to have a look. I know that's the place where we were."

Nagora sat and held her head in her hands. "Everything he told me must have been lies. But I believed him. Why?"

Lars put a hand on her shoulder. "We're just as confused as you, Nagora. There is a power at work here we cannot see."

"Hag is a powerful witch." Yogari pointed at Nagora. "You thought her dead. Now, we've seen her manifest her power. Look at us. See the state we are in. She must be pleased. We must be vigilant from here on. We'll not leave this cave unguarded," said Yogari.

"It's my fault. If I hadn't left the cave, none of this would've happened."

"Don't blame yourself, Nagora. Sooner or later, Pug would have come into the cave. You can't be in every part of the cave at once," said her father.

"But I led him here." Idiot that I am! I failed at my basic duties. Will I ever be able to make this right?

"We don't know that, Nagora. From now on, we'll be on guard." Yogari went to her. He took her hand and lifted her from her chair. He held her. "If Danuka takes us back to camp now, we can be in Cairnmase well before dark. Will you be fine, Nagora? Or do you want me to stay the night with you?"

She looked at Yogari's face as she took a step back. "I'll be fine, Da. Danuka will protect me in the night. You have affairs to see to. The Stone Stander elders will be worried if you don't show up with Raynhard."

Her father reached for her hand. "Don't worry about this, Nagora. Hag fears you and the powers you have. She has used Pug to taunt you. That's all." Da's trying to quell my fears.

"I'll inform Raynhard of the situation. Perhaps he can put his spies back to work, at least keep their ears and eyes open about something that might be of help to us."

Nagora squeezed Yogari's hand. "Tell Geirador too, please. Tell him Pug took Uncle's blades. He might be able to tell Raynhard what to look for should Pug or Hag try to do something with the metal of the blades. In his own way, he's a wizard of sorts."

Yogari nodded. "Good thinking. I'll do that too. Go give Lars a hug to remember you by and we'll be on our way."

Lars held her close. I don't want to let go of you, but I don't have a choice. "Nagora, I will learn to write. I will ask Gabe to teach me. He will send letters to Sagora. I will write to you. The messengers can surely carry two missives as well as one."

"And I will practice my writing too and write back to you. I love you, Lars."

They kissed, and then Nagora bent to tussle with the big hounds to hide her tears while she helped them get into their harnesses and then onto Danuka. As they flew away Nagora held her hand out to them until they disappeared in the sky. Then she let herself cry with her head resting on the stone wall of the cave bowl. Her crying shook her, and she fell to her knees letting the sobs bend her over as she tried to catch her breath. What have I done?

That night, after Danuka had retrieved her eggs and they had gone through the inspection ritual and she had eaten, Nagora made her way to her small cave. She crawled in and set about cleaning it up. She piled the broken spear pieces just outside the entrance, along with Pug's cut shirt and leggings.

I'll burn these tomorrow.

Then Nagora knelt on the floor, took off her sheepskin vest, laid it down before her, and unfastened her right legging from the string that held up her undergarment. She pushed the legging down to her knee. She bent, reached into the pocket of her vest, and brought out King Bernhard's hunting dagger. She placed it on her vest and contemplated it.

Raynhard had given it to her along with the sheepskin vest. They had belonged to his father. Raynhard's words echoed in her mind. "These are for you, Nagora. Reminders of your chosen duty to your king. I want you to accept them as a symbol of the trust I have in you."

Nagora pulled the dagger from its sheath. She held it by the blade as she examined the golden handle. A dragon's spread wings, body, and tail curled around the handle. The dragon's neck and head completed the handle's pommel, with the dragon's open mouth holding a crown. The workmanship was studied and so fine as to make the handle comfortable to hold.

Nagora grasped the handle in her right hand, closed her eyes, and brought the point of the blade to the side of her thigh, just below where her legging had been tied. She pressed and pulled while clenching her teeth to help her bear the pain. At the same time, she uttered an oath. "I will not fail in my duty again."

Nagora wiped the dagger's blade on the front of her thigh before putting it back in its sheath. Then she pulled up her legging and fastened it in place. She returned the dagger to its pocket. It was the first cut on her thigh. It will not be my last.

Family Secrets
Pêyakôskân Kâtamawewak

The next morning, Nagora stood on the ladder and looked out over the lip of the bowl. The mountain air was crisp. The sun patiently wiped the night's frost from the leaves whose green dresses had turned to tarnished shades of red, yellow, and orange. They were ready to dance their last dance with the wind before the coming of winter.

Of late, she had spent as much time as she could in the bowl while the sunlight was there. Maybe I'll regain some of the color I lost from that first month spent mostly in the cave.

It had been almost two months since the hunt for Hag and Pug. Nagora had her own calendar to mark the passage of those days. Since that fruitless search, she had only seen her father on brief unscheduled visits.

Once, Yogari had spent most of the daylight hours with her to set iron rings on pintles along the side walls of the cave entrance and on two lines along the ceiling. The ceiling rings converged at the back wall of the entrance chamber of the cave.

After they had hammered the pintles in place and attached the iron rings, they worked to assemble the hide curtains. Her father had made a sketch of the cave's entrance chamber to show Geirador. It looked like a sock laid on its side. The toe section was the area Nagora lived in. The heel section was where Danuka spent her nights. The bowl of the entrance went from the toe to the heel and out from the bottom of the foot. The curtains met at the top of the foot in the middle.

That way, when Danuka landed on the bowl's lip, she could fold her wings in and down as she stepped into the chamber. Then, as she turned right, she could push past the curtains to go to her side.

The curtains on Nagora's side were far enough from the firepit for Danuka to move them without danger.

Next to Yogari's sketch, Geirador had drawn the layout of the hides so she and Yogari could assemble them in the proper hanging order.

One of the hides hanging from the ceiling on Nagora's side had a flap opening at the top so the smoke from the firepit could escape. Another hanging hide had a flap near floor level to help control the draft of air to the fire.

Geirador had given each curtain a big patch of translucent pig skin hide. These patches allowed daylight to shine though so Nagora wouldn't feel she was always in the dark behind the curtains. How thoughtful of Geirador. I must thank him.

Over the past several weeks, the only time Nagora had been out of the cave was to bring in the firewood her father dropped from nets at the valley entrance. Danuka and Yogari had made almost a dozen trips flying the firewood to the entrance. Nagora stacked it all at that end of the cave. Going to get firewood each day would become one of her chores to help pass the time.

Nagora had written two letters to Lars and placed them in the missive pouch of one of the bags tied to Danuka's harness. Whoever Danuka flew to would check pouch and forward the letters to couriers, traveling to the Land of Skulls. But she had not yet received a reply. *I know it'll take time, but a reply is something I look forward to receiving.* She had also written to her mother and sister and Paruline.

A meeting date had finally been arranged, but Yogari wouldn't be there. He would guard the cave. She was to spend two days in Cairnmase with Tagnyoriva and Sagora at Geirador's. It would be her second and third nights away from the cave.

I feel just as apprehensive about meeting Mum and Sagora as I had on my way to meet them for the first time in the Land of Skulls. I know what's causing my fear. She ran her hands over her belly. She could feel it. *Is it starting to show? I want to keep it a secret for as long as I can.*

All secrets become known eventually. Secrets only exist when they aren't known. Like where Danuka hid her eggs. It was no longer a secret to Nagora. She had finally spotted where in the cave's ceiling there was a fault in the rock, creating the shelf upon which Danuka would place the pouches. That was only because one day, one pouch strap had fallen over the shelf's edge just enough to catch Nagora's eye. *At least they're well out of reach. To reach that high, she would have to make a long ladder. Something I hope I'll never have to do.*

...

A cool mist of rain fell on the morning of the planned family meeting. Nagora had dressed warmly for the early morning ride and threw her waxed woolen rain cape over her shoulders as she waited for Danuka to return with her father. To fly from Cairnmase wouldn't take long. Soon Danuka filled the entrance like a huge shadow.

Yogari slid down from Danuka's wing. He brought his arms out from his cape to give his daughter a hug. "You didn't wear your cape for nothing. I'm happy to have one to wear too. I wish we could all be together, Nagora."

"It won't be the same without you, Da."

"Another time, Nagora. I'm here to do my duty." He kissed her cheek and helped her up onto Danuka.

When her cape was snug around her and she was secure on the saddle, Nagora took hold of the reins. "Ready, Mother. Let's go."

Danuka set down at the same place as the last time she had brought Nagora to Cairnmase. In the twilight, Nagora had seen smoke rise from the chimney of Geirador's smithy. Soon he'll show up to greet me. Sure enough, he approached holding a hide over his head to fend off the rain. "Nagora, you're a welcome sight this rainy day! I'm so happy to see you." Geirador draped an arm over her shoulder and pulled her to him, sticking a damp, bearded cheek next to hers. "You must be cold. Come, we'll go wake the house and get a warm breakfast on the table for you."

"Geirador, I'm happy to be here. You're looking good. Busy as ever?"

"Aye, busy as always, but I've set aside time for you today."

"Thanks again for all you've done to help get our cave ready for winter."

"I'm just happy to help you. I have something else to help you stay warm on the coldest days. I'll show you later."

As Geirador helped Nagora remove her cape, Paruline came through the cellar door. She set a cloth-covered plate on the table and then ran to Nagora. "Nagora! I'm so glad you are here. I miss you so much."

Holding Paruline in her arms made Nagora's heart swell. She wiped a tear. "And I miss you, my first big sister."

Paruline hugged her even tighter. "Da, you're going to have a rough time of it these two days. Four women are going to be talking. You'll hardly get a word in!"

"Don't worry about me. I know how to make myself heard. I can show you right now. Want me to wake those two up there?"

"Da, we'll let Nagora do that." Paruline led her dear friend by the arm to the loft ladder. "Let's get this day rolling. Go get them out of bed."

The two days passed by quicker than Nagora had expected. Her mother and sister seemed truly happy to see her again. They spent most of the time with Paruline in the kitchen, cooking and baking. The variety of biscuits, dried fruit, nuts, and smoke-cured and salted meats would have her larder in the cave overflowing, along with the sacks of oats, barley, flour, combs of honey, and the small keg of mead they had also set aside for her. I can't believe I'm going to have all this food to take back with me.

Will I remember all the cooking tips they've given me?

When they weren't cooking, they were eating. Tagnyoriva and Sagora were also getting their fill of home-cooked food, as they were still traveling from one village to another to help the people with their water supplies. Her mother said she wanted to make sure the People of the Danu were healthy. In her words, good health started with the water you drank.

I'm an outsider, a listener, and an observer of the conversations going on about the work Mum and Sagora do and the people they meet. I wish I had more to tell them about my existence in the cave. Should I tell them about the essence of The Dragon's Kiss and how I experience it? What I feel it has done to me? It's better I keep it a secret. Would they even believe me or understand?

They too have secrets. I can sense it when they won't talk about certain things in front of me. But some of those slipped out and at those times, the tension rose as the smiles from their faces left. I've learned Sagora is intent on returning to the Land of Skulls to be with Gabe for the winter. And that she has agreed to return in the early spring as soon as the snow melts. Though, this seems to still be up for negotiation. I sense it's a running source of conflict between Mum and Sagora.

I see the fatigue on Mum's face. I know she's completely taken by her work to help the people, perhaps trying to get too much done before winter, the vulnerable season for young and old, especially if they have no access to clean water.

But something more is eating at Mum. I should've guessed it that first morning when I went up to the loft to wake them.

The possibility of what it was fell into place on the second day, in the morning after breakfast. Geirador had convinced the others to allow him to steal Nagora away to his smithy to show her something he was making for her.

"So you got this idea while working here in the forge?" asked Nagora.

"Aye. I had the idea come to me a long time ago, by way of the Little People."

I see your smile. I'm not going to challenge you on that. If anything, I'm going to get a good story or a useful tool.

He brought her over to one of his workbenches on which stood an overturned clay flower pot that rested on a metal stand. A stubby candle sat on the stand beneath the pot. "This, Nagora, is going to help keep you warm on the coldest days of winter."

"That little candle down there?"

"Ah! Ha! Thanks to what that little candle does when it burns."

"I know it gives off heat when it burns, but maybe only enough to warm my hands."

"Aye. But if you get your hands too close for too long, what happens?"

"I'll get burnt."

"Aye. And that is because your body is not equipped to hold the heat the candle produces. What holds heat and releases it slowly?"

"An iron pot or skillet taken from the fire?" she said.

Geirador pointed to the hammered head of a sizeable iron pin that protruded from the hole in the bottom of the pot. "This big pin rests on this flattened iron ring, keeping the pin from slipping through the hole. I call that flat ring a spacer." Geirador carefully inverted the pot.

Two smaller pots rested inside the outer one.

"I put six spacers on the pin between each pot. Inside the smallest pot, I loaded the pin with spacers until I came to the hole that crosses the pin. Then I slipped a wire through the hole to hold all the spacers in place on the pin."

"Okay. So the candle is going to heat the big pin."

"That's right." Geirador turned the pots over again so the rim of the biggest pot rested on the three-point metal stand. "The candle heats the pin, and the pin releases heat to warm the air in the spaces around the pots. Warmth radiates out from the pots. Come with me, I'll show you."

It was the room where the warriors had been set up together while they recuperated from their wounds. "See, here in this corner, I curtained off a space around one of the bunks. Your father slept there last night. Go see how warm it is."

Tar piss! Mum and Sagora were sleeping in separate beds in the loft. The double bed was empty. Does Da have a sleeping problem that keeps him away from Mum, or is it a greater problem, like his talk of returning to sea that's causing a strain?

Nagora pushed the curtain aside, and the warmth contained within the space enveloped her. The small space the curtain surrounded was only occupied by the bunk, a chair, and a small table; still it was warm in there. "Wow! That's the heat from one candle?"

"Aye. I don't know how many you'll need to warm up your space at the cave entrance as your father described it to me. Two of these in the small cave he told me about would be more than enough."

"Geirador, I don't know how to thank you. You've done so much for me."

"Your smile is plenty thanks. Let's hope I can pack them so the pots get to you in one piece. If any show up cracked, don't use them. They could break when heated. Pieces could get thrown."

"I'll keep that in mind when they arrive." Nagora ran her fingers over a clay pot as she looked along the workbench.

"I see you are making pulleys. They're just like the ones I saw on the Sea Wolf."

Geirador held a finger to his lips. "Not a word to Tagnya. Yogari went for a sail on the Wolf shortly after his first visit with you at the cave. He went out for three days. He's getting me to make spares of certain parts. He's itching to go to sea. If not with Tagnya, then he plans to go without her. He'd sail with his crew in pursuit of the mercenaries that sailed away with the dragon's gold after the Isle of Smoke battle."

I would love to be with Da on the Wolf. But he didn't invite me. Most likely won't. I can't impose. My duty is here.

"Geirador, does he sleep well?"

"Not much. He works himself hard to bring sleep, but he's not getting what he needs. Look at him well. You'll see he's lost weight. I'm worried. Tagnya is too. All those years waiting and hoping took a toll. Now he's free and paying the price in another way. He has to find himself again."

"I'm worried about him too. I think Mum is heartbroken to see him that way."

Geirador took her in his arms, "We all are, lass. You're about to endure a small fraction of what he went through. You watch out for yourself. I lost your uncle. I don't want to lose you. If you need help, let me know."

It was the first time she had ever seen Geirador's eyes water.

"Go look in on Storm. The sky's clearing. You'll want to go for a ride this afternoon before you leave."

"I will. Thank you again."

In those two days, Raynhard's name came up three times.

The first time was when Nagora had stayed behind with Paruline to help finish the last of the kitchen chores. Tagnya and Sagora had just headed to the corral to fetch their mounts and saddle them up. The last time Nagora had seen Raynhard with Paruline was here, outside Geirador's home. Her dear friend and the king were holding hands. Nagora seemed to have detected quiet complicity between the two. And Raynhard was definitely giving Paruline attention. Nagora remembered feeling happy for Pare.

However, after her night in the cave with her king, Nagora wondered about Paruline's relationship with Raynhard. She decided to ask. "Pare, I have a personal question to ask you."

Paruline finished wiping her hands on her apron. "Ask away. I'll do my best to answer."

"Well, it's about your relationship with Raynhard."

Her friend's eyes focused and pursed lips took the place of her smile.

"The last time I saw you two together, I thought something romantic was developing between the two of you."

With a slight nod of her head, Paruline inhaled. "So did I. But something happened that night he and I spent together here. The freed girls I had brought back from Yhorgal Fortress were asleep in the loft. With Da being in the Dragonwood, Raynhard took his bed, and I set up a cot near the fireplace." She pointed to a spot to the left of the hearth and shook her head. "Nagora, I don't know if I should even tell you this." Paruline brought her hand to her mouth, and with that gesture, the scene from months earlier flashed into Nagora's mind. Now she was seeing it in another light.

"Nagora, I am so glad to see you again." Raynhard's eyes had immediately gone to her brand and then to her eyes and back to the Tiwaz. He reached out to embrace her. His breath on her ear where it met her cheek and her neck brought back the memory of the last time he had held her, but the feeling was not the same.

"Raynhard, I'm glad to see you."

He held both her hands. "I'm a lucky king to have subjects like you and Paruline. Both of you have shown immense courage in your actions." He let go of one of her hands and took up one of Paruline's, bringing her next to Nagora. Then he bowed before them. "'My Ladies of Valor' I call you today, and I bow before you in thanks. Someday, I hope to bestow greater reward on you."

Nagora looked to Paruline and smiled. She was biting her lip again and staring at the ground.

Am I blushing too?

Geirador approached, grinning. "The man hasn't got his crown on his head yet and he's already taking his job seriously."

Dangor nudged Geirador. "Shows he's been well brought up by King Bernhard and Queen Julianna. They would be proud of him."

Geirador scratched his beard as he looked Raynhard up and down. "True. True. I'm proud of him too."

Paruline was shaking her head. "Da, you're embarrassing me."

"Sorry, my dear, for making light of the moment. It was that or cry again. I did plenty of that last night."

"Never be embarrassed by your da, Paruline. Like Dangor would say, 'He's worth his weight in horseshoes,'" said Raynhard.

Nagora shook her head and smiled as the three men bent over, laughing and pointing at each other like young boys.

Raynhard spoke first, barely getting his words out. "Sorry, Geirador, without my crown on my head, I couldn't let that one go by." Their laughter continued.

Paruline took Nagora's hand. "And they want to put him on the throne. Come."

Paruline's comments had brought on another wave of laughter and it followed her and Nagora back to the hut.

Paruline had picked up the pace and her smile left her face. "Pare, what's wrong?"

She opened her mouth as if she were about to speak and then brought a hand to her mouth. Then she took it away. "I must be tired and all these events. What happened to the girls. What happened to you and to our village here. So many things could have turned out worse. All this has finally caught up with me."

Nagora hugged her. "I know the feeling. You'll get over it."

Something had been bothering her friend that day, but she had hid it. Why? "Pare, you stopped yourself from telling me once before, right here, outside." Nagora pointed at the door. "And now that I've brought it up, I can see it's still bothering you. Perhaps if you share it, you'll feel better." She reached for Paruline's hands.

Paruline shook her head. "I don't know, Nagora. It's just so strange. It changed the way I see Raynhard, and it's made me worry about him." Her jaw locked, and she bared her teeth. "Damn it! Nagora, I've lost trust in him because of what I witnessed."

"Pare, tell me. It'll make you feel better. I'll keep it to myself."

Paruline let go of Nagora's hands, crossed her arms below her bosom, and closed her eyes. When she opened them, she looked at Nagora. "I trust you. I've told no one about this, not even Da." She swallowed and took a breath. "I was awake in my cot. I hadn't been able to fall asleep. I heard a shuffling noise and looked to see where it came from. It was Raynhard as Chive. His leg and ankle twisted out. His hair let down over his face."

Paruline uncrossed her arms and waved both hands once down the front of her body. "And he was naked. He approached the fireplace." She pointed to it. "There were hardly any flames, mostly dying embers. His eyes were shut. He seemed oblivious to my presence." She waved a hand before her face. "I realized he was walking in his sleep. He knelt before the embers and began to speak as Chive in that gibberish way that's not understandable. I couldn't make out what he was saying. A sound or part of a word I did make out was 'rin'. Everything else was slurred.

He seemed to be speaking to the flames, leaning toward them a bit whenever he paused."

Something in what Paruline said stirred in a drawer at the back of Nagora's mind. *What puzzle pieces are trying to connect?*

"Then he'd speak something more I couldn't understand. It was strange. It seemed to have a pleading tone to it."

Paruline paused and lowered her gaze. She took a breath and continued. "He was still on his knees. The last of the flames had died. He cried and let himself fall back onto his heels. He bent over and put his face in his hands. When he spoke again it was as Raynhard." Paruline paused and looked at Nagora.

"What did he say, Pare? You can tell me."

Her friend's lips twisted and trembled, like the lips of someone about to share a hurtful secret. "Nagora, I can't remember the words exactly, but enough to get a sense of who he was talking about."

"Go ahead tell me what you recall."

He said, words like ' ... always wanted her ... saved ... need her ... my country ... her strength ... make her my queen.' His hands on his face became fists, and he struck at the hearthstone and said, ' ... how ... how ... convince Nagora ... my queen ... how ... rule without her ... ,' words that referred to you, Nagora."

The events of the night in the cave with Raynhard came flooding back into Nagora's mind. At this moment, she wondered if the shame she felt was about what she'd done with Raynhard or the hurt she'd inadvertently caused her dear friend.

Paruline went on. "He stood and one hand wiped at his face. I thought he was awake, but when he leaned his ear toward the embers and laughed as Chive, I realized he was still asleep. He took no notice of me and shuffled back to his room, giggling."

Paruline reached out to Nagora and took her in her arms. "I don't blame you, little sister."

"Pare ... "

Her friend put a finger on her lips to silence her. "In a way, I'm glad I learned this from the one I thought I was falling in love with. At the time, I wondered how much credence I should put in witnessing our king's desire for you to be his queen. Nagora, Raynhard obviously has feelings for you. After all you've done for him, it only makes sense he would. You can most likely confirm what I've told you, though I won't ask you to. I know you'll tell me when the time is right. Knowing you, you're probably carrying a pain greater than mine."

Nagora held Paruline close. *Tar piss! By the stars! Pare if you only knew what he did with me. You're right. I'll not share it with you now, but at an appropriate time.* "Pare, I see why you worry about Raynhard. Now I'm worried too. And I can understand why you've lost trust in him. That is strange behavior, and it could very well be pointing to something we don't see or can't yet understand. Could he be ill? Had his taking on Chive's identity become too much for him?"

Or does Hag have control of him in some way? I dare not speak that question aloud.

Paruline pulled back to look at Nagora. "I've asked myself those same questions. And I'm sorry to say it, but I question his fitness to rule. I probably shouldn't question his ability based on a single sleepwalking incident."

"Perhaps not, Pare, but still, I think we should take it as a warning sign and keep our eyes open. Will we ever know what he lived through as Chive, Hag's idiot gatherer of herbs and mushrooms, living in Yhorgal Fortress? What you've told me will have me on the lookout for anything that might help explain that behavior. If I find something, I'll let you know. Trust me, Pare."

"I trust you, Nagora. I feel better now that I've told you. A ride on our horses will do us good. Come. Let's go before the others come for us."

Then, on two occasions, Sagora brought up Raynhard's name. The first time was on their ride back to Geirador's corral that afternoon. Nagora caught Sagora's slip, which Tagnyoriva tried to cover. They had been talking about what it was like to ride a dragon compared to a horse.

Sagora had said Raynhard hadn't been flying with Danuka as much lately, as he had found a more pleasurable riding companion in Aliza.

Her mother had been quick to add: "Aliza's father was one of the Dragon Riders Yogari had trained, and one of the twelve riders hung at the Isle of Smoke Bridge by Raganora. She's a good-looking woman, almost Raynhard's age."

"Let's race to the corral. Winner doesn't have to brush her mount." Paruline's call had come at the right time.

Nagora didn't want to comment on the woman in Raynhard's life; so she kneed Storm, and the others had followed.

In the stable, she took her time as she brushed Storm, even if she had won the race. The others had already taken their mounts back out to the corral.

Sagora came back in and watched her. "You must be lonesome in that cave, little sister."

"I am, but I have many things to help me pass the time. I'll do my duty."

"You must miss Lars."

Nagora smiled. "I do. I've written to him. I'm waiting for a reply. I know he'll want to reply himself rather than have Gabe write for him. Have you received news from Gabe?"

"Two weeks ago, I received his last missive. Nothing since. I consider myself lucky if I get news once a month."

Should I ask for news? If there was something worth sharing, Sagora would have done so by now. Nagora rested an elbow on Storm's hip. "When do you leave for the Land of Skulls?"

"Soon, within two weeks at the latest. Mum has insisted Geirador and two others escort me back to Godomor's hunting lodge and wait for the patrol to meet me. Geirador will hunt on the way back. He's hoping for a light snowfall to be able to track deer."

Nagora tapped Sagora's upper arm. "Big sister, I want you to kiss and hug Lars for me. And Aydan and Lyam too. And give Lars a jab in the stomach. Tell him not to get too fat over the winter. I heard the stories about all the eating and drinking that goes on in Skull Bay when they're snowed in."

Sagora laughed. "It's not as bad as it sounds. Don't worry, Gabe will keep him busy. Do you think Lars'll come back here?"

"He said as soon as he could be freed of his duties for a time, he would come back." Nagora reached for Sagora's hand. "Sagora, see if you can get Gabe to assign him to escort you back here in the spring. That would be great."

Sagora shrugged. "If I come back, I'll do that for sure." She sighed. "I don't know that I want to come back."

"Why is that?"

"I'll not lie to you. Being with Da and Mum is not all I thought it would be. Even for Mum. She hasn't found the man she knew all those years ago. And he's trying to find himself. We all change." She waved an arm.

"I was raised over there. As much as I like working with Mum here to help the people, I miss being a healer in Skull Bay. To be honest, I feel like I'm part of the family in that community. My loyalties are there. I don't have that same feeling of attachment here."

Sagora raised a hand. "Don't get me wrong, I've come to love and value Paruline and Geirador."

And then Nagora's twin brought up Raynhard a second time. "And I was for a time, I'll admit, quite taken by Raynhard while we were in Windhaven. To hear him talk about his vision for his country and its people was inspiring. I guess the passion he has to fulfill his father's dream makes him appear to be a dynamic leader. At least when I compare him to Gabe, who's simply a prince helping manage the affairs for Godomor and not yet that country's ruler."

Sagora crossed her arms. "No, Gabe is my man and as the days go by, I realize how much I miss him. Raynhard needs a queen from the Land of the Danu. Someone to help him inspire his people. I might look like Edana, but I'm not her."

Nagora looked into Sagora's eyes. "Are you saying I should be Raynhard's queen?"

Sagora held up her palms. "No, no. I'm sorry. I expressed myself badly." She shook her head. "What I was trying to say is that he needs someone like Edana. Nagora, I've been to many of the villages and towns here. Believe me, Edana is still being talked about. All her appearances on the unicorn, on the plain, and her battle on the Isle of Smoke Bridge, they are all legends now. Raynhard needs a queen who will embrace that, take pride in it, and build upon it.

"Mind you, if Edana were to become his queen, that would make her a truly inspiring legend. The Dragon-Warrior Princess comes to free the dragon and becomes Queen of the Land of the Danu to sit at King Raynhard's side, the rightful heir to the throne. And she's a Dragon Talker on top of that! Admit it, looked at that way, it sounds like one of those happy-ending stories. But that's not the reality of the situation, is it, little sister?"

What seed are you trying to plant in my mind, Sagora? A seed to grow with the one Raynhard planted in me?

Nagora wagged the grooming brush at Sagora. "No. The reality of the situation as it stands right now is that one of the Dragon Talkers is dedicated to guarding Danuka's eggs. She has no time to fly around the country to attend royal functions with her king. And she loves a man other than her king."

Though, I'm almost certain I bear my king's child. What would Sagora say if I spoke that out loud?

Sagora reached a hand over to Nagora's arm. "I'm sorry. I didn't want to upset you. I was just sharing my perception of the situation. I don't want you to feel in any way you should take on the role of Queen of the Land of the Danu."

"I'm not upset." Nagora dragged the brush across Storm's back several times and then stopped to face her sister. "I'm tired. My task is a burden. I have no choice. I was gifted with it. I wear the Dragon Talker's amulet. It comes with great responsibilities. I shirked them once, only once, and have paid dearly for it."

Nagora waved the brush. "None of you brought it up, so I'm bringing it up with you. I'm sure you all know about the theft. I want you to know it brought home the weight of my role in the future of the Land of the Danu. I will not falter again."

Sagora put an arm around her. "Nagora, none of us are blaming you for what happened. None of us. Do you hear me? Nothing points to you as being at fault. It could have happened while you were in the cave. Don't blame yourself. We have great admiration for what you are doing. We all wish we had the strength you have."

Nagora put her arms around Sagora. "Thank you. It's good to hear."

She let go of her sister. "I'll be with you in a moment. Soon as I finish with this big boy."

Sagora smiled.

Nagora gave Storm's mane a final pass with the brush and let him nuzzle her as she wrapped her arms around his neck. She put the brush on the shelf and led Storm to the corral. "You be a good boy. It'll be awhile before I see you again. Go!"

Nagora put an arm around Sagora's back and they walked back to the house, arm in arm, without a word.

After the evening meal, the women set about filling the big leather bags Nagora would bring back to her cave. When Danuka set down, Nagora went to get the dragon, bringing her closer to the bags that waited to be tied to her harness. These bags are heavy. I'm happy to have help to tie them on. Da will help me take them off.

It was time for good-byes. After long hugs from Tagnyoriva and Sagora, Geirador came forward. "I let you ladies have a good time of it these past two days. Before Nagora goes, I have something for her and for her sister." What could it be?

His hands were behind his back. "They actually arrived three days ago, so the delivery is late, but appropriate since I think you might want to read these in private." He held out one hand. "For Nagora." It held two letters.

"For Sagora." His other hand held a single letter.

The sisters rushed forward. Geirador raised his arms so they had to hug him and pull his arms down to get their letters.

Nagora held one in each hand. "I don't want to lose them."

"Put them in your scrip," said her mother.

She did and Paruline came to her, put her arms around her, and whispered in her ear. "When it's time, let me know. I'll be there for you."

Nagora's eyes teared up as she hugged Paruline tighter. She had shared the double bed with Paruline. The four women had talked most of the night. Paruline had caressed her belly when Nagora had said her stomach was full from supper.

Did you guess, Pare? You did. You have the healer's gift.

When Nagora let her go, she nodded and climbed up on Danuka's wing. In the saddle, she adjusted her hat before taking hold of the reins. She waved and patted the dragon. "Ready, Mother. Let's go."

Lies
Kiyâskimowewin

"Nagora, you've been crying," said Yogari when she stepped off Danuka's wing at the cave entrance.

"Just too happy with my visit. Da, you've no idea how much it means to me."

"I can imagine. If you're happy, then so am I."

"Da, the bags are loaded and heavy, and more are to come. Can you help me unload and empty them before returning?"

"Of course."

"I'll spread hides on the floor near the larders. We'll empty the bags on them. Tomorrow, I'll try to get it all sorted and stored away."

Nagora looked at the piles of food on the hides. "They've truly taken good care of me. I ate like a pig for two days. The food was so good."

"You can't go wrong at Geirador's. Paruline is one of the best cooks in the land," said Yogari.

"I know, Da, and we spent most of our time cooking with her."

I want to ask him about the Sea Wolf and how he felt when he returned to the sea to sail for the first time in so many years, but I won't. I'll let him keep his secret.

"What did you do to keep busy?" asked Nagora.

"Look at this." Yogari brought her to her side of the entrance where the curtain was attached. Between two of the pintles, he reached into the space behind and pulled out a net. "See, this end's attached to this ring." He kept pulling until he had the other end in his hand. "You hook this end to the ring on Danuka's side, and you've got a hammock. It'll be a comfortable spot to lie in the sun. And when you go behind the curtain to your side, you'll see I hammered a pintle with a ring to the wall over near your shelves. That way, you can hang the hammock there. You could use it to sleep in if you want, or just to rest."

"So that's why you left the nets from the firewood here."

"That's right. But for another reason as well. I hung a net in the water at the lake where you marked the entrance from the other cave. It might catch Pug if he comes back into the cave that way."

"Good idea."

"When Danuka comes back, the bags won't be as heavy. You can always send a message if there's anything else you need. I'm not sure when I'll be back. Surely before it snows." Yogari hugged her and climbed up onto the saddle. "You're sure you'll be fine? You don't want me to return to spend the night?"

"I'll be fine, Da."

...

While waiting for Danuka to return, Nagora pulled the two letters from her scrip. She held them to her cheek and then smelled them. Lars, I want your scent. If I read them right away, I won't be able to savor them like in daylight when my eyes can take in every detail of the script crafted by your hand. I want time to read them over and over again, to hear your voice as I read each word. I want to feel your presence as my fingers trace the words you wrote. I need time to do all of this, to cherish them. I'll wait until tomorrow.

Nagora brought the letters to her bed and laid them near where she would rest her head.

Now how might I be able to raise the leather curtain on my side for more daylight to read and work while the weather's not too cold? A good length of rope looped down and under from one side of the curtain to the other and threaded through the iron rings would allow me to lift the big curtain enough to allow light in. I'll check my supplies. I think I have one that just might be long enough.

When Danuka returned, Nagora unloaded the bags from the harness without too much difficulty. She emptied them after Danuka had inspected her eggs. Then she headed for her small cave.

Nagora crawled into the cave with a lantern. The clay pot heaters will provide plenty of warmth if I build a stick frame to hold a piece of hide, closing off the entrance. I could use the broken spear pieces.

She removed her vest and knelt for what had become her nightly ritual. Tonight she would cut twice.

Nagora let her fingertips find the place of the first cut. When they had, her eyes recorded the spot. She pulled the dagger from its sheath, found the spot between two previous scars, and placed the tip there. She straightened, took a deep breath, closed her eyes, and pulled. She sucked in more breath with her oath, "I will not fail in my duty again."

She opened her eyes, turned at the hips so the fingers of her left hand could search for the second spot. They found it between previous scars in the blood that seeped from the cut above. Again her eyes marked the spot, and she pressed the dagger's tip in place. "I will not fail in my duty again."

Nagora wiped the blood from the dagger on the inside of her thigh before pulling up her legging.

After fastening the empty bags to Danuka's harness, Nagora stepped back out of the way to let the dragon disappear in the early morning haze. While waiting for the sun to rise, she prepared to install the rope that would be used to lift the curtain.

First, she had to lash two ladders together to reach the iron rings on the ceiling.

Then she had to lash two poles to the long ladder to make it stable enough to climb.

Where the two poles crossed each other, Nagora lashed them to a high rung on the ladder. Lower on the ladder rails, she tied a rope that ran out to first one pole, then to the other, and back to the other ladder rail. She used locking hitches on the poles to keep the knots from sliding. With the rope in place, Nagora could splay the poles outward to support the ladder wherever she positioned it.

The toughest part of setting up the pull rope was moving the ladder from one side of the curtain to the other. Once she had the rope in place, it was a heavy pull for her to get the curtain up, but it was doable. She left it up.

Nagora went to her bed for the letters and brought them over to the table. She pulled out a chair and sat with both hands on the letters.

Which do I open first?

She chose the one under her right hand. She examined the folded vellum and the seal that held it closed.

A circle. Inside it, Tiwaz and Algiz. We share the Tiwaz brand on our foreheads. The branded twins. Algiz, the one that most resembles your sword is "Protection.". Lars, you chose well. What rune symbols will I choose for my seal? Tiwaz and what other? I'll think on this.

She turned the folded vellum over and let her fingers trace over the letters of her name.

You wrote with a brush, not a quill.

Nagora took a small knife from its holster and slid the blade's edge between the seal and the vellum until the seal released. She set the knife on the table and took hold of the missive with both hands. She closed her eyes, unfolded it, set it on the table, and tried to let her fingers see what was on the page before opening her eyes. No words came into her mind. I thought my fingers would feel at least one symbol. Yet for some reason, they're feeling a multifaceted story. Facets of a part of my life.

Nagora brought her fingers to the edge of the page and opened her eyes. Her eyes teared, and she swallowed as she was taken by the image before her. It was a drawing of her with her arms wrapped around Aydan's neck. Aydan was rendered in ink almost the same color as his red hair. She was drawn in black contour lines. She was smiling and Aydan too. She wiped her tears. How can an image do that to me and evoke so many memories of moments shared with Aydan and Lars?

"I never knew you could draw like this," she said aloud through her sniffles as she wiped her nose on her sleeves. How can this picture give me so much joy as I look upon it? Lars, it makes me think of you in so many ways.

This is more precious than gold. Where will I put it so I can see it often? On the wall opposite the firepit. I'll find a way to keep it open and hang it there.

Nagora set the picture aside, then took her knife and lifted the seal on the other letter.

☨

My Nagora,

I think of you each day as I practice my writing. Now I am satisfied how I write the symbols so I will write to you.

It was cold here for a few days. We had snow on the ground two days ago. It is gone now. Winter is coming.

We are almost finished rebuilding the main bridge. Godomor wants to call it Edana's Victory Bridge in honor of the Hundred Best who helped in her victory.

Gabe and Godomor send you greetings and wish you strength and courage. There is much talk of what the warriors saw in the Land of the Danu. Many people wish to see you return so they can welcome their hero.

Gabe is newly respected among the warriors here. He proved he is a commander. Gabe looks forward to Sagora's return. He plans to be on the patrol to meet her.

I was singing a song about you and Aydan looked for you everywhere. I had to go find him at Umma's place. He was waiting for you next to the door. I told Umma to send him back next time. I changed your name in the song, but think of you when I sing it.

I draw pictures of you so I can see you. I sent one to you. I hope you like it.

Until the next letter,

Lars

‡

Nagora read the letter again and again, running a finger over the symbols as she read them, seeing and hearing Lars as she read them. She folded the letter and held it to her breast.

It was many days later as Nagora was practicing her writing when a chill ran through her body. She had been writing the names of all the people she could think of. She had begun to write the names of enemies too. For some reason after writing "Erin," she wrote "Aliza".

Tar piss! This can't be. Wait. It can be. Trust your hunch. It's "Alizarine!" And then Nagora recalled what Paruline had told her of Raynhard's sleepwalking as Chive.

It has to be. It's Hag. She's been at work right under our noses. For how long? She's in her other body. Raynhard is in danger. He has to be warned. Is it too late? I'll write to him. But will he believe me? Not in a letter. I must talk to him. He has to come here. How do I get him to come here as soon as possible?

Nagora looked at the stack of vellum pages in her writing kit. She set a fresh page before her, dipped her brush in the ink, and wrote:

‡

My King Raynhard,

Your queen requests your presence tonight at the latest.

Edana

‡

When the ink was dry, Nagora folded the page. Next, she pricked the tip of a finger to draw a drop of blood, letting it fall on the page where she then poured the wax from the lit candle. As the wax clouded over, she pressed the seal she had carved onto the side of one of the handles of her throwing knives.

Nagora had chosen Tiwaz and Dagaz inside a circle. Dagaz resembled a dragon's wings in its shape, and one of its many meanings was "Disappearance." A dragon in flight had the power to become invisible.

When the imprint of the seal in the wax had hardened, she wrote, "To King Raynhard." It would leave with Danuka the next morning.

Danuka returned alone the following night. Nagora read Raynhard's reply.

‡

Edana,

I cannot come today. I will come in three days time. I

will bring important news for Danuka.

Raynhard
I hope I'm not too late.
‡

Tar piss! For all I know you are too late!

After Danuka had finished her egg inspection, Nagora questioned her. "Mother, I need to speak with you." Danuka touched the Tiwaz brand on Nagora's forehead with the tip of her snout.

"Mother, have you seen Aliza in Windhaven?"

From afar.

"So she has never ridden on you with Raynhard?"

Never.

"Is Raynhard strong?"

Yes.

"Is he looking for a place for you?"

Yes.

"If I want to make him see something from my past, is there a way for me to do that?"

Union of the amulet with his forehead and mine while we join.

"You mean ... "

Yes.

"Thank you, Mother."

If that's what it takes.

The next day, Nagora prepared her small cave. If Raynhard was to spend the night, he would spend it there with her. That way, she would be away from Danuka as she tried to convince him of the danger he was in. She swept her small cave clean and spread a few hides and sheepskins. She lit one of Geirador's clay pot heaters.

That night, Danuka came with a message from Raynhard. Danuka was to return with him the following day before mid-day and then leave before nightfall.

"Raynhard! Finally, you've come!" He stepped down from Danuka's wing and stood before Nagora with arms at his side. He's not embracing me. I wonder why.

"I'm sorry, Nagora. I couldn't come sooner. I had important things to see to and the information I bring you today is part of that." He looked around at the entrance chamber curtains. "This place has changed. Yogari told me he had helped you install these. Are you happy with them?"

His mind is elsewhere, and he's already thinking of leaving. Could that be?

"Yes, they'll help make winter bearable. It'll be upon us soon." She led him over to her side so Danuka could push past the curtain to her part of the cave.

He watched the curtain slide back into place. "True, soon enough there'll be snow here in the mountains. Yogari tells me you are prepared."

"Yes. A wooden snow shovel arrived last week. It'll be of help when the snow comes."

"It's the least we can do. Your father and Geirador have worked hard."

"As well as Pare," Nagora said.

"I hear your visit with Tagnya and Sagora was productive and joyful."

"It was, and I'm sure I owe you a measure of thanks for that."

"Here." Raynhard handed Nagora two letters. "Sagora left yesterday, later than she had planned. She wrote to you before leaving. The other is from your mother."

Nagora held one in each hand. Two more letters to add to those she would reread daily. "Thank you for bringing them. I'll read them later."

The ring on his finger seemed out of place. He's king after all. It might've belonged to his father. He can wear what he wants. Dare I ask about it?

"So Nagora, what is so urgent that you wanted me to be here the same day?"

"Raynhard, this will not be easy for me to explain. It will take time. I've cooked a stew and prepared a space for us where we'll be comfortable to talk. If you will, come with me."

Nagora led him past the leather curtain on Danuka's side. Danuka moaned.

Nagora brought along one of the two lanterns she had hung next to the passageway, leading to the lake. They took the long path around the lake. "This is where the lake opens to the cave Pug came in from. Did Da tell you about the net he placed here?"

"He did. I see."

Raynhard's not showing much interest. Had Da's explanations been enough for him? He must have greater concerns on his mind. And here I am about to ask him to crawl into my small cave.

...

"The stew smells good, and it's warm in here. We've plenty of light with these candles. You're right, Nagora. We'll be comfortable here." He leaned his back against one of the rolled up and folded hides that made a seat and backrest against the stone wall.

Nagora removed her vest and knelt before the cooking pot that rested on one of the stands meant for a clay pot heater. The candle that burned on the stand beneath the pot kept the stew warm. She filled a bowl with stew, placed a spoon in it, and handed it to Raynhard. "I have bread here." She placed a cloth-covered plate not far from Raynhard, and then she served herself.

Nagora sat back on her hide and stirred the stew in her bowl as she watched Raynhard. He had been letting the bowl warm his hands. She waited for him to taste it.

"Your stew is good." He licked his upper lip as he looked at her.

"Thank you. I feel I may have shown you disrespect in my letter. I'm not your queen and, even if I were, I have no right to give you orders. Please forgive me."

A hint of a smile touched his lips. "You are forgiven, Nagora." He sighed and set his bowl down. "The matter must be urgent for you to want to get my attention in that way. Speak frankly."

"I feel awkward about what I have to tell you, yet I think that I am justified in doing so. At least, I believe so."

"I'm listening."

You say that, yet you seem so distant. "During my visit at Geirador's, I learned of Aliza, the woman who has recently come into your life."

Raynhard tilted his head, the thumb of his ring hand caressing the amber jewel on the ring as he continued to listen. Would I describe his look as stern or concerned? It straddles the border between those two. He's not speaking, and it's making me uncomfortable. Nonetheless, I'll continue.

"Raynhard, I believe Aliza is not the person she appears to be."

His eyes closed for a brief moment. "Have you met her, Nagora?"

"No, I haven't. But ... "

"But you are ready to claim she is someone else." His voice was ice.

"Raynhard, please, hear me out. Hear why I say this."

"I'm listening." He pursed his lips and stared at her.

You're taking this as an attack. "Are you aware of all the facts of my interrogation of Pug?"

Raynhard pushed his bowl away on the floor. His eyes didn't leave hers. "He escaped, and what you learned from him were empty lies that led you nowhere. And now somehow, you are going to try to link Aliza to him."

Nagora had never seen Raynhard so angry, so impatient. Tar piss! He thinks I made up that information. Don't take his bait. Stay calm. "I'm not trying to link her to Pug, but I am trying, if you will let me, your Majesty, to link her to Hag."

His face reddened as he clenched his teeth beneath closed lips. He motioned with a hand for her to continue.

"Do you know the details of my encounter with Hag in the cave down in the vent shaft on the Isle of Smoke?"

Raynhard nodded. "I do." His thumb flicked the amber stone on his ring.

"Even if you do, let me remind you of one thing, just to make sure you can hold it in your mind for a moment. I saw Hag transform into another person, her true self, a younger self, a raven-haired beauty; and she called herself 'Alizarine.'" Nagora raised her hand and a finger. "Now hold on to that name, 'Alizarine.'

"When I questioned Pug, I asked him the name of the old woman who had read his fortune. He told me her name was 'Erin.'" Again she held up her finger. "And hold onto that name too.

"Pug also told me the old woman, Erin, transformed into another. In his words, 'She becomes a black-haired beauty with black eyes and a body with skin as white as snow. Her lips glow red. She wears a scarf of fine red silk that barely covers her.'

"That, Raynhard, is the description of who I saw Hag transform into—Alizarine."

His eyes narrowed. "Nagora, I don't see how you can link Aliza to Hag. How are you making that connection?"

Nagora took a deep breath. "On the day I wrote to you, I was practicing my writing. I was writing the names of all the friends I had made. I ended up writing the names of enemies I made too. I had written 'Erin' and then 'Aliza.' When I reread them out loud from the bottom up, my body chilled. 'Aliza' 'Erin'. I heard 'Alizarine.' That, Raynhard, is how I am making the link."

Nagora pointed at him. "I fear for your safety. Your mother and father were poisoned by Hag. You witnessed yourself what the poison did to your father. I saw what the poison was doing to King Godomor. Luckily, Mum was able to cure him and purge the poison from his body. Raynhard, I don't want you to meet the same end as your parents."

His face was red. "How can you say Aliza is Hag and possessed with the will to do such evil to me? You don't even know her. You make such an accusation based on coincidence that her name resembles part of Alizarine's. You expect me to heed your warning based on that?" He pointed at her. "To make an assumption such as you have is naive."

Nagora pointed back. "Tell me about Aliza. Describe her to me."

Raynhard took a deep breath and shook his head. "Yes, she is a raven-haired beauty. Yes, her skin is white as snow. Yes, she wears black and a scarf of red. But do you know why, Nagora?" He shook his head. "No! You don't! I'll tell you why.

"Her father died on Raganora's orders, hung from the Isle of Smoke Bridge because he was a Dragon Rider. Trained by your father, by the way. She wears black as she and her mother have done since her father's death, to mourn him. And she wears red as her mother did, until she died of grief. Like her mother, she swore an oath to wear red until justice is served on Raganora for the death of her father and the eleven other riders who died on the bridge that day. Now you know." He crossed his arms.

Nagora lowered her gaze to the bowl in her hand. She put it down and waited a moment before continuing. "Can I ask some questions about her?"

Raynhard shrugged, held both hands palm up, and looked to the ceiling. "Ask."

"Has Aliza promised you anything?"

Raynhard's face showed he was puzzled. "What? Why would she promise me anything?"

"Has she offered you anything?"

"Only her friendship and advice when I've asked for it."

"What advice did you ask for?"

"I asked her where she thought a dragon would best care for her eggs?"

I can't believe it. "Why would you ask her that?"

"Because of all she learned about dragons from her father as she grew up. He had taught her many things about their habits and ways as he learned them when being trained as a rider."

Raynhard sounds so sincere. "Is this connected to the information you want to give me?"

He almost smiled. "It is. I've been exploring possible places where Danuka would be safe to hatch her eggs."

I don't like this. "And what advice did she give you?"

He shook his head. "More of an opinion. In the past, the Isle of Smoke seemed to be the preferred place for the dragons to congregate. But with Raganora stripping the island of most of its trees, most of its caves and vent holes were filled in with the erosion of the land on its slopes. Still, I thought it might be worth exploring to see if any of those caves were still accessible. Her father had been familiar with which parts of the island those caves could be found. Aliza shared what she knows, and your father completed that information with his own."

Now all kinds of possibilities flashed through Nagora's mind. "Have you found a spot yet?"

"No. I have teams still searching the island on foot. I'm waiting for them to report. I had one team report on the possibility of demolishing the vent house and the beamed floor structure built over the original vent hole. With it gone, a dragon could fly in and out of that vent."

"Was Da part of that team?"

"He gave his opinion. He said he would never return to that cave below in the vent hole, no matter how freely he could come and go. He doubted Danuka would return there."

That's a relief. "Can you blame them?" I went down there once. That was enough.

"Not at all. Though, it's a possibility to be considered for the future, for other dragons."

"If your teams find a suitable cave, then what?"

"Your father and Danuka would have to approve of the best cave. If they approve, then she would move her eggs, and only after no one is left on the island and the rope bridge is removed. Danuka would have to feel completely secure. Your father believes if she does, she will have the instinct to care for her eggs by herself. A Dragon Talker would be needed only later on, to approach and tame the young dragons."

"So my father and me would have time to ourselves?" I could be with him, or I could be with Lars. I would have time with Storm. And Pare. Maybe visit Moreena.

"That's why I wanted to share this news with you. You might not have to spend the whole winter here. Right now, searches are slow because the locations we have are approximate and some digging is involved, along with evaluating the surrounding terrain to establish how safe the caves we discover are, or if they can be made safe. We're looking long-term to set up future safe nesting sites for the dragons. Nagora, we're doing this for you."

Nagora glared at him. "For me?" She shook her head. "No you're not! You're doing this to make Danuka comfortable. You're holding up the possibility that I might be free. That will only be so if you succeed. Until then, I stay put. No wonder Da hasn't spoken to me of this! At least he has the courtesy to wait until it's a sure thing! Perhaps if he had, I might feel hopeful."

Raynhard held up his hands. "Please, Nagora. Try to understand. We wanted to be sure we found a place before telling you. Perhaps we'll locate one within another five or six weeks. The weather is milder on the coast than here in the mountains, giving us more time to search. We didn't want to get your hopes up and then say, 'Too bad, you have to wait longer.' Now you're aware of the situation, so don't be surprised if we do have to say that to you."

I won't get my hopes up. Aliza has me more worried than hopeful. "Thank you again for thinking of Danuka. I understand what you are trying to do. As for myself, I won't get my hopes up. What does Aliza know about Danuka?"

Raynhard sighed. "She knows what most common people know about her."

"Does she know how many eggs Danuka has?"

Raynhard hesitated before answering. "Yes."

"Does she know what a dragon's egg looks like?"

"Yes."

I knew it! "Does she know the difference between an egg that has a young dragon and one that doesn't?"

"Yes."

Of course! "Does she know about me? That I'm a Dragon Talker?"

"Yes."

"Does she know me by my name, Nagora?"

"Yes."

"Does she know Tagnya is my mother and Sagora my sister?"

"Yes."

"Does she know Sagora and I are twins?"

"Yes! How many of these questions are you going to ask?"

My enemy knows more about me than I know about her! "Does she know your other identities, Chive, The Watcher?"

"No."

"I don't believe you."

Raynhard leaned forward and jabbed a finger at her. "If you know the answer, why do you ask?"

Stay calm. "I have to hear the answers from your lips."

He leaned back against the wall. "She knows about my past life. She doesn't know that you called me 'The Watcher' before you knew who I truly was."

Tar piss! She knows too much. "So she knows you were Hag's idiot gatherer of herbs, and that you saved me from drowning when I swam from the dungeon sea cave?"

He struck his knee with a fist. "Yes, damn it! What do you think two people interested in each other talk about?"

Somehow, you're in her control. "Has your interest in Aliza taken you into her bed? Or have you taken her into yours?"

Raynhard was on his knees and moving toward Nagora. "How dare you ask such a question about my private life?"

Nagora reached over to the pocket in her vest and pulled out the royal hunting dagger, still in its sheath. She held it in front of her with both hands, her right hand on its handle. "Because of my chosen duty to my king!"

He froze where he was, staring across the dagger's sheath into her eyes.

"Because I fear for the safety of Danuka's eggs. Because I fear for the future of my king and his kingdom, the Land of the Danu. Because I fear my king has let his guard down and is blind to the danger he courts. Because I love my king."

Nagora pulled the dagger free of its sheath. "Strike me in anger, and you do so in accordance with Hag's plan, though you be blind to it. Strike me and you lose the last line standing to defend your realm. You think you have won your crown back. But you are wrong, Raynhard. The battle has not yet been won. The attacker is on your doorstep, beneath your nose, in your bed, ready to kill you like she did your parents who ruled this land. Yet you are blind and do not see."

Raynhard backed down. "Nagora, have you gone mad? What is wrong with you? Are you jealous? Is this what these questions are about? I asked you. I begged you. I even ordered you to be my queen. But you refused. Now that I have a woman in my life, you make up this drama. No, Nagora, I fear you are the one without vision."

Nagora dropped the sheath, reached into the neck of her sweater for her amulet, and pulled it out. "You recognize this, Raynhard? You took it from around my neck and placed it around your own to give you strength to row me back to my beach, that night you saved me from drowning. You took it because you knew it had power, but what power exactly, you could not even guess and you still can't because even I have not finished discovering its powers."

Nagora jerked the amulet in his direction. "Hear again, Raynhard, the words you spoke to yourself aloud on the beach after you had made soup to feed me. 'Soup fit for a king and his queen. Let's go see if my queen is awake.' I did not hear you speak those words until you returned my amulet to me. When I put it back around my neck, all the images of all the actions you performed while wearing the amulet came to me in rapid succession, as well as all the words you spoke out loud."

Raynhard's jaw dropped.

"I saw you climb to take the gull eggs from the nests. I saw you fish for the flounder in the shallows. I saw you draw the heart on the gull's egg with the charred end of a stick from the firepit in the hut."

Raynhard blinked as he stared at her, open-mouthed. "You never spoke of that, Nagora. Why do you bring this up now?"

"I thought I was not myself then. I couldn't believe what I was seeing and hearing. For a while, I thought I had drowned and returned to a different world. I feared what others would think of me, so I never spoke of it until now. Now I'm still learning the power of my amulet."

Nagora paused for a moment to touch her amulet to her forehead. "With my amulet, Raynhard, I have the power to show you Alizarine as I saw her and fought her in the cave on the Isle of Smoke. With my amulet, I can bring you to that moment to see her. Then, Raynhard, you can compare her to your Aliza. If she is not one and the same, then I will be wrong, and you can move on in the knowledge that your realm is still safe."

Raynhard held up a hand and shook his head. "Why should I believe all this? You weren't under the curragh when I returned with the soup. You could've followed me, watched me do all those things, heard me speak those words."

"Ask yourself why would I have done so. Why wait until today to tell you? The truth, if you will believe it, is that I awoke under the curragh and feared for my life still. I had no idea it was you who had brought me there. I was weak. I wanted to flee, but didn't have the strength to stand. When I saw the other overturned curragh nearby, I propped up the one I was under and rolled over to the other, propped it up, and rolled under it. I lost consciousness again from that effort. When I awoke, the smell of the soup you had left under the first curragh brought me back to it. Why you hadn't looked for me under that curragh, I don't know. And why you left the soup, I can only guess."

He held a finger to his head. "In my mind, you were hiding somewhere, watching me like you did so many times before when I came to watch you on your beach. I figured if I left the beach, you would come back to the curragh. How many times in the past had you fooled The Watcher you had never met? I felt you had fooled me again."

"And you think I'm trying to fool you today?"

"I think you're motivated by jealousy and reasoning based on coincidence."

Nagora put the dagger back in its sheath and pulled her sweater over her head to show her naked torso. She ran her hands over her belly. "I carry no jealousy of your woman, Raynhard. It is my duty that pushes me to question who your woman truly is." She held up her amulet again. "If you are so sure of Aliza, then why not eliminate all doubt, if only to satisfy me so I may better carry out my duty?"

Raynhard stared at her belly.

I can guess what you're thinking.

"Who is the father?" His eyes remained on her belly.

"So now you ask a question about my private life." She undid the strings that held up her underpants and let them fall. "I will answer you Raynhard if you join with me, so I can show you Alizarine. You will then tell me who Aliza truly is, and then I will tell you who the father is."

He looked up at her. "I have no desire to join with you, Nagora."

"Raynhard, let me take care of that. It won't be long. Then we'll both know. Come. Lay down here."

Raynhard submitted to her mouth and when he was ready, Nagora straddled him and guided him in. Then she leaned over him and brought her amulet to his forehead. She looked in his eyes as she focused on the memory of her encounter with Hag in the cave. When it was clear in her mind, she closed her eyes and brought her forehead down onto her amulet to let the scene play out for Raynhard.

"No," said Raynhard as the scene ended and he went soft and slipped from her. "No, that is not Aliza."

Aliza controls you. I don't know how. Like she controls Pug? The witch has that power. A lie for a lie. "Lars is the father."

Back at the main cave entrance, the silence that had settled between Nagora and Raynhard was palpable. Whose lie is more painful? Which will have greater consequence?

Unless you've been blinded by Alizarine, I hope that now you are forewarned and will act accordingly. You cannot say you weren't warned. I can't protect you from this cave. May your kingdom survive.

Danuka rose from her side of the cave and pushed past the curtain of hides to the bowl's entrance.

Just before Raynhard climbed onto Danuka to leave, Nagora reached out to hold his arm. His eyes on her hand spoke the words he did not say: How dare you touch me? She let go of his arm. "Please, Raynhard, if you can, I would like my condition to be kept secret. I don't want Mum and Da to worry about me. And I want Lars to hear about it from my lips."

Raynhard nodded. He climbed onto the saddle and patted Danuka.

She spread her wings and pushed off the cave's lip.

Will I ever see my king again?

Nagora went to retrieve the letters Raynhard had brought her. She sat cross-legged on the floor in the daylight of the cave entrance to read them. Sagora's brief letter promised she would write in the winter to send her news from the Land of Skulls. Her mother's letter gave her a message of encouragement, news of what they were preparing to send her, and a wish she might get permission to visit her daughter at the cave. That won't happen, Mum. You're too busy.

Nagora put the letters away. She would read them again and think on the words she read and on the words not written, but that were hiding behind those on the page. It was the mystery of unwritten and unspoken words. From her experience, those words held the seeds of trouble or uncertainty or heartbreak.

Winter held the mountain in its embrace, and when the wind changed direction and blew past the cave entrance, it warned snow would soon be on its way. The hide curtains kept snow out of Nagora's and Danuka's sides of the cave, but the cave bowl entrance where her dragon landed filled with snow. It meant Nagora had to spend much time with the shovel, heaving snow up and over the bowl's lip and through the crack, when light and dry and fluffy enough. Her belly was growing, and it forced her to take her time with the shoveling task.

Storms and cold, windy days meant Danuka would stay in the cave, curled around her eggs, moving only to be fed.

In the late days of fall, Danuka had brought sizable pieces of smoked meat wrapped in sheepskins. Nagora had stacked the meat like firewood at the cold valley entrance of the cave.

Nagora had disengaged the trap at the valley entrance since the first snowfalls had stayed, blocking the exit.

The stream had frozen over there, and icy fingers stretched along its shores toward the lake. Will they reach the lake? She had fashioned a sled to drag pieces of the meat to feed Danuka. Nagora could have let her feed at the other end, but Danuka preferred the meat to be warmed over the coals of the fire. If I told people a Dragon Talker is also a nursemaid to her dragon, they wouldn't believe me. It meant making a bigger evening fire, but Nagora didn't mind the extra heat.

The piece of firewood that floated on the edge of the lakeshore, marking the underwater access to Pug's cave, was frozen in a sheet of ice which had spread out into the lake almost touching the island. Nagora kept her eye on the progress of the ice. For now, it had stopped its spread.

Will the depth of the lake rise or fall? For now, it too was constant.

There must be a trickle under the ice and snow in the stream outside still letting the water flow.

On cold, clear days, Nagora would climb the ladder and look out over the lip of the bowl. She could often detect miniscule dots of movement in and around Yhorgal on the white background of snow.

I wonder what Pug and Aliza are up to.

What are you doing to my king, Aliza? Have you started to poison him?

Have you spent all your gold, Pug? Do you have any left? Will you come again? If you dare, I am ready for you.

Are you still blind, my king? Or did I succeed in opening your eyes?

Spring will bring answers to my questions. I fear those answers. Thinking of the possibilities darkens my days. They usually start in brightness. Best I occupy my hands to banish those dark thoughts.

Nagora continued with her daily exercise routine, even if her growing belly interfered with some of her movements. To it, she added time each day to work on leather garments. She planned new leggings, shirts, and slippers for herself. Belts, knife sheaths, and scrips were her choice as gifts to make to thank all those who'd helped her.

Nagora always had a piece of knitting to work on to change the pace from writing, reading, and working on her leather projects. Knitting let her mind work out problems she encountered in her leather projects, and come up with things she could write about to Lars, Sagora, her parents, and Paruline. Each one she wrote to had their own challenges, Lars being the easiest, and her mother, the hardest.

How many times have I thought of writing to you, Raynhard? Too many. I'll not write until you write to me first. I don't want to give any information to Aliza through you.

That was what tempered her letters to her father and mother.

I trust what I write to Pare as she will not share in specific detail. I trust her and Sagora.

That old issue of trust still haunted her. Her uncle's words would surface: "Don't trust anyone but yourself." How many times have I mulled over those words? How were they to be taken, to be interpreted, and in what context? They applied in some cases but not in others. I've had to fight to learn to trust in others and to gain their trust. Some gave it without question. Others always called it into question. I've counted on my fingers those whose word I can trust. The fingers of one hand count them all. When I think about that, it makes me uneasy.

Who does Lone Wolf trust? Who trusts Lone Wolf?

My answer to those two questions gives me a list of those worthy of trust.

Each night, Nagora drew a bucket of water from the lake and brought it to her small cave to bathe. The hide over the entrance and the two clay pot heaters make me feel like I'm on my beach again on a warm summer day, soaking up the sun's warmth after a swim in the bay's cool water. Thank you, Geirador.

Being naked as she washed her body had become the most enjoyable moment of her day. The clutching feeling had changed. It was no longer caused by the essence of The Dragon's Kiss, but radiated from her.

Washing her body was sensual and enjoyable and energizing. What used to be uncontrollable desire for sexual release had become a warm, radiating energy that spread up from her loins into her growing belly in rhythmic waves, making her want to rock back and forth as she knelt with her buttocks, resting on her heels before the bucket of cold lake water. It was her time to marvel at the changes in her body.

Caressing her belly with her hands and forearms delighted her. Do I have that look of serenity I've often seen in women bearing a child? They always looked so beautiful. I feel at peace, and at the same time, I feel powerful. An infant is growing inside me. "Magical" is the only word I can think of to describe what's happening to me. "Mystery" is the word that comes to mind when I think of the birth of the infant I carry.

A boy or a girl? What will it be? What would my king desire? Surely, a male heir. Can I grant him that? No, I do not have that power. At least I am not aware that I have it. Just as well some things remain a mystery.

But the mystery she carried, cloaked in a lie, filled her heart with pain and only the pain of her nightly ritual cut helped soothe that pain.

"I will not fail in my duty again."

Lure
Mîcimihkahcikan

The worst of winter's cold had abated for the past ten days, or at least been lulled into sleep by the sun, the same sun in which Nagora had taken to basking in her hammock spread across the bowl. She kept her boots, hat, and winter clothes on just the same, but her hands were bare and warm as she shuffled the pages of the letters that had arrived in a bundle a few days earlier. Reading them once again provided her with the company she had been longing to have.

Paruline had verified Nagora's calculations as to when the baby would arrive. Based on a series of questions Nagora had answered, Paruline confidently estimated the time of birth close to the time her friend had calculated.

From what Nagora gathered from the missives of Sagora and Lars, they would arrive before she gave birth.

Who do I want to be with me at the birth? Pare or Sagora? Or do I want to be alone? Pare advises I not be alone. So many things could go wrong. Yet all could go well. Though it would be easier to predict if I'd had a child already.

Do I want Lars to know that I'm to give birth? And what about Sagora? Has Pare told her? She doesn't say so in her letter. I trust she will keep my secret. Though, I have yet to tell her who the father is. I will in time, depending on how my plan unfolds.

Then she came to the drawing of Godomor sitting by his fire.

Lars, if only you knew the memories of my talk with Godomor that day and the story he shared with me. I'll have to tell you someday.

Nagora could hear Godomor speak her name to her, "*Ka Peyakot Mahihkan*," from the page. She wiped the tear it brought as she said his name, "*Ohtawimaw*."

Father, Lone Wolf carries a child. May my child have your wisdom. I fear for its destiny, Father. I fear my child will be born and set on a path like mine. A path I have had no choice in.

Next was the picture of Lars standing between his two beloved hounds, Aydan and Lyam. His hand was outstretched and reached off the page to her. He was smiling like he did when he had looked in her eyes, just as he was in this picture. Oh Lars, to be lost in your eyes away from this cave so I can take your hand and walk by your side. The wind was blowing in his hair. The handle with the crossguard of his great sword peeked over his shoulder. This time, Nagora's eye caught Skull Rock in the background, at the sea entrance to Skull Bay. It was as she had seen it that time he had held her by his side, protecting her from the cool wind that first day they had met.

He's calling me back to him. He wants to hold me close to him, to protect me.

Nagora set the letters on her belly and reached her hand out to Lars. Her sobs shook her in her hammock, and the letters fell to the rock floor.

Yogari and Danuka showed up unexpectedly early that afternoon. Nagora was at her table working on a leather belt, carving out the fine interlaced knot pattern with a shallow v-gouge. She had raised the leather curtain on her side to take advantage of the daylight. It was cold. She wore her hat and a sheepskin coat over two sweaters.

"Da!" Will he see my belly? Will he even notice with what I'm wearing? "I'm so happy to see you! This is so unexpected."

"Nagora, I've come to make a delivery." After stepping onto Danuka's wing, Yogari unfastened one of the bags and brought it down with him. He reached across it and kissed her cheeks. "And I have news for you."

Nagora held onto his arm. "What is it, Da?"

He patted her hand. "It can wait. Here, let's get this bag open. Paruline has been baking for you."

Nagora removed her tools and belt from the table to make way for the contents of the bag.

Yogari pulled out a fresh loaf of bread and two cakes. "She said you'd be happy to have cheese. Here you go. Goat's cheese. And this." He set the waxed cloth-wrapped parcel on the table next to the cheese. "Open it."

"Honeycomb! I've been dreaming of this! With the cheese and the bread. Oh! My! I'll eat only that until there's no more."

He smiled at her. "Paruline said you'd say something like that."

"What news do you bring?"

"Well, besides the greetings and good wishes everyone sends you, I want to inform you of what's coming."

It can't be bad. He's not showing signs of concern. "What's coming? I know spring is coming. What else?"

"Danuka is going to start laying eggs soon, and in quantity. They will be the blue eggs with the red veins."

Wow! "The ones without babies inside? The ones young dragons will feed on?"

"That's right, Nagora."

"Does that mean you have found a place for her to hatch her eggs?"

He scratched his forehead. "Yes and no. We've found a place with good potential."

Where? "On the Isle of Smoke?"

"Aye. But we're waiting for the spring melt of the snow higher up to see what will happen. That, and what the rain brings. We need to see if there'll be runoff and mud and debris sliding down the mountain."

Is that hope I'm feeling? "Was the entrance clear when you found it?"

"It was partially. We've left it that way for the time being. We put markers all around it to see how they fare after the runoff. If the situation in the cave isn't made worse, we'll plant larch and other shrubs along that slope above, around, and below the cave. So by early summer, if all looks well, it could mean a move for Danuka."

By early summer, that would mean ... "And what about the inside of the cave?"

"It's big. Not as big as the network you have here, but plenty big. And it shows signs of dragons having used it in the past. There's a dry basin in the back."

"A dry basin? For?"

He held up a hand. "That's the other thing I have to tell you about. In that cave, the basin would be filled with water by a dragon occupying it before the time of the shedding."

Shedding? "What's the time of the shedding?"

"It's important you know about it, Nagora. It's the time when a dragon sheds its skin to grow into a new skin because, well, because it's growing, getting bigger."

"Are you telling me Danuka will be shedding?"

"Aye. She'll shed her whole skin, in one piece."

Is that possible? "Truly? In one single piece?"

"I know, Nagora. It doesn't seem possible, does it?"

How? "So she'll need water?"

He nodded. "True, and that makes this cave ideal with its lake. Plenty of water to make her shedding easier."

I'm going to see that? "So you've seen her shed before?"

"Oh! Yes! Many times."

"How did you get water for Danuka on the Isle of Smoke?"

"I had to beg to have some sent down in sufficient quantity to help her. With all the water in the lake, you won't have to worry about helping her. Danuka will be able to shed on her own."

On her own? "What happens when she sheds?"

"You've seen what looks like a seam that goes from her belly back to the base of her tail?"

Can't miss it. "Yes, whenever I'm here to see her land on the lip of the bowl, it's visible."

"Well, the shedding starts with that seam splitting open. When it does, she'll go into the water to let the water in under her old skin. She'll come out and roll around or rub against the cave walls, return to the water to let more in. She might even roll over in the water many times to work more of it in between the new and the old skins."

If Da weren't telling me this, I would never imagine Mother doing that. "Is it painful for her?"

Yogari shook his head. "It won't be with so much water available to her. But it will tire her immensely, and she will be in a weak and vulnerable state for at least three days afterward, and she'll be hungry. If Danuka has enough to eat, she'll quickly regain her strength. And you'll be surprised how much bigger she'll have grown."

She's going to get bigger? "So with the water between skins, how does she get out of the old skin since she is so much bigger? The old skin must be tight over her new skin?"

"Like your skin, hers too can stretch. The water helps it stretch. So when she feels it has stretched enough, she backs out of the old skin from its open belly seam. It's a long and slow process. Danuka will work more water in between the skin. Her belly, back legs, and tail come out first. Her tail will go to work pushing and pulling at the skin along her neck and at her head. When she works on her front legs, you'll know they'll come out soon. And when they do, she pulls her neck and head out."

I can't wait to see that. "What about Danuka's wings? That must be difficult?"

Yogari smiled. "Surprisingly, no. At least it doesn't seem to be. She'll flap them gently a few times and then just shrug her new wings free.

"Finally, Danuka will reach back with her mouth and gently grasp the old skin on her back and lift the whole thing off in one big piece, almost like she's lifting a translucent shadow of herself."

Wow! I'll believe it when I see it. "It must be amazing to see happen."

"It truly is, Nagora."

Nagora put a hand on her belly. "So when will Danuka's shedding take place?"

"Like I said, she's going to be laying eggs in quantity, more than she'll need to feed her young. When the laying stops, ten to fifteen days later the shedding starts. It can last up to three days, though with the water she has here, a whole day at the most I would say. So I'm guessing, in eight to nine weeks from now. Spring will be here and the leaves coming to the trees."

Oof! A week or two after I give birth. I should be fine. And I'll have a baby to care for too. "So the most important thing for me to do then is to make sure she'll have plenty to eat after her shedding?" I should be able to do that.

"That's right. Do you think you'll have enough to feed her? That's the other reason I've come."

"Come, Da, we'll go check her food supply right now."

On their return to the entrance they went around the long lake path. "See, Da, where you set the fishing net. The ice has receded by half. During the coldest days it almost reached the island."

Yogari took her hand. "You must be happy. It's a sign the weather is warming. We might have an early spring. I doubt we'll see many awful cold days from now on. We may yet have a good snow storm or two. Danuka will spend fewer days at the cave, so we'll be feeding her. From what I've seen, you'll have plenty of food left for Danuka. Keep the smoked and salted pieces for her shedding time in the spring. It'll be warmer in here by then."

Better for my baby and me. "What should I do with the eggs she lays?"

"You can eat some if you want to."

Whoa! "Truly? I could?"

"Sure. Cook one like you would any other egg. Mind you, it's a damn big egg. Boil it. Cut it into pieces. You'll have enough for a few days. Or you could mix one in with a stew to make it nice and thick. Stir it until it's all cooked and mixed in. They were a welcome part of my food fare in the cave. Even Danuka liked to eat a cooked one now and then."

Back at the cave entrance, Nagora had more questions.

"Do the shells break easily?"

"Compared to the other kind, they do. They're resistant to breaking, but have a soft spot on their big end. It allows young dragons to break them open easily. The eggs with babies don't have that, from what I've learned. I've never tried to break one of those."

That makes sense. "Okay, should I put those eggs some-where special? Do I have to hide them? Will Danuka want to inspect them?"

"No, you won't have to hide them and she won't want to examine them. Let her pick her spot to lay them. She'll nudge them all together with her snout. Don't be surprised if they end up in a pile. They'll be fine."

"Da, you told me Danuka had mated before her capture, and years later she released the seed from its receptacle inside her to create the eggs with dragon young because there was a time limit to how long she could hold the seed inside her."

"That's right. I did."

"So do you know what the time limits are for both types of eggs?"

"From what I've learned, Nagora, the limit for both is twenty years. It's a lucky thing that is so. The twenty year limit has helped dragons survive over the centuries. Right now, we're in an extreme situation, with Danuka being the last of her kind. Lucky for us, she coupled before captivity and has been able to survive to lay the eggs of future dragons. Let's hope there's a male dragon among those eggs. If not, these hatchlings will be the last of their kind unless a male dragon can be found somewhere else."

"What are the chances there'll be a male?"

"It's a one-in-two chance, usually, from what I've learned. Though, some dragons have had no males among their hatchlings. A rare occurrence. But it happens."

"Let's hope the chances are on Danuka's side."

"Yes, Nagora, let's hope for that. May the stars let the chances be on her side."

Nagora looked skyward out of the cave entrance. "May the stars let the chances be on Danuka's side." To that prayer, another silent one: May the stars let chance be on my side for a healthy baby. Uncle, watch over us.

"Da, if I had known you were coming, I would've wrapped these. I've made something for you." Nagora went to the shelf where she had placed her finished pieces. She handed one to her father.

"Nagora, this is beautiful." He held up the lamb leather hooded shirt, cut and sewn together so it would slip over his head. The back panel was longer and curved up at the sides to meet the front panel. He hugged her.

She returned to the shelf for the next gift. "This is for Mum." It was a scrip with a fold-over flap on which she had scored an intricate dragon with its wings spread as if about to take flight. Her father's mouth hung open as he examined it.

"I made one for Sagora and one for Pare too. Sagora's is black. Pare's is the rusty red one." She set them on the table.

"Nagora, they will be amazed. You work so well."

"And this is for Geirador." She took it from the hook on which it hung.

"Nagora! How thoughtful! It's about time he gets a new smithy's apron. Why he hasn't taken the time to make himself one is beyond me. This one is stout and heavy. His old one is in shreds and holed in too many places. He'll be a happy man."

She pointed. "Do you think he'll like the pocket on the chest? I noticed he often looked for his small marking files. I figured the slotted pocket would keep them at hand for him."

Yogari was smiling. "Oh, he'll like it for sure and ask why he's gone without one all these years."

"These are but small thank-yous I owe to all of you for your help. Hug them all for me. Tell them I miss them."

As Yogari went to pack them into the leather bag, he found something that had remained at the bottom of the bag. "Oh! There it is. I thought there was something missing. Here. Guess what's in this?"

Nagora took it and brought the wax-sealed edge of the cover of the jar to her nose. "No! Pickled herring!"

"They went ice fishing in the bay. Paruline swore if they caught something, she would pickle some for you. When you're done with this one, send a note with the empty jar. She'll send back a full one. She has many more."

Nagora hugged her father a last time before he climbed into the saddle. She waved him away. Da's not blind. He must've noticed my belly, even with my coat and sweaters on. Did Pare tell him? If she did, she held him to secrecy and reassured him. Or, Danuka told him. Would she have reassured him? She'll not tell me. Perhaps that's why Da came to inform me of Danuka's laying and shedding. We're both to be mothers. And even if Da noticed today, he would most likely want me to announce it.

I know what my evening meal will be today. I'm so happy with Da's surprise visit. To be with him, and to learn about Danuka laying eggs and then shedding. I can't wait to see that. This must be one of the Dragon Talker's privileges.

And there'll be the birth of my child. My king's child.

It was almost a month later while walking along the cave lake that a wet net flew over Nagora's head and covered her face. She was violently pulled into the lake. As she sank underwater, she fought to keep calm. So Pug's come back. I didn't expect this surprise. Stand. Your head will be above water.

Nagora stood. "Pug!" She gasped for air as her feet found the bottom and she moved toward shore. "I've been expecting you. What's taken you so long?"

"Thought you'd catch a big fish, did you? Look who's in the water now." Pug brandished her uncle's skystone blade before him.

"My da set that net to stop you from coming in here from your cave. I knew it wouldn't be enough to keep you away." Nagora climbed out of the lake, up the bank, and onto the path. She pulled the net from around her head and kept her eyes on him. "Pug, you can't believe how much I've wanted you. You've been in my dreams every night. Only you can deliver me from a fate I have no desire to live. Let me put my blades down."

He pointed the big blade at her neck. "Easy as you undo that."

Nagora slipped the straps from her shoulders and let her blades slip down. She transferred the sheath to her left hand and set it next to her feet. "I'm going to remove my vest." I want him to better see my belly. "You have to help me. Please, Pug, you're the only one who can." She raised the edge of her wet sweater up over her swollen belly. "Please. You have to help me get rid of this." Her left hand caressed her belly and her right hand pulled her sweater higher to show her breast.

Pug lowered the blade. "What do you want me to do? I had nothing to do with that." He pointed to her belly.

"Oh! No. If it was yours, I would keep it. It's the king's bastard child. He raped me, Pug. He did this to me. You can help me be rid of it so it looks like a natural death. Please, Pug, say you will." She reached a hand out to him.

He stared at her hand as it came to rest on his chest. She kept her touch light and locked her eyes onto his.

"I don't know how to do that for you."

"Your mistress does. I know Erin does. She has the poison to do that. I know she does. She used it on three occasions on the unborn infants my mum carried many years ago. I have no wish to be the mother of the king's child." She moved her hand up so it touched the skin at the opening of his shirt. "Pug, please, you can get that poison for me."

"For someone who wanted to off my balls and feed them to me, you've changed your song. What trickery are you up to?"

"Does this look like trickery?" She reached for his free hand and placed it under her sweater on her belly and held it there. "If I could, I would cut it from me. Believe me, Pug. My intentions were to do to you as you say; but when I saw the magnificence of your cock and felt its power, I wanted it inside me. How I resisted when I had the chance, I don't know. I'm sure every other woman who's had the pleasure to lay her eyes upon it and hold it did not deny herself. Is that not so, Pug?" She moved his hand to her breast.

Pug smiled. "Dragon Warrior Princess, I came here with revenge on my mind, for this," he brought the blade up and held the handle before her face so the stub of his middle finger touched the tip of her nose, "and these." With his thumb, he pointed to the slim pink scars that ran across his face.

Nagora pushed his hand aside with her nose so she could look into his eyes. "Go ahead, Pug. Take that blade and cut my breast off. It's sharp enough to do that. You'll have a prize you can turn into a scrip to carry your coins. What a brave heroic tale of revenge you'll be able to tell those who buy you a mug of ale to hear it. But you won't do that today because you know I need you, and you need me. I know you've come for more eggs. Erin needs them, doesn't she?"

Pug lowered his blade and let go of her breast. "Aye, I've come for the eggs."

Nagora reached to her hair with both hands and leaned her head sideways to wring water from it. "Erin is desperate, and I'm desperate, Pug. How desperate is Aliza, Pug?"

"She needs the eggs. Badly. I'm not to return without an egg."

In her mind, Nagora smiled. You do know Aliza. Erin and Aliza, one and the same—Alizarine!

"Listen to what I'm going to tell you, Pug. And believe me when I tell you this. There are no eggs here in the cave."

Pug grabbed the neck of her sweater. "What do you mean, there are no eggs? There have to be!"

"Easy, Pug. There are eggs, but not the kind you are looking for. I'll show them to you."

He let go of her sweater.

"You can take some of them to Aliza if you want to. They might be able to help her until I can find out where the eggs of the dragon young are."

He grabbed her sweater again. "Explain, and it better be good."

"Pug, I'm not lying to you. Believe me. I've searched every crevice of this cave. We can search again together. Since you stole those eggs, the dragon has hidden the others. I don't know where. Since I've looked everywhere in here, I suspect somewhere outside the cave."

"So how are you going to find them?" He let go of her sweater.

"Follow me, Pug. I'll show you."

...

Nagora led the way toward the valley entrance of the cave. "I don't know about you, but I'm starting to get cold. After I show you this, I want to go change into some dry clothes. I can give you a blanket."

"Get on with it. Show me."

"Can I take that lantern or do you want to bring it, Pug?" She took it.

"Look." She pointed to the mound of blue eggs with red veins leaning against the wall opposite the stream that flowed from the lake. She held the lantern closer to them.

"Shit! There must be a hundred of them," said Pug.

"If you want, you can look through them to see if the others are hidden among them. Or I can move them for you."

"Why so many?"

"To feed the dragon young, Pug. It's their first food. It makes them strong and gives them a healthy start in life. Would you like to eat one? I can cook it for you."

Pug made a face.

"I've eaten one. They taste good. You've seen what they do to Erin when she eats one. Maybe that's how she was able to take that cock of yours for her satisfaction.

"Pug, I've just had a thought. These eggs are fresh. I know Erin has some like this, but they are probably much older and no longer fresh. These could be more potent. Not like the ones with dragon young, but still worth a try. Bring her as many as you can carry."

He jabbed a finger at her. "That doesn't tell me how you're going to find the other eggs. How're you going to do that?" He lifted the blade before her face.

"You don't have to keep waving that blade about. I'm not going anywhere in my condition. I'm not armed. I won't attack you."

He lowered his blade.

"This is the situation. The dragon is laying all these eggs to feed her young. As you can see, lots of them. She doesn't inspect them or even count them. But her eggs with the dragon babies are another thing. Those she counts and checks every night."

He waved his hand. "Come on! Get to it!"

"When she's done laying eggs, she's going to shed her skin."

"Stop!" His eyes narrowed. "Do you mean like a snake?"

"Exactly. She's going to have to be here in the cave for at least three days. That means she'll have her eggs with her. The thing is, we don't know exactly when, and neither does she. So she'll probably bring her eggs back here before time. Believe me, Pug I will be watching her."

"How do you know this?" He poked the side of his head with a finger.

"From my da. He's not only a rider but a Dragon Talker, like me. He knows more than me. With all the time he spent as a prisoner with the dragon in that cave on the Isle of Smoke, he knows these things. He's witnessed them many times, except for the laying of the eggs with babies. He's only seen that once."

Again, he jabbed a finger at her. "So how does that help you find the eggs?"

Nagora held up a hand. "I'm getting to that. My da told me to mark the day the laying starts. See, over here on the wall."

She lit the marks she had made on the wall. "She's been laying for twelve days and will continue for as many. So in twenty-two to twenty-seven days at the latest, she'll shed her skin. My da warned me. It'll be a most dangerous time, even for me, to be near her. You've seen what she can do when she's mad, Pug. Remember, I saved you from her that time. I doubt I'll ever be able to do that again."

Pug swallowed.

"You remember it well, don't you?"

Pug's mouth twisted on his face. "So when do I return for the eggs?"

"Pug, I'm cold. Can I go change? I'll tell you over there."

He waved her toward the main entrance.

Nagora waddled along as fast as she could. She stopped where she had dropped her sheath of blades. "Will you bring these with you, Pug? If you allow me, I'll carry my vest."

"Take your vest."

Behind her leather curtain, Nagora lit another lantern. "Put them where you'll feel safe, Pug. As long as I know where they are after you leave."

He looked around as she threw a dry sweater and leggings on her bed. Underpants and socks and slippers followed. She brought a blanket over to one of her chairs. "You can sit and wrap yourself in this. It'll help warm you."

On the stone shelf, Nagora found an empty hemp sack with drawstrings and set it on the table. "Before you leave, you can put eggs in this, as many as it'll hold, if you like."

Then she undressed, starting with her boots and socks, then her leggings. She hung them on the back of the other chair. Pug sat in his chair with the blanket over his shoulders, watching her every move. She unfastened the drawstring of her undergarment. She was facing him. Is he remembering what he did to me with the help of his four cronies? They had held her and pinned her to the ground.

Nagora lifted her sweater over her head and brought it over to a hide on the floor. She took her time with her back to him as she spread it out to dry. When she returned to the shelf to get a cloth to dry herself off, Pug placed the blade on the table. His eyes were on her body. She took her time patting her body dry.

Then she sat on the edge of her bed with her legs spread to accommodate her belly when she bent over. "As I was saying, Pug, the dragon should start to shed anywhere from twenty-two to twenty-seven days from now. But my da said because she's in better shape than when she was captive in the cave, she might shed before that. A sign would be how many eggs she lays per day. From what my da told me, I can see she's laying more eggs in a day than what he told me she laid when she was in the cave with him.

"So, if I were you, I would come back in fifteen or sixteen days, seventeen the latest. I promise you, Pug. I'll know where the eggs are by then, and you won't leave here without at least one. But you have to bring me what I asked for. Just explain to Erin. She'll know what I want. If you bring the poison, she'll get her eggs. I promise."

He was shaking his head. "Come back and walk into a trap? Do you think I'm that stupid?"

Nagora held out an open palm. "Pug, you're no idiot." Then she pointed to her head. "Do you truly think I was stupid enough to leave you alone in that small cave, unguarded, so you could escape? Sure, I had two men tie you as I wanted you. But later, when I questioned you and touched your strength and held it and watched it manifest its power, do you think I didn't realize you were too strong to be held by those ropes alone? Why did I let you escape intact, Pug, despite my promises? Why?"

Nagora reached down and held the bottom of her belly. "Because of this, Pug. I knew you would escape. I knew it had to look like a true escape. But, I knew something else. I knew you would return. I wanted you to return because you are my only hope of ridding me of this royal egg I carry. It must not see the light of day with its heart beating." She reached for a sweater and pulled it over her head and shook her damp hair free.

Pug stared at her.

Nagora lay back on her bed and spread her legs even more. She let her fingers play at the bottom of her belly and caress the hair that spread across its stretched skin. "Pug, you have to believe me. Come back when you like, at your own risk, to face the mother dragon, if you feel you have the strength to face her."

Nagora held out both hands to him. "Before you leave, Pug, come take me with that beautiful cock Erin gave you. I want to see it, hold it. I want it inside me so the child I bear can feel the strength of my liberator. I will not be forced into becoming queen to a man I despise, a man who raped me."

Pug stood and unfastened his crotch piece, letting it fall away between his legs. It grew in his hand as he approached and knelt between her legs. She reached for it and guided it. "Oh! Pug! Take me!"

His fingers dug into her hips. "What are you going to find for me?" He was leaning over her bulging belly as he pumped in and out of her and stared into her wide open eyes. "What? Tell me what!"

"Oh! Pug! Give it to me! The eggs! All her dragon-young eggs! I'll get them all for you. Pound me, Pug! Take me!"

He bared his teeth as he looked down at her. "Promise me no tricks! No traps!"

"Oh! Pug! I promise! No tricks! No traps! I promise, Pug. Give it to me!"

He fell over her and then she rolled with him onto her side. She had her leg pulled up so her heel pressed into his lower back. His cock pulsed with a spasm, filling her with the warmth of his semen. Her left hand grabbed and pulled at his shirt. "Oh! Pug! That is so good! I promise you anything you want. Oh! That was worth waiting for! Just bring me the poison, Pug. That's all I ask."

"Would you promise to kill the dragon for me?"

Nagora did not hesitate. She pulled Pug closer with both her hands and leaned her face into his. "Fuck! Yes! I would promise you that, Pug. It would be my greatest revenge on my king! Can you bloody well imagine that? First, I kill his unborn infant, and then I kill his beloved dragon. I would go from heroine of the country to the most hated whore in the land! Oh! Fuck! Yes! Yes, I would do that for you, Pug!" She shook him as hard as she could. She snarled as she said it. "Fuck! Yes! I'd do that. Make me promise, Pug! Make me promise! Take me again and I'll promise!"

He pulled from her and rolled her off the bed so her knees were on the floor and her arms and chest on the bed. He took her from behind. "Promise! Promise! Promise you'll fucking kill the dragon for me! Promise you'll kill the dragon for Erin! Promise me!" He pumped her with each word. The faster his strokes, the faster he spoke.

"Oh! Fuck! Aye! Pound me, Pug! Yes! I promise I'll kill the dragon for you!" She was screaming the words as loud as she could. "I promise I'll kill the dragon for Erin if her poison rids me of the king's offspring. I promise, Pug! Take me! Take me! Give it to me!" If Hag can hear me or see me somehow through Pug, am I convincing her?

Nagora fell back on her heels. Her belly almost touched the floor. Her right cheek rested on the back of her hand as she looked back at him. "Fuck." The word came out of her mouth in a low croak. "Pug." His name was a squeak. She had lost her voice. Her left hand had reached back and held onto him, pulling at the shaft to milk it of the last drops. What he had spilled in her oozed out onto the floor.

"You promised," he said between breaths.

Nagora nodded and spoke the word "Yes" almost silently. She let go of him and rolled onto her right hip so her back rested against the side of the bed. Her legs were splayed. Her right bent at the knee. She leaned her head back as she smiled at Pug. She swallowed and managed to say, "If I didn't fear the dragon's return, I would ask you to take me again."

He smiled back at her and licked the corner of his mouth.

Nagora let her head fall back onto the bed and closed her eyes for a moment. Then she opened them. "Pug, you'd better go." She reached out a hand to him. "I don't think I'll be able to stand."

Pug took her hand and reached down to hook his other hand under her arm. He lifted her.

Nagora stood before him. "Shall I help you with that?" She reached down to take his crotch piece, but he was not yet in a condition to allow it to be tied in place. She smiled coyly at him.

"I'll be on my way," he said.

"No tricks, no traps when you return, Pug. I promise. Shall I go with you?"

"I know the way." He picked up the big blade from the table and brought it over his head to find the mouth of the sheath and slide it home. He took the hemp sack and left.

Nagora sat on the edge of her bed with her elbows on her knees and her head in her hands. Her shoulders shook as she bit back her sobs. Did I convince Hag? Or did I just give Pug what he's always wanted? She buried her face in her palms as shame washed through her.

That night in her small cave, Nagora knelt and put the tip of the royal hunting dagger to her thigh with greater resolve than ever before as she spoke her oath. "I will not fail in my duty to my dragon and to my king."

In the light of the lantern on her table, she composed, with great care, a coded missive to Geirador describing her plan, listing her needs, and setting out the instructions she wanted him to convey to those who would be involved.

‡

Geirador, please read my plan carefully before you convey my instructions to the people mentioned in this letter.

My instructions:

To Lars:
Be patient. Come only when I send for you. Only when Pare tells you, come to me. Wait for me outside the cave at the valley entrance.

To Da, Mum, and Sagora:
When Geirador tells you to, go to the Dragonwood. Da, you will bring Danuka there with her eggs. Sagora, Pare will bring you a basket with instructions. Follow them.
Mum, keep your family in the Dragonwood until I arrive or until Lars arrives. Your lives depend on doing what I ask of you.

To Pare:
The time approaches. All is as you said it would be. I will send Danuka to bring you to me. In my plan to your da, I tell who the father of my child is and the reasons for my actions. Share with Geirador what you told me. It will help him, and you, understand the why of my plan.

To Geirador:
You said if there was anything I needed, I could call on you. Today, I do that. Please read my plan and share it with Pare. She has more information that will most likely confirm my reasons for this plan. My plan lists what I need. If you can provide those things, I will be forever grateful.
If you can deliver my instructions to the people I love and ask them to trust in me, no matter what, we stand a chance to save our king and his kingdom.

Your Nagora,
EDANA
‡

Nagora folded and sealed her coded letter. In the morning, it would be in the message scrip. She would instruct Danuka to take it to Geirador, first thing.

The day seemed to drag on even as Nagora occupied herself with tidying up her side of the cave, finishing a pair of leather slippers, and preparing what would go into the cooking pot that evening. I hope Geirador will sense the urgency of my requests. Or will he think I'm unreasonable? Perhaps he'll think I'm not well in my head. Will he believe my plan? Geirador, I'm putting all my trust in you.

Ladder
Kihcêkosîwinâhtik

Whoa! I wasn't expecting that! Nagora's heart stopped for a moment. Danuka had dropped onto the lip of the big bowl at the cave entrance where Nagora stood. Usually, she rose from below over the tops of the trees to land. Nagora backed out of the way. "Welcome, Mother. It is good to see you return."

Nagora climbed onto the wing the dragon had lowered for her. She unfastened the single bag tied to Danuka's harness.

Geirador must've kept the other two. Maybe he'll send them back tomorrow.

Danuka went off to lay more eggs.

Nagora rushed to her table to open the bag. Attached to the message scrip was a parcel about twice the size of the scrip. There was nothing else in the bag. She opened the scrip and took out the folded letter with Geirador's seal on it. She lifted the seal with one of her knives and unfolded the missive. It was in code with enough space below each coded word for her to transcribe the key to them. She unfolded her key and wasted no time unlocking Geirador's reply.

‡

Nagora,

Pieces of gold leaf are in the package with instructions and ingredients you will need. That was the easy part.

Yes, I will instruct the people you love as you have directed me. I cannot help you with the rest of your plan. Trust me, I know who can—The Little People. I know you see my smile as you read this. I know you speak the *Language of The People* as do the Little People. Summon them to help you. Pay them with gold. You are lucky, you have gold coins, and you will have the dragon's shed skin to offer them. It is most prized by the Little People.

To summon the Little People do the following:

Take a gold coin. Pierce two holes in it like a button. To do this, use your big skystone blade. Heat the tip with the flame of a candle until it begins to change color. Place the tip on the coin. Hold the blade by its pommel and turn the blade. Do not press on the pommel. Let the weight of the blade do the work. Take your time. The holes will appear.

Thread a string of hemp or linen through one hole and then back through the other. Tie two knots on that side of the coin. Tie the string to the handle of your skystone blade just above its crossguard. The coin must hang down and touch the blade on its centerline. The string must not touch the edges of the blade to get cut.

Bring the blade to the stream. Find a spot where you can stick the blade in the current of the stream. Stick it in gravel, or silt, or in a crack in the rock, and stick it at an angle in the water so the current moves the coin on the blade. The sound of the coin striking the skystone blade will call the Little People.

They will come to you. It may take a day or two, but they will come. They will come in the dark. Your cave must be dark. They will carry small lights. There will be many of them. If one should allow you to see him or her, it will be like looking at a mirror image. Like a mirror image, you cannot touch them. Don't be afraid if they touch you. No harm will come to you.

Explain how they can help you. They will ask you what you offer in exchange. Spread your gold coins on the cave floor before you. They will take what they believe is fair for their help. If they ask for more, tell them all the dragon's shed skin is theirs. Trust them, Nagora. Let them work their magic. You will know they are there. No one else will.

Paruline and I support you in your brave plan. May the stars be on your side.

Geirador
‡

Tar piss! I wasn't expecting this. I've heard so many strange stories about these mysterious people. Most tellers of those stories call into question their existence. To be working with them almost frightens me, though Geirador's words reassure me. I don't have a choice. I trust him. Since he tells me to trust the Little People, I will. If they provided Geirador with the skystone to make my blade and knives, they will be my best hope to help me carry out my plan. And I speak their language, so that will help.

...

Danuka had just left when Nagora hoisted her leather curtain to let the daylight strike her table. If I'm to see what I'm about to do, I'll need good light.

First, though, she performed her ritual morning exercises. For the first time, the weapon she chose was a brush. Not the finest one she used to write with, but the next one up in size. According to Geirador's instructions with the gold leaf, it would be the best to use for the gilding process. This morning's hundred slow, deliberate repetitions will help my concentration to replicate a dragon's egg.

When Nagora finished, she took an empty hemp sack with her to the egg pile at the other end of the cave. She piled some of the eggs, which Danuka had laid the night before, further along the cave wall, stretching the pile out to keep part of the path clear. Then she chose three and placed them in her sack.

Geirador's instructions were on the table under two bowls. Nagora set the sack on the other chair at the table, removed two of the eggs, and placed them each in a bowl. Then she brought a clean cooking pot to the table and went for the two remaining ingredients, the jar of honey and the pot of salt.

Nagora examined each egg with its blue and red veins embossed in the blue surface. The blue veins on the feeder eggs were devoid of gold. Filling them with gold leaf would give them the appearance of eggs with babies—blue eggs with red and gold veins. She turned the eggs over and over in the bowls, making sure there was no dirt or dust on them, especially in the recessed veins.

Good. They're clean. She went to her firepit and started a small, hot fire beneath the grate upon which the cooking pot would rest. I'll feed the early flames with many pieces of kindling.

Nagora returned to the table with a small glass, which she set next to the honey jar.

After removing the last egg from the sack, she examined it for dirt, and then made the sack into a nest on the chair. Good. It'll rest secure. She picked up the egg and held its big end up to pierce it with one of her knives. She pecked at the egg with the knife point until a tiny hole appeared in the shell. Geirador's instructions were clear. Avoid piercing the red egg yolk. She blew away the miniscule debris of shell.

Nagora tilted the egg and measured out a glass of egg white and poured it into the pot. She repeated this six more times. Then one glassful of honey went into the pot, followed by half a glass of salt.

Before Nagora began to mix and heat the ingredients, she cleaned the windows of the three lanterns and gave them fresh candles. Then, in case a breeze might come into the cave and blow a gold leaf onto the floor and render it useless, she lowered the leather curtain and reattached it to the rings on the walls. Her hands needed to be clean, so she took the time to wash them with care and dry them.

Nagora reread the instructions.

☦

Mix the ingredients well.
Set over the flame.
Stir with a freshly cut piece of dry wood the size of your brush. Stir until the salt has dissolved.
DO NOT LET BOIL.
Remove from flame.

> Continue to stir until cool enough to touch.
> The mixture should be clear.

Nagora followed the instructions. I wish my copper pot was smaller, but it'll do.

> Pour into a glass jar.
> Set next to a lit lantern.
> It is ready to use.
> ‡

Nagora set the jar of glue next to a lantern. Now, she was ready. She sat in her chair, pulled the bowl with the egg close to her, dipped her clean brush into the mixture, and painted the recessed veins with the glue. On contact, the glue would hold the gold leaf in place. Without the glue, the gold leaf would not hold. Once she finished painting the recessed veins of the two eggs, she cleaned her brush and prepared her table for the gilding.

Nagora set the package of vellum pages on the table next to a bowl. A single gold leaf rested between each page. Geirador's instructions told her she had enough to gild two eggs, possibly three, but promised to hammer more gold into thin, light leaves. If she needed more, she just had to ask.

Does Geirador have special tools to do this? Perhaps a special hammer and anvil? This master smithy must know every metal-working secret there is. He's truly a treasured friend. I hope I won't disappoint him.

Nagora moved the three brushes to the right of the vellum pages so they were at hand near the table's edge. The bowl with the egg was on the other side of the vellum pages. She lifted the first page gently, slowly, to reveal the first gold leaf. It was no bigger than her palm. She held her breath as she brought the tips of the wide brush hairs to the edge of the leaf to lift it from the page. Its weight was imperceptible, lighter than the smallest feather she had ever held. She placed a single finger on the rough edge of what Geirador had called an uncut leaf, one that had not been touched or cut to any shape after being hammered, but left as it was, coming off the anvil. Just as well, he had written, for the use she was putting it to, to gild the irregular, intertwining, and sometimes gnarled recessed veins. No two eggs were alike.

Nagora let the leaf touch down on the egg's surface. Once it had settled, she held it with a single finger as she gently brushed its surface with the hairs of the brush. As soon as a piece of the gold leaf contacted the glue, the rest of it above the recessed veins sunk right into place. She brushed over the sunken leaf parts with the smaller brush to attach them firmly in the recesses. The rest of the thin leaf not held by the glue tore away. She picked it up with the big brush and moved it to the next section of veins. She repeated this until she had no more leaf left.

When she finished gilding the veins of the first egg, she took a break to stand up, walk around, and rub her neck. It looks good, like a real one. Though on close examination next to an egg it imitated, I would see the difference. Pug won't. He won't have another to compare it to.

After gilding the second egg, I'll paint over the gilded veins with a glaze to seal the gold leaf in place. Geirador had sent her the missing ingredient to make the glaze. The recipe was like the glue mixture, but with less honey. I'll just have to add the hardener Geirador sent. It was a thick white liquid which would become transparent when mixed and heated with the other ingredients. When applied, it would dry hard and protect the gold leaf.

I've got two eggs gilded and enough gold leaf for about half of another. I'll ask for more. I'll want to have four gilded eggs ready in case of a mishap with one. No time to lose before Pug returns.

If all goes well, I must convince Danuka to go along with the next part of my plan. Will she? That question kept coming back to her.

Just tell her the truth. She'll believe me. Do I tell her before or after she sheds her skin? Before, just in case I have to come up with a new plan.

Days later Nagora heard the squish of wet boots. He's taken my advice. "Pug? Pug, is that you? I heard that, Pug. Have you brought me what you promised?" She lit the lantern she carried with the candle from the lantern on Danuka's side of the cave. She had just approached the lantern when she heard the wet footsteps, two of them, squishing water from the seams of boots. "Pug, I know you're there. Show yourself."

Nagora drew her blade, slipped the lantern's carry handle onto the end of it, and then drew a knife from its holster. "You think this is a trap? It's not. I have something to show you. It's something that will make you happy. And there are more where it came from, waiting for you to take them. Pug, if you don't show yourself, I can't give it to you and show you where the others are. And, if you don't have what you promised me, then you better leave. Our deal is off."

Nagora waited and listened. "You've checked the other end of the cave. You want to be sure this end is clear too and that I'm alone. Is that right, Pug? I can't blame you. Tell me what you want me to do."

"Put your knives away. Drop your sheath there where you stand. Turn around. Walk back with your arms held out straight."

Nagora set the lantern on the cave floor and did as he asked.

"Hands behind your head. If you move them, you're good as dead."

A hand moved under the back of her sweater and then up her left side over her breast to emerge at the collar where it grabbed onto the sweater. Then the cold skystone blade rested against the right side of her swollen belly. "If there's anyone else here with you, tell them to show themselves. If they don't show themselves or try something, you'll die."

"Pug, I will not speak to someone who's not there. I'm alone in the cave with you. Believe me. Take me over there, and you'll see it's true. Then we can get on with our business."

After making it behind the leather curtain on her side of the cave and Pug had a good look around, he let go of her.

"I'm glad that's done with.

"If I were you, I wouldn't trust me either." She smiled at him.

"Show me the eggs."

"The egg. One egg. You'll have to get the others yourself. In my condition, you're lucky that I was able to get one for you. You'll see why later."

"Where's the egg?"

"At the other end, in the small cave."

"Let's go."

"Not so fast. You want more than one egg, don't you?"

Pug nodded.

"Put that blade away then and give me a hand. You'll need a ladder. If I had known you were coming today, I would've left it standing. I didn't want the dragon to find the ladder. Now we have to put it together again." She pointed to the ladder leaning on the far wall of her side of the cave. "Bring that ladder and the pieces of rope hanging from the rung. We'll tie it to the other ladder that rests on the lip of the entrance." She held aside the leather curtain for Pug to bring the ladder out.

"Pug, do you want us to lash them together here in the daylight, or do we bring them into the cave?"

"Here."

"Set that one down. Get the other and bring it. We'll lash it to yours."

As Pug set the other ladder down, he looked to her for instructions.

"I overlapped the bigger one by three rungs. I was just able to reach the shelf where the eggs are. I had to climb real slow because the ladder was springy."

"And you think this will hold me?"

"I think so, Pug. What do you think? Do you want to go cut spruce poles to reinforce it?"

"I have little time. I'll try it and see."

"It wasn't an easy climb in my condition. I climbed up one rung and waited for the ladder to stop swaying before moving on. It scared me because I had no choice but to set the ladder steep."

Pug looked at her. Doubt covered his face.

"At least you'll have me to hold the ladder for you. And you don't have a belly the size of mine to get in the way."

"Move aside. I'll tie them together."

Pug went to work. *Your knot work is sloppy.* Working with Uncle had taught her all the intricacy of knots and their appropriate use, especially when lashing things together. *It'll hold. How well remains to be seen.*

Pug stood up and pulled up on one of the top ladder rungs. He looked back at his lashings, and then at her. He must've felt the ladder he's holding move against the other.

"Go ahead, Pug. I'll pick up the other end."

On the lakeshore path near the shelf location, Nagora called for a halt. "We set the ladder here."

Pug stopped. He looked up. "I don't see a shelf."

"Neither did I. I looked up all along this cave's walls many times."

"So how'd you find it?"

"I watched every night since our last meeting, from my small cave. I lay on the floor and looked out and up this way. I saw where she lifted the pouches, but the recessed shelf in the rock was never visible."

"So you climbed the ladder to have a look?"

"That's what I did this morning. Luck was on my side. The strap of one of the egg pouches stuck out over the edge of the shelf, just enough to be visible. I was able to reach it and pull it down."

Pug looked at her. "I don't trust you."

"Tie a lantern to the ladder, Pug. Hold it up there. You'll see the shadow where the shelf is."

Pug shook his head.

"Let me get the egg from the small cave. You'll see. Take that one. Forget about the others. Shit, I'll have enough problems when the dragon realizes one of her eggs is missing. I'll have to explain that to her. It'll be easier than explaining why all her eggs are missing."

"You talk too much. Get the egg."

"Did you bring what you promised me, Pug?"

"It's right here." He patted his scrip, which hung on his right hip. "Get the egg."

As Nagora left for the egg, she looked back. Pug was lifting the ladder in place.

Nagora handed the pouch to Pug and held up her lantern so he could examine it. His eyes widened as he turned it over in his hands. He smiled as he put the egg back in its pouch and lifted the strap over his head, hanging the pouch over his left shoulder.

She held out her hand.

Pug reached into his scrip and took out a small linen-wrapped cylinder and handed it to her. "You'll find a glass vial inside. It's sealed in wax."

"Do I take it all? What does Erin say?"

"A single drop in some tea should do the trick. If you take it in the morning, you'll know before nightfall. Birth pains will start. The infant will be blue at birth. Dead.

"And she says not to forget your promise to kill the dragon."

"If this doesn't kill me, but works as Erin says, I'll keep my promise, Pug. It'll be my liberation.

"Pug, you could leave with that egg now and come back with Erin for the others, after I've killed the dragon."

Pug shook his head. "No, my orders are to bring them all back." He placed one hand on a ladder rung. "Up you go."

Nagora hesitated for a moment, the time to place the poison in her scrip. She put a hand on the rung next to Pug's and looked up. Then she looked at him. "You'll hold the ladder. Don't rush me, Pug. Like I said before, one rung at a time. I'll wait for the ladder to stop swinging before going up another."

Pug smiled at her.

Nagora started her slow climb. By the time her hands reached the top rung of the lower ladder, it swung in an increasing back-and-forth motion. At each rung, she had to adjust her belly first and face sideways, waiting for the motion to stop, and then face the ladder to climb another rung.

While Nagora waited again for the ladder to stop moving, Pug called to her.

"Come back down. This is taking forever. Come on. Stick your ass out there and come down. I'm holding the ladder."

Nagora set her foot on the ground. "You see what I was talking about, Pug?"

He pushed her aside. "Just hold the ladder."

He almost ran up it until the middle and then stopped to let the ladder settle from its back and forth motion. Then he continued up two rungs, waited, and climbed two more. "I see the shelf." He climbed another rung, paused, and looked up again. At the next rung, he reached out the fingers of his left hand to touch the edge of the shelf. He brought his hand back down and climbed to the next rung.

As he reached again for the shelf, there was a sharp cracking sound. His feet went through the rung. His right hand held the ladder rail and the tips of the fingers of his left hand held onto the edge of the rock shelf. "Shit!"

Nagora stepped aside as Pug's feet and legs grappled with the ladder wobbling beneath him. "Be careful, Pug! Hold on!"

The ladder twisted, and so did Pug. When his fingers let go of the shelf, the ladder pivoted on one leg. For a moment, it stood vertical. Pug reached out for the rock wall with his right hand. As soon as it touched the wall, he and the ladder fell backward. Somehow, Pug had placed his right arm behind him and freed his right foot, possibly hoping to jump from the ladder or at least land on one foot.

When Nagora got to him, Pug was on his back, unconscious. His bowels and bladder had emptied. Blood leaked from his left ear. She had to move him. Take your time. You can't rush in your condition. She pulled away the ladder. Then she knelt at his left side and pulled his hip toward her, holding him with her left hand as she pulled his right arm to his side. The way it moved told her the arm was broken, possibly at the shoulder. She pulled the flattened egg pouch out to the side.

Then she switched hands and worked with her left hand to straighten his leg. Pug groaned. When she released his hip, his foot twisted at a strange angle. The fall must've broken his ankle as well.

Nagora unfastened the buckle on each strap of Uncle's sheath of blades. She lifted the straps above Pug's shoulders.

If you come to, Pug, you'll be in pain. Maybe I have something for you.

Nagora returned to the ladder and undid Pug's lashings. She brought the top ladder next to Pug so that his feet were level with the bottom rung. After placing her left foot between the rungs opposite his thigh, she went down on her right knee so it rested on the ladder rail.

Next, she bent over to grab him at the hip and by the shirt beneath his armpit. In one motion, she pulled and rolled him over face down on the ladder, pulling her foot free just in time. Now to bring his right leg over so it rests on the rungs.

Nagora tied a piece of rope from one ladder rail to the other, over Pug's backside. Before she did the same at his shoulders, she lifted Pug's head and pulled the straps of his scrip and the egg pouch free. The left side of his head rested on a rung. Blood from his ear dripped. She tied the end of a rope to the rail below that rung, gauged the length of the free end and tied it to the rail on the other side.

Now she had a loop of rope she could step through and place at the back of her neck, over her shoulders, and down her sides. This caused her to bend at the knees. Okay, take it slow. You're already carrying extra weight.

When Nagora took hold of the rope and stood straight, the ladder lifted. She dragged Pug to her small cave, stopping several times along the way to rest. When she stopped near the stream that flowed from the lake, she left Pug there while she went for a bucket and a cloth in the small cave.

When Nagora returned, she cut away his leggings and undergarment before filling the bucket to rinse the excrement from Pug's backside. She washed him with the cloth as best as she could before dragging him to her cave.

Nagora crawled inside and pulled him in as far as she could. With several hides set next to the ladder, she leaned

over him, grabbed the ladder, and rolled him over onto his
back. Next, she untied the ropes and pushed the ladder out. As
she caught her breath, Nagora sat back on her calves with a
hand resting on her belly.

The bleeding from Pug's ear seemed to have stopped.
Nagora made a pillow of a sheepskin hide, lifted his left
shoulder, and reached under his back to lift him so she could
slip the pillow under his shoulders and head. Tar piss! He's
heavy.

Nagora walked back to the cave entrance to get a blanket,
smaller hides, a waterskin, and the other egg she had gilded.

When Nagora returned, she poured water on Pug's lips.
Then she slipped two fingers between them and poured a few
drops more. Pug coughed up blood. She tilted his head to help
clear out the bloody spittle. She dribbled more until he drank a
tiny bit. She unfolded a cloth between his legs and reached
under his legs to pull it out on each side of him so she could
then pull it up under his buttocks.

Then she placed the gilded egg on Pug's chest. She draped
his left hand over the egg. Hag, if you can see this somehow,
here's one of the eggs you wanted.

Finally, she covered him with the blanket.

What'll I tell Danuka?

There's no point trying to hide what happened. Now it's
time to inform her of my unfolding plan. Danuka will witness
the first part on her return. Will she cooperate like Pug did?

I hope she will.

. . .

In the meantime, Nagora returned the ladders and raised the curtain on her side of the cave. She placed the smashed egg pouch in a bowl and set Uncle's blades on a chair. I'll clean them and the holsters later. Her own blades were on the table. I prepared a poison of my own many months ago. I used one. Are the other three still intact?

Three of the four knife holsters each held a small wax cylinder to the flat side of the knife blade it carried. Each cylinder was half the length of her little finger and not quite as big around. Inside each tiny wax cylinder was a thorn from a hawthorn shrub.

Many months ago, with tweezers from Tagnyoriva's medical scrip, she had barely touched each thorn's tip to the liquid in the vial of her mother's "healer's secret," as Sagora had called the poison medicine. After, she placed each thorn inside a piece of bark from a twig before filling the space around the thorn with wax melted from a candle.

Now she carefully pulled the first throwing knife from the edge of the holster that held the knife's handle in place. Then she tilted the holster and tapped it. An intact cylinder fell out. The other two cylinders from the other holsters were also intact. Good.

Sagora had explained how Tagnyoriva used the poison medicine. "If ever a warriors suffer too much from wounds Mum judges are fatal, she could give them a drop of this to allow them to fall asleep and go peacefully to the stars."

...

I know there's not a drop's worth of the "healer's secret" on a thorn tip, but certainly enough to keep Pug comfortable. I'll only use it if he's conscious and in obvious pain. How long it'll allow him to sleep, I don't know. I hope there'll be enough for my needs.

Perhaps I'll ask Geirador to send medicine from his cupboard.

Nagora returned the cylinders to their hiding places and put on her blades.

Then she set Uncle's blades on the table to clean them. All the blades were in fine condition. The main sheath needed to be cleaned and re-oiled. While she was at it, she re-oiled the straps and small knife holsters.

The entrance bell tinkled. It brought Nagora to her feet. She had been waiting and resting on her bed. "Welcome, Mother. I have good and important news for you today. I have captured the one who stole your eggs."

Danuka brought the tip of her snout down to Nagora's forehead.

"No, Mother, I am afraid we will not get your eggs back. But with your help, we will put an end to the witch who sent him to steal your eggs. She is Hag, the same witch who has sought the death of all the dragons in the Land of the Danu. She still wants your death, Mother. And the death of your unborn dragons. But I can stop her. I can save you. I can save our king. And I can save his kingdom. Mother, I can only do that with your help. I will tell you how later. I think we should go see the thief. He is in no condition to flee this time."

...

Nagora crawled into her small cave and Danuka's head followed. It hovered over Pug's body, smelling his body, each of his limbs, the gilded egg, and his head. She placed her snout on Nagora's forehead. Nagora whispered, "Outside," and motioned she wanted to leave the small cave. I fear, somehow, Alizarine can hear what Pug hears.

Outside and well away from Pug, Danuka again touched Nagora's Tiwaz. "Yes, Mother, an arm and a leg are broken. His head too. You are right. He may never wake up again. If we can keep him alive, I know my plan will work. Yes, later I will tell you about it and what I will need you to do."

After Danuka had laid more eggs and had inspected her eggs, Nagora explained how she had trapped Pug and what she planned to do. She was sitting between Danuka's folded wings with her legs crossed. Danuka lifted the tip of her snout away from Nagora's forehead and brought her head back to look into Nagora's eyes.

Is she weighing what I've asked her to do? Perhaps trying to see into the future to weigh the consequences? Or to decide if she'll trust, or not trust, her Dragon Talker?

And then, Danuka raised her head and brought it back in a graceful arc before lowering it until the tip of her snout lifted Nagora's sweater and touched her distended belly button. She let it rest there. The beautiful iridescent scales on the top of Danuka's head spread out, fan-like, to her ears. I rarely get to see this part of her. What is she doing?

When Danuka lifted her head away, her red eyes stared into Nagora's eyes again. She's looking inside me and I can't read anything beyond her eyes. Danuka touched Nagora's forehead again.

"I will give birth to my child sooner than expected. And your shedding too will happen sooner. You are sure of this, Mother?

"I will feel it. Sagora will not have arrived.

"Will you bring Pare to help me, Mother?

"As soon as it is time. Thank you, Mother. And my plan, Mother?

"You agree to give me an egg in exchange for my child. I must place my amulet around my child's neck. I must give my child my blades. I must give my child to Sagora. If my plan works and I return your egg, you will give me back my child. Those are your conditions.

"Mother, I agree to your conditions. I thank you for giving me an egg. I promise I will return it.

"Now? In the dark? Yes, Mother, I will get ready now."

Danuka sat back and brought her wings to her sides.

Nagora uncrossed her legs and leaned onto one hip and then to one knee to get up.

Nagora crossed over to her side of the cave and removed her blades and vest. She pulled on another sweater, her blades, her vest, the vest Raynhard had given her, and her sheepskin hat.

When Danuka returned from hiding her eggs on the shelf, she set a wing down so Nagora could climb onto the saddle. There, Nagora lifted her sweater so her belly rested against the base of the back of Danuka's neck. The cold on her belly quickly turned to warmth.

Nagora tied herself to the saddle with the straps made for that purpose.

Then she undid the laces holding the earflaps of her hat, brought them down over her ears, and tied the laces snug under her chin.

Finally, she pulled the sleeves of her two sweaters over her hands before grasping hold of the reins. "Ready, Mother."

Danuka climbed to the edge of the bowl, spread her wings, and pushed off into the cool spring night air. It was the last condition Danuka had stated, and she wanted it carried out this night. She wanted to take Nagora and her unborn child for a ride.

Nagora was to hold onto the reins and let Danuka fly. It was Nagora's first true night flight. Danuka climbed higher and higher in the sky in ever widening circles as she pumped her wings.

"Mother, my heart is beating faster." At that moment, Danuka turned on a new course and started a long, slow glide in a straight-line descent that brought them out over the sea, away from the coast until they were skimming over the dark waves.

Danuka flapped her wings and increased her speed over the water. I've no choice but to close my eyes and hang on. "Mother, my body is getting cold." Danuka's wings stopped their pumping as she settled into a glide. Nagora looked right, to the coastal shoreline along which Danuka glided. As she looked ahead, she spotted the fortified wall of Skull Bay in the distance.

Why is Danuka taking me here?

They skimmed over the water. Danuka kept parallel to the coast as she flew past the entrance to Skull Bay. Nagora glimpsed the skull-shaped rock at its entrance. A wisp of an image of her standing on the dock in Lars's arms slipped in and out of her mind.

Had Danuka not told me to be a passenger in the saddle and enjoy the ride, I would have used the reins and my mind as a Dragon Rider to have Danuka set down in Skull Bay. No, I wouldn't do that. Not in the middle of the night. It could be costly.

Enjoy the ride. This could be part of the future chosen for me. I better not dwell on that possibility. Though, Danuka surely has a reason for this flight.

Skull Bay disappeared behind them, and Danuka maintained her course and speed along the coast until she reached the farthest tip of the coast of the Land of Skulls.

Danuka tipped her wings and turned left, heading further out to sea where she climbed higher. It's like she's trying to reach the moon above the horizon. It's so big and bright. I don't recall ever seeing so much detail on the moon's surface. "Thank you, Mother, for showing me this."

And then, Danuka slowly turned back toward the coast.

Nagora kept her eyes on the rising sphere until it fell behind her right shoulder. If I were someone on the coast watching Danuka's silhouette grow on the background of the moon, what would I be thinking?

Again, Danuka skimmed the waves and, as the coastal cliffs approached, she slowed her glide. To the right in the distance, a small, sandy cove beach, bathed in moonlight, came into view. To the left on the tall steep cliffs, Nagora saw the distinct opening of a cave. Danuka banked and pumped her wings once as she flew up and past the big cave opening until she was above the cliff. There, Danuka flapped her wings again and circled higher above the cliffs and the sea.

Nagora looked down on the rock strewn landscape above the cliffs. It differed greatly from the rocky, shrub-covered landscape opposite it, above the small beach cove. A valley separated the two different plateaus and wound its way down to one side of the small cove. *Now I remember it! It's the cove Sagora had brought us to on the day we trained with the fire baskets. It was the first time we tried to look like Edana on a horse with flaming hooves.*

Danuka slowed her flight over the cliff and gently flapped her wings so she descended in a smaller, tighter circle across the cliff face. They passed the cave entrance again. *Wow! That's a big cave.*

"Mother, if you wanted to, you could fly into that cave."

Danuka pitched and turned away as she dove toward the waves below, pulling up just in time to keep Nagora from closing her eyes. *Thank the stars! I thought she was going to dive into the water.* The dragon climbed toward the moon. Over Nagora's shoulder, the cave entrance on the cliff face receded in the distance. Danuka banked left and flapped her wings harder.

The ride's going to get cold again. She held on tight and hugged her body as close as she could to Danuka. Behind her, moonlight glinted on the surface of the waves.

Danuka slowed and climbed again in a long graceful circle that brought them back over the land on the coast and then out over the sea again. Danuka climbed ever higher over the land and the sea, straddling the liquid mirror of the sea and the solid black of the land.

"Mother, my body is enjoying the sensation and my mind can't believe the wonder it sees." How peaceful I feel up here. From here, everything below seems so peaceful too. Will I ever feel this way again? Why has Danuka taken me so far? Will she tell me? I mustn't ask. If she doesn't tell me, then I'll know it's our secret.

Nagora hugged Danuka and let the wind pull the cold tears from her eyes.

After they landed at their cave, Nagora stayed on Danuka's back with her cheek resting against her scales. She patted the dragon. "Thank you, Mother. I will never forget this night."

Danuka moaned, and Nagora climbed down onto the outstretched wing.

While Danuka went for her eggs, Nagora removed her big vest and her hat, prepared her medical scrip, and set out a small bowl to brew tea. Danuka settled into her side of the cave with her eggs. Nagora left with the scrip and bowl for her small cave.

Pug was still unconscious. He had a fever. Nagora pulled the blanket off him and prepared willow tea on a candle heater. She wet a cloth and bathed his face and neck. Then she rinsed the cloth and set it as a compress on his forehead. He hadn't moved since she had left him. His right shoulder had swelled, as did his elbow and wrist. She unfastened his boot. Because of his swollen ankle, she had to cut down its side to remove it. She removed his other boot to compare the two ankles.

The right was at least three times the size of the left, and it was blue.

Once the willow tea had cooled enough, she made him drink a mouthful from a small bowl.

Before leaving, she placed a hand on Pug's chest and said to him, "I'll be back to keep watch over you. Sleep well, Pug."

Then she covered him with the blanket and left.

Nagora went to the spot where the stream emptied from the cave lake. On her knees she set her lantern on the ground near the stream to prepare for her cut. She sat back on her calves and took her time to find a space on her right thigh. With the tip of the dagger in place, she brought herself up on her knees. She caressed her belly with her left hand as she pressed and pulled the dagger tip against her thigh and spoke her oath, "I will not fail again in my duty to my dragon and my king."

When Nagora sat back on her heels, she stared at the dagger's point she now held before her face. The hope I have in my plan is as slim as the invisible filament that holds this crimson tear of blood to the royal dagger of my pledged duty. At least I have not lost all hope.

Her eyes moved to the pommel of the dagger. The golden dragon held a crown in its mouth. Danuka, you have agreed to help me. I prefer not to think of the cost. Knowing you are on my side gives me strength.

As Nagora looked back to the blade, a solitary drop of blood fell from its tip onto her belly. Let the battle come. She bent and rinsed the dagger in the stream.

Little Wolf
Piwi Mahihkan

Three nights later, when Nagora awoke in her small cave next to Pug, she could not control the trickle between her legs. It did not smell of urine. The pain in her back had become more intense. The baby had settled lower inside of her. She crawled out of her cave and waddled her way to Danuka as the trickle continued.

"Mother, it is time. I have some of the signs Pare told me about. You must bring her as soon as you can."

Danuka brought the tip of her snout to Nagora's belly. Nagora lifted her sweater for her. After keeping her snout to Nagora's great belly button for a good moment, she lifted it to Nagora's forehead.

"Yes, Mother. I will prepare what Paruline will need. I will be ready for her when you return. Thank you, Mother."

Danuka left to hide her eggs, and Nagora went to her side of the cave to start a fire and put a pot of water on it to boil.

Then she waddled over to her bed and laid out large clean linen cloths, clean washcloths, and the baby clothes. She brought the woolen blankets and tiny garments she had knitted over to the table. She had made a sheepskin carrying pouch with straps that crossed over her shoulders at the back to allow her to carry the baby at her front.

When Danuka returned, she pushed her head past the leather curtain and over to Nagora. She was carrying one of her recently laid eggs in her mouth. She held it for Nagora to take. Once Nagora had it in her hands, Danuka touched the tip of her snout to Nagora's brand.

"For my child? To drink along with my first milk to give it strength? Mother, I believe you. Thank you for this gift. I am sure my child will enjoy it. Yes, Mother. I am almost ready. I have set water to boil. My bed is ready. I await your return with Pare. Let me put the message in its pouch, and then you can leave."

Nagora went to her writing kit and opened the box to retrieve the letter she had written for Paruline the day before. Had Danuka not predicted the earlier birth, I might have waited longer before writing the letter. I'm glad I wrote it sooner.

Danuka pushed off and glided away in the early morning darkness. Just a hint of twilight eased its way into the night's star-speckled blackness. Nagora looked to the stars. A few nights ago, Danuka brought me and my unborn child closer to you. I had never seen you so bright. I wonder which of you will become the star of my child.

Uncle, I know you are up there looking down on me. I ask you today to keep watch over me as I bring this child into the world, and thereafter, to keep watch over my child. Knowing you are will give me strength.

"Nagora!" Paruline stepped down from Danuka's wing and opened her arms to embrace her.

"Pare, I'm so happy you are here. Just seeing you has taken away my fear."

Paruline stepped back and placed a hand on Nagora's belly. "Are your contractions regular?"

"On a full count."

"Where do you feel pain?"

Nagora placed a hand on her lower back. "Here and when the contraction comes, it moves to here too." She brought her hand around to the front of her abdomen.

"And your water?"

"Still leaking, but not as much as when I woke up."

Paruline hugged her. "Let me get my scrip. Then we'll get you ready to be a mother." Paruline unfastened the leather bag from Danuka's harness. "Where are we going to do this, Nagora?"

Nagora held the curtain aside to show her side of the cave. "I can raise the curtain if you prefer more daylight. It'll warm up."

Paruline had a quick look around. "Yes, let's do that. We don't know how long this will take."

While Paruline set out her medical scrip on the table, Nagora asked, "So you've not had any letters of late?"

"No, Nagora. Da thinks Sagora and Lars will deliver the next ones when they arrive. He's expecting them to show up any day now."

"It's colder up in the Land of Skulls. Spring must come later," said Nagora.

"That's what Da says. But he thinks Lars will travel as soon as conditions permit, that is, if Gabe has no pressing work for him."

Nagora sighed. "Well, spring always seems to bring lots of work."

"True, but don't forget, Sagora promised to return as early as possible to help your mum. She doesn't want to head back to Gabe as late as last year."

And here I am about to throw an unexpected newcomer into their plans. What will they think of me when they find out? Or do they already know?

I don't want to question Pare's discretion. But I want to let her know what's coming in case Geirador hasn't already.

"Pare, has Geirador talked to you of my plan?"

Paruline looked into Nagora's eyes with sincerity and concern. "He did, Nagora. He had me read your plan, and we discussed how you linked Pug to Hag, how your plan grew from that, and how you also linked Aliza to Hag.

"When I learned who the father of your child is, I told Da of Raynhard's sleepwalking incident as Chive. We agreed that your suspicions about Hag are founded and that our king is in danger, but that he doesn't realize it."

Paruline reached for Nagora's hands. "Nagora, only when your child is born will I be able to confirm who the father is for sure. From what you told me, even if Lars took those precautions, he could still be the father. Even if you feel sure that it is Raynhard, I want you to know that withdrawal is not foolproof."

"I believe you, Pare, but I'm sure you'll confirm my feelings."

She let go of Nagora's hands and smiled at her. "We'll know today. Da told me to expect to be updated. What's the situation now?"

"I've captured Pug, a key to my plan."

Paruline's eyes grew wide. "You have him here?"

"Yes, Pare. He confirmed my suspicions of Aliza."

"How?"

Nagora explained how she had seduced Pug, convinced him she needed a poison from Hag to rid herself of her baby, and how Pug had not reacted when she slipped Aliza's name into their conversation instead of Erin's.

"You did that, Nagora? In your condition?"

"I had to. I had to trap him like I did Prince Acindor. I did it for my king.

"Pare, he's injured. He's not conscious. I need to keep him alive to carry out the rest of my plan. Can you examine him?"

"Of course, we have time before you give birth."

"I want you to listen to me before you do. What I tell you will seem strange, but it's the only way I can explain it."

"What is it, Nagora?"

"I don't know how, but I think Hag has some kind of control on Pug from a distance. Somehow, she can see or hear what he does, no matter where he is."

Paruline frowned as she listened.

"I know how strange that is. But I think it's possible. She has made him into an instrument for her use. She has even changed him physically, to be used for her own pleasure and as a reward to him."

Paruline's head pulled back on her neck with a question on her face. "How so?"

"You'll see, Pare, when you examine him. His penis is unusual in size, so much bigger than what it was when he assaulted me, especially when it's erect."

"You're sure of this, Nagora? Perhaps he's just grown as a man."

"You'll see. Then you tell me."

"Okay. I believe you. I'll examine him."

"When you examine him, if I'm right about Hag being able to see or hear what he does, then you mustn't open his eyes or speak near him."

"Okay, but you'll have to tell me what his eyes look like when you peer into them. I want you to describe the dark centers. Their shape, and how they react to candle light when you bring it near his eyes."

"I can do that."

"Good. We'll do that first. Then I'll examine his body." Paruline pulled out a chair and sat across from Nagora and motioned for her to do the same. "Before we go, tell me how he was injured, when, and what you've done so far to keep him alive."

Nagora told everything that had happened that day.

"How much of the 'healer's secret' have you given him so far?"

"I pricked him twice, a thorn every two days. He's due for another today. You know about this poison?"

"My Da was a medic in the good king's forces, remember? I'm sure he's the one who gave the recipe to Tagnya. You're lucky you haven't killed him. I'll give you something else to use. I have to examine him first."

Paruline stood and walked over to Nagora's side of the table to help her up. "I think you have another contraction coming on. Do you prefer to wait for it to pass before we go there?"

"I'll be fine. I can take the pain. I'm not too fast on my feet though."

Paruline waited outside the small cave as Nagora examined Pug's eyes. When she crawled out, Paruline helped her up and took her aside.

"His eye centers are round. They get smaller slowly when I shine the light in them."

"Okay, my turn." Paruline crawled into the cave with her medical scrip.

When Paruline came back out, she took Nagora's arm and led her aside. "You're right. That is unusual. I'm surprised he's so calm and without fever. Did you give him some willow tea?"

Nagora nodded. "Yes."

Paruline smiled. "That's why. Well, he's not going anywhere on his own. That's for sure." She handed Nagora a small vial. "I put a single drop of this on his tongue. He must get it once a day. If he becomes agitated, give him two drops."

Nagora took it. "I'll keep it in my scrip."

Paruline walked Nagora back to the cave entrance with an arm around her.

...

Back at the bowl, Paruline asked, "Nagora, have you done your exercises today?"

"No. With my water leaking, I didn't want to take a chance."

"Were they to be the fast or the slow ones?"

"The slow. Why?"

Paruline looked around the entrance. "Is there a rope or something you could hold on to while standing up?"

"I have a hammock I can hang across the bowl here." She pointed and went to the curtain edge to pull the hammock through.

Paruline took the hooked end and walked it over to where Nagora had indicated. She set it in place. "Okay, this will do, but I have to shorten it so it hangs higher. I'll tie this end around a piece of firewood and then hang it." She handed the end to Nagora. "Hold it. I'll get the wood."

Paruline pulled with all her might and hooked the hammock to its iron ring. Now the net hung across the bowl in a horizontal line. It was just above Nagora's head when she stood beneath it. "Perfect," said Paruline, and she went over to Nagora's bed to bring cloths and blankets over to the bowl. She set them on the stone floor beneath the middle of the hammock.

Then Paruline went to the firepit to stoke the embers beneath the pot and add several pieces of wood. "I need a bowl to scoop out water to wash our hands."

Nagora pointed to the shelf on the wall behind Paruline. "Take your pick from those on the shelf. There's a dish with soap further over."

Paruline held the bowl in one hand and the soap dish in the other as Nagora washed her hands. When Nagora finished, she did the same for Paruline.

Then Paruline emptied the bowl and returned to the pot on the fire for more. "Ooo. That's hot now." She hurried to set the bowl on a chair and added cold water from a waterskin. "I'll wash between your legs. You can either pull up that sweater or take it off. After I wash you, you'll do your exercises."

The inevitable had come. Paruline would see her right thigh. I won't even try to imagine what she'll think. I'll find out soon enough. Nagora pulled her sweater over her head and dropped it on the blanket on the floor and waited.

Paruline bent to one knee before Nagora as she set the bowl and soap dish in place on the floor. She had a washcloth and larger linen cloth draped over her shoulder. She was motionless as she looked at Nagora's leg. Paruline placed a hand on Nagora's hip as she turned her sideways to have a better view. Next came the tentative examining touch of her friend's fingertips as they explored the scars and fresher wounds. A single finger deliberately traced a crooked path on the unscarred skin of her thigh.

Nagora swallowed and waited, submitting to the unspoken questions of Paruline's fingers.

Paruline stood and without a word, put her arms around Nagora and pulled her tight as she brought a cheek next to

Nagora's. She held her like this until Nagora reached her arms around her. Paruline shook as she sucked in her breath through her nose and pulled Nagora even closer. "Little sister, I want you to know that from now on, you are not alone. I know the pain you give yourself helps you overcome another pain you are trying to survive. Know this, Nagora, if you are to survive the birth of your baby, this must stop until you regain your strength. If you do not, you could put your plan in jeopardy."

Paruline placed a hand at the back of Nagora's head and pulled it to her shoulder. "Do you look at your leg when you do this, Nagora?"

"No, Pare. I let my fingers find the places."

Paruline brought her hand from the back of Nagora's head to her chin. She looked into Nagora's eyes. "You've created a maze on your thigh, almost a map of sorts." She hugged Nagora to her again, and then kissed her cheek. "Will you be careful, Nagora?" She let go, stepped back, and held Nagora's eyes with hers.

She's waiting for my answer. "I will, Pare. I promise."

Paruline smiled, wiped away a tear with the back of her hand before kneeling again to wash Nagora.

"What weapon do you want for your exercises?"

"I'll take my bow."

Paruline brought Nagora her bow and stepped back to watch her. "Just pretend I'm not here."

Ward off, rollback, press, push, pull, elbow strike, shoulder strike, advance, retreat, look left, gaze right, center balance. She repeated the warrior's dance a hundred times, slow and deliberate, as her contractions came in waves at closer and closer intervals. Her body sweat as she fought to subdue her pain.

Paruline guided her to the hammock. "Reach up. Hold on. Spread your legs. Let your knees bend as the hammock takes your weight. You'll be squatting. Breathe deep. Push with the contractions. Don't worry. I'm right here behind you on my knees."

Paruline adjusted a folded blanket and clean cloth between Nagora's legs. She rubbed Nagora's back and encouraged her with each push she made. "That's it. Push. Hold it. Relax." Now and then she reached around and placed a spread hand on Nagora's abdomen.

Nagora took another deep breath and pushed. "It's coming. I can feel it."

"Can you hold on?"

"Yes. I'm holding on. It's coming. It's coming! It's coming!" Pain seared through Nagora's lower back. Paruline must have expected it because she rubbed it away. Then a deep cramp, like the worst ever of her bleedings, seized her insides and twisted them. And then it was over. The release from the pain was a pleasurable contrast. "I've done it!" she cried.

"Yes, you have, Nagora!" Paruline held the baby. "It's a girl, Nagora. Hold on. I'll clean her eyes and nose and mouth. Look, Nagora." Paruline reached forward between Nagora's legs, leaning against the back of her legs as she held the infant. She turned it onto its stomach in her left hand.

"I have to make her sing, Nagora." Paruline's right hand gave a quick sharp slap to the baby's bottom. The baby cried. "Listen to her sing! See those blue spots at the base of her back and on her bum? Her father is definitely from the line of the First People of this land, like Raynhard. She has his black hair. She'll have his dark skin in summer. Your feelings are confirmed. With time, the blue spots will disappear."

Paruline turned the baby over and set her down on the blanket. "Admire your daughter, Nagora. Hold on. I'll come around to finish cleaning her face and help you."

Paruline wiped birth fluid from the baby's eyes, mouth, and ears before holding the baby to Nagora with one hand as she placed her other arm around Nagora's waist. "Help me hold her to you. Can you stand straight, mother Nagora?"

Nagora stood and placed one hand on Paruline's shoulder as her other reached over to her daughter.

"Can you walk over to your bed with me?"

Nagora nodded. "Pare, she's so small."

"She looks healthy, Nagora. She will be strong like you."

Paruline had Nagora lay on her bed with her baby to her chest. "I will tie off the cord, Nagora, and when your daughter's first coat comes out, I'll cut the cord. Then we'll place it with the coat in the fire as an offering to your star ancestors."

Nagora witnessed this simple ritual once before when Geirador and Pare had helped deliver a baby in Cairnmase. Now it's my turn.

Paruline covered them with a knit blanket. "I'll get some warm water to clean both of you."

You are so small, my daughter. I will call you Sarah. Nagora touched Sarah's tiny pink, wrinkled face. She placed her little finger in Sarah's hand and Sarah held on tight. She smiled at her daughter.

You are so tiny, yet so strong, *Piwi Mahihkan*, Little Wolf.

Paruline washed the baby and just as she started on the mother, Nagora said, "I think her coat's coming out."

"Let me cut the cord first. There, I have it. To the fire." Paruline stepped over to the fire and let the newborn's first coat and cord slip from her hands. "May your daughter live a long life and only find her coat for her final journey to the stars."

"Thanks, Pare."

After Paruline had finished washing them, she propped folded blankets around them and placed Danuka's egg at Nagora's side. "So it will warm and be ready for the feeding. Now you have to rest. Try to sleep a little. I'll watch over you. When you wake, you'll feed your daughter."

Nagora had dressed and was sitting cross-legged on her bed. She slipped her left arm from the sleeve of her sweater and let it fall behind her shoulder. Then she brought baby Sarah to her breast and rocked back and forth as Sarah sucked at her nipple.

"She's always hungry, Pare."

"That's good. Let her feed as often as she wants. Here, I've filled the rabbit-leg teat again with more of the egg."

Nagora placed the feeding skin against her own skin above her breast. She had made it from the skin of a rabbit's hind leg, scraped clean of its fur. She had stitched the long seam to close it, folded it over, and stitched it again. This gave her a little bag she could fill through the ankle opening with the help of a funnel. A drawstring closed it off. This allowed Sarah to suck out the contents.

...

The tiny bell hanging from the cave's ceiling tinkled. Sarah stopped sucking for a moment as Danuka landed on the lip of the bowl. "Welcome, Mother," Nagora called from her bed. "Come see my baby."

Danuka folded her wings and brought their curled talons down onto the cave floor as she stepped down into the entrance. She turned in Nagora's direction with her great tail wrapping itself around her belly. The dragon stretched her neck out and brought her head down over Nagora's baby, smelling it. Danuka moaned. She brought the tip of her snout against Nagora's forehead.

"Yes, Mother, she is small, but she is so strong. And she is getting stronger with your gift. She drinks it with my milk at every feeding. Watch."

Danuka pulled her head back far enough to see.

Nagora pulled her own nipple from Sarah's mouth and gave her the rabbit-leg teat. Sarah sucked away at it, as content as at her mother's breast. "See, Mother. She is feeding on your egg. Thanks to you, she will grow stronger."

Danuka touched Nagora's brand again.

"I call her Sarah, Mother. She is my *piwi mahihkan*, my little wolf."

Danuka lifted her head away and looked to Paruline. She had been standing by the firepit, watching and listening. Her mouth hung open. She must've heard me say the baby's name. Paruline's eyes were blinking away tears.

Nagora held out a hand to Paruline. "Sorry, Pare, I didn't ask you. But I've always loved your mum's name."

Paruline went to Nagora, hugged her, and placed a hand on Sarah's head. "Thank you, Nagora, for honoring Mum's memory. Da will be so happy."

Danuka touched Paruline's hand with the tip of her snout and moaned.

"See, Pare, Danuka likes my baby's name too."

On the evening of the third day of Paruline's stay with Nagora, Danuka told Nagora: "My shedding time approaches. Prepare Sarah. She leaves with Paruline tomorrow morning."

"You're sure you still want to go through with this, Nagora?" Paruline held her hand.

"It's my choice, Pare. I brought this upon myself. It's my plan now. It's my battle. It'll be my chance to redeem myself, to make up for my actions and choices. Who else will get rid of Hag? She'll not stop until the last dragon is dead. I've sworn to protect Danuka and her eggs. The future of the People of the Danu depends on it. Our king's future depends on it, even though he's blind to the danger he courts. I have to make him see again."

The early morning air was cold. Nagora hummed as she nursed Sarah for a last time. Paruline tied a scarf over her head and was ready to leave. She watched Nagora.

Nagora placed Sarah in the sheepskin carrying pouch. "Danuka wants you to give her to Sagora." She pointed to the front of the pouch. "Here in the pocket is a letter for Sagora. She's to open it if ever I don't return with Lars to get Sarah. But I'll return. It's just in case." She picked up her daughter and rubbed her nose against Sarah's. "Aye, Mummy will miss you. You're in good hands. Pare will find someone to nurse you, and she'll bring a few of Danuka's eggs too. It won't be long before Mummy comes to pick you up again."

Nagora held Sarah to her cheek and closed her eyes. "Pare, if for some reason I don't come for Sarah, I want you to tell Sagora that I want you to raise her as your own, even if Danuka told me to give my baby to Sagora; because, right now, Sagora, Tagnya, and Yogari are so busy. Not that you aren't too, but you've always been the person I trust the most. I trust you'll take good care of her, and when she's old enough, you and your da will train her."

Paruline smiled. "You'll come for her, eventually. In the meantime, I'll care for her as if she were mine. Da will be happy to have a little Sarah at home."

"Pare, thank you so much for all your help. I don't know how I'll ever be able to show you how much I appreciate what you've done for me and Sarah." Nagora held out her four-day old baby so Paruline could put Sarah's arms through the pouch straps that would cross over her shoulders.

Paruline lifted the top flap of the pouch and kissed Sarah's forehead. "You're going for your first ride on a dragon, little one. Enjoy it. Danuka will have us home in no time."

Danuka brought the tip of her snout to Nagora's brand.

Nagora didn't say a word. She swallowed and nodded as she reached into the neck of her sweater to her amulet, pulled it up over her head, and went to Paruline. She placed the amulet around Sarah's neck and kissed her. *Now the witch will know I'm defenseless.*

Then she removed her skystone blades and rolled them into a neat bundle and placed them in the leather bag attached to Danuka's harness. "Pare, my blades are for my daughter. Tell that to Sagora." She hugged Paruline and then helped her up to the saddle.

Nagora stepped down from Danuka's wing. The dragon climbed to the lip of the bowl. Paruline looked over her shoulder and nodded to Nagora.

"They're ready, Mother," she called.

Nagora waved to Paruline. Her hand trembled as she did.

Danuka is out of sight. I'm alone again. Already I miss you, Sarah. What am I doing? Should I go through with this? Do I have a choice? I've set it in motion. I must follow through. No turning back now. I best get busy.

I must call the Little People.

Nagora went to the shelf where she had set Uncle's blades, took them in her hands, and brought them to her chest. She put her cheek to the walrus hide handle of the big blade, walked over to the entrance, and looked out to the sky. "Uncle, give me strength. Watch over Sarah." She slipped the holster straps of the sheath onto her shoulders and returned to the table.

From her scrip, Nagora took the gold dragon coin she had prepared and turned it over in her hand. Each of the dragon wings had a hole. On the other face of the coin, each hole had taken out a star. Then she took a fine leather lace and threaded it through one star hole, pulled it through to thread into the dragon wing hole. She pulled the lace ends to make them equal.

Nagora pulled Uncle's big skystone blade from its sheath and set it on the table so she could tie the gold coin in place on the handle just above the crossguard. Good. The coin rests against the blade's centerline, just above the Tiwaz symbol, and it won't swing to the blade edges to cut itself free. She grasped the skystone blade handle and headed for the stream near the valley entrance.

Nagora found a spot in the stream bed where enough gravel had accumulated to stick the blade in at an angle so the current would make the coin tap out its calling song to the Little People. She remained kneeling near the stream and watched, in the light of her lantern, as the coin hopped and jumped underwater against the skystone blade.

I count on your help, *Mêmêkwêsiw*; please, come to help me.

Nagora crawled into her small cave and crept past Pug. Rolling onto her back, she pushed with her heels into the smaller recessed area to get her pouch of gold coins.

Nagora set the pouch just outside the entrance of the small cave. While on her knees there, before returning to Pug, she, bent and rested her face in her open palms. She took a deep breath. Now Hag, be you Erin, Aliza, or Alizarine in body, if somehow with your witch powers you can hear me, let this be my invitation to you to join me in an alliance you could never have imagined. I'll play this out as best I can, and hope to see results that will best suit my plan.

With renewed hope and resolve to carry out her plan, Nagora crawled back into the small cave. She placed a hand on his left leg. "Pug, can you hear me? I'm back. It worked, Pug. It was hard. It hurt. It hurt me something terrible. But it was worth it. I'm rid of it. The king's runt is no more."

Nagora crawled up alongside him and placed Pug's hand on her belly. "Can you feel what's no longer there? Before taking Erin's poison, I removed my amulet. I'm no longer shackled to the dragon. I'm finally free! I'm free, Pug.

"You should've seen it! I had to pull it from me. I wrapped the lace of my amulet around its neck to pull it out. I almost ripped off its blue head. It was a bitch, Pug. A fucking little bitch I don't have to feed.

"I have so much milk. Do you want to drink it, Pug? It might be good for you." She pulled up her sweater and placed a nipple at his mouth. "Go on, Pug, suck it." She squeezed her breast until milk dribbled on his lips. She slipped a finger between his lips so it leaked into his mouth. "Can you taste it? I wish you were awake. You could drink your fill. Suck both my tits dry." She squeezed more milk from her breast to his mouth. "That poor little blue bitch never got to taste my milk. Isn't that sad, Pug? Imagine when I show that little, shriveled blue body to the king. I'll pick it up by a foot and shake it at him. I'll tell him, 'Here's your little bitch. Isn't she something?' Ha! What do you think he'll say? Do you think he'll cry?"

Nagora pulled her sweater down and sat back on her heels. "I know when he will cry. Oh! Shit! Is he ever going to cry when he sees I've slain his dragon. Pug, he'll lose all hope. He'll fall down on his fucking knees. He won't know what the fuck to do, will he? I'll have dashed all his dreams. Just like that, his dream dashed by the one who's supposed to protect that dream. He's going to regret he raped me and used me."

Nagora placed a hand on Pug's chest, next to the hand holding the gilded egg. "I bet Erin would like to witness the king fall down like that. She'll get what she's always wanted.

She'll become the beautiful Alizarine once again, forever. Alizarine will be irresistible once again. She'll have any man she wants, any king and his kingdom. The world will be hers, Pug. What'll she do for us? Take us on as her faithful servants? I hope she can heal you, so you can get the reward you deserve. Maybe you'll want me too. Whatever happens, Pug, know that you did your best. And whatever happens to me, I'll know I finally did something of my own choosing. I'm free of the king's bitch that was growing inside me and I'm free of the dragon. Now all I have to do is kill the last dragon."

Nagora bent and kissed Pug's forehead. "I'll be back later to give you your medicine."

"Welcome, Mother. Did my Sarah have a safe trip?"

Danuka put her wing talons on the floor as she climbed down from the lip of the bowl. She touched her snout to Nagora's forehead. "My little wolf made the trip well. Geirador was still holding her when you left for Windhaven. He was happy."

This news made her smile. I wish I could have been there to watch Geirador hold Sarah in his huge hands. She must've looked so tiny in those hands. Tiny and safe.

"Mother, has news of Sarah's birth reached Windhaven?

"No one mentioned it. Did you see Yogari?

"You flew with him to the Isle of Smoke. Have they found a cave suitable for you?

"One that shows promise. The entrance will need to be secured from rock slides. And they are looking for another. Moving fallen rock and digging away debris takes time.

"Mother, I am sure Da is doing his best to find the ideal place for you. How many days before your shedding, Mother?

"In two days. Will you have the strength to bring a message to the king for me?

"Good. Yes, Mother. I will set my plan in motion. I will fight the witch and win. If not, I will die trying."

After Danuka inspected her eggs, Nagora took another hide, a sleeping roll, and her small medical scrip to the small cave. She set the hide out on the floor about fifty paces from the small cave entrance and placed her pouch of gold coins on the hide.

Inside the small cave, Nagora washed Pug's body. She prepared the medicine Paruline had left her. She ran the drop down a spoon onto his tongue and then made him drink from the waterskin. "There you go, Pug. This will keep the fever away, and you won't feel any pain. I'll sleep here by your side.

"I've been able to convince the dragon to leave the egg with you until after her shedding. But it will be too late by then, Pug. She'll have no use for her eggs by then. They'll all be for Erin. And she'll give you your reward. You'll be rich. If she gives you the gold from the eggs, you'll be doubly rich. It's the purest of gold." She kissed Pug's forehead. "I'll be back later."

Nagora stood outside the small cave with her hands on lower back as she stretched and took a long breath. There it is—my invitation laid for Hag. Now the question is: Will she take it?

Little People
Mêmêkwêsiw

What is that? Did I hear it or imagine it? I'm no longer alone in the cave. Nagora had spread out the gold coins on the hide and then blown out her lantern to wait for their arrival. She tried to see with her ears in the dark. I'm sure it came from the valley entrance. Should I call to them?

No. They have arrived. They're coming. Hundreds of them. And more following behind them. She swallowed. Stay calm. Believe what you see. Those are the tiniest lights I've ever seen. Smaller than sparks. Pinpoints of light. White light.

Do I believe my eyes? They walked along the floor and on the walls right up to the cave ceiling. They spread in a steady stream, flowing toward her and then past her and all around her.

The lights stopped coming. Nagora held her breath and waited. The lights all went out at the same time. She took a breath, and they all lit up again. She could see nothing else. Not a shadow, not a shape. She reached down and picked up three coins and let them fall. The lights flashed in waves and swirls as if they were dancing.

Nagora spoke to them as she did to Danuka, in the *Language of The People*. "Welcome, Little People, to the home of my dragon. *Mêmêkwêsiw*, I am honored that you have heeded my call in my time of need. My need is great, for I battle a witch who is powerful and who seeks to destroy the last dragon in the Land of the Danu.

"I have learned about you as many of my kind have, through the many stories told about you. And I have learned about you from one I trust who says he has dealt with you in person. He is the maker of the skystone blade I planted in the stream to call you. He told me you would come, and you have. Again, I thank you." She waited.

What Nagora heard covered her body in goose bumps. It was a single voice that came from all the lights in the cave from all around her. That voice spoke clearly, almost as a whisper in her ears and so real it was breath on her neck.

"We come to you in peace, Dragon Talker. We are at your service. We will do our best to protect your dragon and its eggs. Such has been our duty throughout the ages. It is in our interest to continue to harvest the gold of the dragon eggs. Your dragon is the last in the Land of the Danu. We have been waiting for this moment for a long time. Protect you, though, is not something we can do, no matter the price you pay.

"You have already paid with your child for one dragon-young egg, a high price. What can you give us in payment for our help?"

They know? A chill of regret ran through her. She had to take a breath to speak.

"All these gold coins are yours."

"What else?"

"My dragon will give you her shed skin."

"What else?"

"I have nothing else of value."

"The small blades on your back and the skystone blade in the stream. They are yours?"

Nagora hung her head. Uncle. "Yes." She slipped the holsters from her shoulders, brought them to her lips, and then laid them on the hide before her. "They are yours now." Had I agreed to have my arm cut off, it would feel like this.

"The golden hunting dagger in your vest. That is yours?"

"Yes, it is mine. I need it to kill a dragon. And I need it to kill the witch. Afterwards, whether I live or die, it will be yours."

"What else?"

"Tell me what you want. If it is mine, I will give it to you."

"The horn of your unicorn."

"You are in luck. I have two of those."

"We only need one to help you with your plan."

"But you don't know my plan."

For a moment, all the lights glowed with a greater intensity that lit up the cave for the blink of an eye. Then the lights went out; and, in the darkness, a lone voice in her ear spoke every detail of her plan.

They know it and all that caused me to conceive it. I feel so vulnerable before them.

The lights reappeared and the voice from before spoke. "Dragon Talker, you have chosen this path and this plan. We can do our best to help you protect your dragon, but as we said before, we cannot protect you from the unknown. When fighting evil, we always face the unknown. The path you have chosen could end here. From now on, trust us. Let us do our work."

"*Mêmêkwêsiw*, I put my trust in you."

"Dragon Talker, do not fear our actions. We are leaving to prepare and we are here. Do not try to understand how we do what we do. Appreciate what we do."

All the tiny lights swiveled in unison, and then marched off in the direction they had come, fading into the darkness, disappearing into the unknown.

Again I wear the mantle of loneliness. Oh! Sarah! If I could hold you again, perhaps for the last time, to have you suckle one last time, I could bear this feeling.

Uncle, my plan is in motion. Watch over me, please.

Nagora reached into her scrip for the small pouch of fire starter and her flint. My last words to the Little People. Why do I have doubts?

It must be all those stories of their trickery. But weren't those also stories of how our kind wanted to trick the Little People out of their possessions or try to hold them captive?

Nagora moved over to the edge of the hide to where she had set the lantern down. She opened one of its panes and took out the candle. Then she took the royal hunting dagger from her vest pocket, pulled it from the sheath, and dragged it across the flint to spark the fire starter to life. She touched the candle wick to the flame and returned it to its holder in the lamp.

Appreciate what you do? You've left with every last coin I've ever had, my Uncle's blades, and a unicorn tusk. Why do I feel like you've robbed me?

I'm ashamed. How can I think such thoughts?

Why can I, in one breath, profess my trust in you, and then moments later feel like you've deceived me? Geirador told me to trust you. I trust Geirador. I told you I trusted you to help me. So why do I have those thoughts? You seem to know everything about me, everything about my plan, and more. I've paid you. You've taken all you esteem to be of value.

Danuka took my child, my amulet, and my blades. What do I have left?

Nagora held up the royal hunting dagger. I'm defenseless, except for this dagger. It's already spoken for. It's no longer mine. It's my weapon of choice for this battle. My other weapons will be useless.

Mêmêkwêsiw, you are right. I chose this path. My actions led me here. I must follow through. I chose to call on you for help. I must trust you. Without you, my plan is doomed to failure.

Nagora lay down on her bedroll next to Pug. She placed a hand on his cheek, leaned over, and kissed his lips. "Sleep well, Pug. Rest so you can get better." She closed her eyes. That was for you, Hag.

Sarah, I'm imagining you are here with me and I'm watching you feed at my breast. Please, let me sleep.

The next morning at the cave entrance, Nagora couldn't help but notice Danuka's lips had swollen. "Mother, are you well today?"

Danuka touched Nagora. "Yes, Mother, I will prepare my message for the king. You will deliver it tomorrow. The swelling is a sign that the shedding time approaches. Tomorrow will be the last time you fly in your old skin."

"Mother, the Little People, *Mêmêkwêsiw*, answered my call for help last night. I have paid them in part with the gold, Uncle's blades, and a unicorn tusk. Only your shed skin and the royal hunting dagger remain to be given in payment."

Danuka's wings pulled her skyward.

Nagora turned away from the lip of the cave. I hope Mother will be well. Now, to get on with my busy day.

First, her daily ritual exercises. Today, she did them fast, with the royal hunting dagger in hand.

Nagora came away from them with a clear mind, ready to write her missive to the king.

‡

My King Raynhard,

> In five days from now, I bid you to come to what was once our secret place. Come by the valley entrance, like you did the first time with me.

> I bid you to come witness the legacy I will leave to you.
> Come witness the legacy I will leave to your kingdom.
> Come witness the legacy I will leave to the People of the Danu.
> Come witness the legacy I will leave to my child.

> I bid you to come with your companion, Aliza.
> Come with her to witness the legacy I will leave to your dreams.
> Come and witness Aliza rejoice for you and your people.

> Come witness a glimpse of what the future holds for you.

Your faithful servant,

Edana
‡

Nagora reread the missive before folding it. *He won't come by the valley entrance. He knows about the trap.* She pricked a drop of her blood from her finger onto the vellum, poured candle wax over it, and, as the wax clouded red, she pressed her Edana seal into the wax. When she lifted her seal, its imprint sat on the vellum overlap. It was a circle with four parallel lines that cut across it. Two dots sat on the second line, one on the third line, and a single dot on the fourth line. The Tiwaz symbol rose from the first line. *Will Raynhard get its meaning?*

For a higher cause, for a higher cause. I will not fail in my duty again. For a higher cause.

She placed the letter in the message pouch, ready for Danuka to deliver.

Then Nagora went to Raynhard's cache of weapons. She took three short swords and three spears to place in strategic spots in the cave so they would be at hand while she watched over Danuka during her shedding. *I'll bring my bow and quiver too.* And she stuffed a half dozen candles in her scrip to renew the ones in the lanterns of the cave.

After placing the last of the candle stubs in her scrip, Nagora crawled into her small cave with a lantern to look in on Pug. She found the gilded egg at Pug's side next to his left hand.

Are you still alive?

Nagora pulled the blanket from him and watched him for a few moments. His chest rose and fell slightly. She touched his open palm. The fingers twitched ever so slightly. She placed three fingers in his palm and closed his fingers over them.

"Pug, how are you? How are you doing? Can you hear me? If you can, squeeze my fingers. Pug, if you are in pain or hurting, squeeze my fingers."

No response. What caused you to lose hold of the egg?

"You slept well last night. Did you have a bad dream? You've lost hold of your egg. Here, Pug, I'll put it back on your chest. Hold it. You don't want to lose it, do you?"

Nagora raised his head and placed a rolled-up sheepskin hide beneath it. Then she held the waterskin close to his lips and dribbled water on them. She placed two fingers between his lips and poured more until he swallowed. She gave him more.

"You'll get your medicine later.

"It won't be long. In six days, Pug, I'll get my revenge. Erin will come. She'll help you. She'll have medicine stronger than mine. Hold on, Pug. You've got to hold on."

"Welcome, Mother."

Danuka had swelling in the scaly skin around her eyes, snout, ears, on each side of her wing talons, and at the joints of her legs.

"How are you feeling? You look tired, Mother. I am concerned."

Danuka touched the Tiwaz brand on Nagora's forehead.

"Yes, Mother, my message to the king is ready for you to deliver. Your shedding will start tomorrow night. I am not to be afraid.

"Mother, I will not be afraid. Trust me. I will watch over you.

"Yes, Mother, I have prepared the food. I can cut and boil some for you if you wish, like I did for you in the cold days we had this past winter.

"I understand, Mother. I will keep my distance. I will keep out of your way. I won't be afraid. And I will not worry.

"Is there anything else I should know, Mother?

"You will leave in darkness well before morning's first light and return as soon as possible.

"Thank you, Mother. I will be ready for you."

That night, on her way to the small cave, Nagora found a gold coin standing on its edge on the hide she had set out to watch for the Little People.

I'm sure I didn't forget it there. It must be a sign. Are they returning? I'll give Pug his medicine and come back here to wait.

My eyes feel heavy. I must've fallen asleep sitting here cross-legged. Nagora stretched her legs out on the hide. How long have I been sitting here? I should lie down.

Then the sound came, and the pinpoints of light appeared, but not in the numbers of their first visit, yet enough to get her attention. She blinked her eyes and waited. The gold coin still stood on its edge. They surrounded her, and then the voice whispered, "Ask no questions. Do as you are told."

Nagora nodded. Did they see me acknowledge their words? Surely.

"Remove all your clothes. Lay on your back on the hide. Spread your arms and legs. Do not fear. We will not harm you. Breathe, but do not move."

Nagora had questions. Why? What will you do? She obeyed their order and lay naked on the hide. She waited and waited and when she was about to speak, she felt it. It was just perceptible on the skin at her feet and then the sensation repeated itself as it worked upward along her legs to the rest of her body and around her neck and face and forehead and out to her arms and fingers.

Yes. My fingers will know. It's like a fine thread being wrapped around a finger, not too tight, not too loose. By the time the sensation left her fingers, it seemed to lift from her feet and legs and hips and waist, chest, shoulders, neck, face, and arms.

"Get dressed."

I know what they've done. They've measured me. Why? What does that have to do with my plan? Don't speak the questions out loud. Obey.

The pinpoints gathered before her and the voice spoke to her. "Someday, you will thank us. Sleep well."

What does it mean? Why? I don't understand. Those words hold both comfort and foreboding. Which of those feelings should I trust? Is there a warning in those words?

I know I have to trust you, but I dislike trusting blindly.

Transformations
Meskociwepinikewin

Nagora awoke to Danuka's gentle prodding. She was curled into a ball under two sheepskin hides on the spot where the Little People had measured her. Awaking from the deep sleep, she brushed away the misshapen memory of what she had been dreaming. Who covered me with the sheepskins? "Yes, Mother, I'll be with you in a moment."

Getting up was like pulling herself up from a thousand invisible threads that held her down. She lit her lantern. Are there actually threads holding me? Once she was standing, she set herself in motion, stopping to scoop up a handful of water from the stream to splash on her face.

At the cave entrance Danuka was waiting. Nagora lit another candle. The appearance of Danuka's face caused her to step back. Her dragon looked so frightening in the dim light. The swelling hadn't stopped. Can she still see? She was careful in adjusting the bridle and harness on Danuka. She placed the message pouch in one of the leather bags and attached it to the harness.

"Mother, have you eaten?"

Danuka touched her.

"You are sure, Mother? I trust you. Okay. No offer of food for the next three days. I understand.

"I'll be waiting for your safe return, Mother."

The dragon climbed to the lip on the bowl and balanced there with the help of her long tail. Even in the dim light of the lanterns, the swelling was apparent at the base of her tail, along its ridge, and at its tip.

Danuka disappeared on silent wings into the night. I'm worried. I promised her I wouldn't. Will she return safely? This is the first time I worry about her, but I've never seen her in this condition.

Nagora looked to the stars. Please bring her back safely.

This dark morning, Nagora wrapped two blue dragon eggs with red and gold-leaf-gilded veins in a small woolen blanket she had knitted for Sarah. They were the last of the four dragon eggs she had gilded. She started the slow hundred repetitions of her exercises, holding the two eggs in one arm, as if they were Sarah. Her other hand held the royal hunting dagger to ward off, rollback, press, push, pull, elbow strike, shoulder strike, advance, retreat, look left, gaze right, center balance. I'll focus on protecting Sarah in each position.

It had never taken her such effort to complete the set, and when she did, she fell to her knees in tears. She dropped the dagger and cradled the eggs to her. Her tears gave way to heaving sobs. "My Sarah, what have I done?" The question came out of her as a hoarse, strangled scream of desperation. She stared at the woolen bundle in her arms and shook her head as she tried to regain control of her breath. When she did, she set the eggs aside.

Then Nagora unfastened her right legging and pushed it down as she brought herself upright. Through the watery haze of her eyes, she bent and picked up the royal blade with her right hand while the fingers of her left hand groped in search of a scar-free strip of skin on her thigh. When it found one, she guided the tip to the spot.

"Sarah, forgive me for what I have done."

Nagora took a deep breath and swallowed.

"I will not fail in my duty again."

She pressed and pulled to plow another furrow for her pain.

Nagora fell over onto her side and lay there until daylight crept into the cave entrance and her tears had dried.

After eating for the first time that day, Nagora prepared packets of dried fruit and nuts. She cut fine strips of dried smoked meat and wrapped them in pieces of clean linen. She set these back in the food cache.

Nagora went to Danuka's reserve of dried and salted meat at the other end of the cave, bringing back selected pieces to cut up for boiling. Before doing that, she set a pot, filled with root vegetables, on the fire to boil. They would be for her. By the time they would be ready, the meat for Danuka would be ready to take their place in the pot.

...

Just as she put the pot of Danuka's meat on the fire, the tiny bell tinkled. Danuka settled on the lip, folded in her wings, leaned in on her talons, and hopped to the floor. "Welcome, Mother." I don't know what else to say. Can she still see from the slits of swollen skin? I can barely see her eyes. Don't ask. Get busy. Remove her bridle and harness.

As soon as she finished, Danuka left the entrance and headed deeper into the cave. Nagora set the bridle and harness down to follow her from a distance.

Danuka eased into the lake and submerged. Nagora counted. At two hundred, the dragon's head surfaced. She snorted water from her snout and went under again. The water must bring her some relief. I wonder if she is in pain. Does her skin itch? What does old skin pulling away from new skin feel like? Painful like a fresh blister?

Danuka surfaced and slowly swam around the island once before climbing out of the water. She rubbed the length of one side of her body against the lone stone pillar that stood on the island like a gigantic inverted carrot growing skyward. She repeated the rubbing on the other side of her body, and then returned to the lake to disappear underwater again. This time, hundreds of bubbles, in small groups and then big clumps, popped and gasped on the water's surface. Nagora smiled. Reminds me of Geirador's ale poured to quickly in a mug.

When Danuka climbed back onto the island, she rubbed the whole length of her neck against the pillar as well as the edge of a wing, raising it as high as she could before dragging it back down. As the base of her tail came alongside the obelisk-shaped pillar, the rest of it wrapped halfway up and around it. As she moved on, she pulled her tail while keeping a certain tension on it as it slipped free of the pillar.

She repeated the same slow dance against the pillar for her other side.

Only a narrow strip of the dragon's skin was attached to the length of her backbone. The skin around the length of her neck was wrinkled almost all the way up to the back of her ears. The skin on her tail was also loose and sagging.

Danuka crawled back into the lake and swam slowly around the island a dozen times before letting herself sink beneath the surface again, staying there for a count of five hundred. All that time the water above rippled with bubbles rising and popping.

On Danuka's third climb onto the island, she pulled herself across it so her front rubbed from her chest area along her belly to the base under her tail.

Then Danuka folded her wings to her sides, rolled over onto her back, and spread her wings out. Wow! I've never seen her do that! Like Aydan rolling over to have his belly scratched. My! Her belly seam has a slit the length of my arm.

Danuka twisted and reached her head back to the stone pillar. Tar piss! She's biting on it! Small fragments of stone fell and Danuka swept them into her mouth with her tongue. Then she pushed up with her wings as her long neck arched up and over her belly like a cat about to lick itself. Instead, she breathed in and out through her open mouth, cradling the stone fragments on her blood-orange tongue. Her breaths came quicker as her belly expanded, splitting the seam further.

The skin around Danuka's eyes now hung like loose bags, and that of her lips around her open mouth drooped limp as flags on a windless day.

Danuka stopped breathing, brought her head back so her snout pointed at the cave's ceiling, and shook her head from side to side. Do I hear the stone fragments striking Danuka's teeth? Is she setting them in place between the upper and lower teeth?

When Danuka breathed again, she did so through her snout, but she only breathed in. Her belly grew and grew so the seam split more and more. The new belly skin scales appeared to be white, the color of newly frozen wavelets on a lake, in contrast to the lush green tones of her old skin.

A strange wheezing noise came from Danuka's snout as she expelled the air she had breathed in. Her old belly skin sagged away from the new. She crossed her wings over her chest, rolled onto her side, and then pushed her front up with her wings as her tail helped raise her rear so she could slide her hind legs under to stand.

Danuka closed her mouth and began quick intakes of breath through her snout. Ripples of unattached skin the width of Nagora's saddle traveled along Danuka's backbone and neck. Danuka raised her long neck in a graceful curve so it bent back over one of her outstretched wings. As her giant belly expanded, she flapped her wings and took in more air, and now her chest and neck expanded as well.

Danuka chewed and sparks were flying from between her biting teeth as she exhaled to release a giant belch that ignited into a flame, streaming out of her snout and mouth in a plume of orange and red. It licked across the water to the opposite shore, making a rushing noise like a storm wind along the sea coast.

Nagora stumbled backward. That's the biggest burst of flames I've ever seen in my life! Her heart was beating like a drum. Tar piss! The fire power of a dragon! Her heartbeat slowed. Is this something dragons only do when they shed, or can they do it at will?

Danuka moaned as she settled on the island rock in the middle of the lake. She brought her head back so it rested on the taloned joint of her right wing. A single red eye looked over the drooping face skin at Nagora.

"Rest, Mother." Nagora left for the cave entrance.

How will the Little People manage with Danuka's shed skin?

What had Geirador written in his letter?

Nagora remembered: " … and you will have the dragon's shed skin to offer them. It is most prized by the Little People … Trust them, Nagora. Let them work their magic."

So much of the old skin has come loose and it hasn't broken except for the belly's seam. Only parts of the skin at the tail, legs, wings, and around the neck near the head still held on.

I'm sure the lake water has made it easier for Mother.

Back at the entrance, Nagora picked up the bridle and the harness with its small saddle. She took the time to inspect them before hanging them on their pegs on Danuka's side of the cave. Geirador's handiwork with the leather was holding up well thanks to his attention to details that made both the rider and the dragon comfortable. Have I given enough thought to the details of my plan? How will I fair as it unfolds?

At the back of her mind the words of the *Mêmêkwêsiw* ruffled her: " ... we cannot protect you from the unknown. When fighting evil, there is always the unknown. The path you have chosen could end here." Have I truly chosen this path, or has my dragon set me on it? Have I ever had a choice?

Nagora climbed the ladder that leaned against the lip of the bowl at the cave entrance. She looked out over the growing carpet of green leaves on the trees in the valley below.

They are getting their new skin too.

Nagora looked at the backs of her hands and rolled up her sleeves to see the skin on her arms. Still so pale. I can imagine my face. In the past years, the sun had always burnished the winter white of her skin until it shone with the light, golden brown tone she would wear until late fall.

For a moment, an image of her walking with Sarah in her arms along her beach at Sandy Hook Bay washed into her mind like a gentle wave lapping at the shore. That image disappeared when the wave pulled back into the bay. Will I ever walk along that seashore with Sarah? She had walked her beach all those years, without her mother, believing her mother had died giving birth to her.

What will my daughter believe about me?

Time to go back and check on my dragon.

The sound of splashing woke Nagora. Her head snapped up from her chest. She had tried to stay awake as she kept watch over Danuka. She had been sitting on the cave floor near the lake with her back against the stone wall, knees drawn up, her strung bow resting over her knees and an arrow in her hands.

Danuka had her wings spread out and was dipping them in and out of the water.

Nagora reached for an arrow on the floor. How long was I asleep?

The dragon climbed back onto the island, slowly bringing one leg up, then the other, and finally her tail. The skin on her legs and tail had released. Danuka stood still as the water dripped from her.

Then, one after the other, she lifted a leg from the ground and moved it in a small circle. She did this several times until her legs came free of their old skin.

With the help of her tail, she pushed the old sleeve of skin from her neck and head, and then she brought the finned-ball tip of her tail around and held it in place with a front claw as she pulled her new tail free. These were easy feats for Danuka, considering the length of her tail that wrapped completely around her when she rested her belly flat on the ground.

Finally, Danuka spread her wings wide, brought them up and flapped them, first, in small arcs that she widened, and then in bigger and bigger arcs. Gracefully, she pulled them back at her sides, brought them down to the ground, and stepped out of them.

Danuka stood proud in her glistening new white scaly skin. Her new skin was almost translucent. All the muscles beneath her skin rippled with clear definition as Danuka flexed her wings again. Oh! My! Mother is beautiful!

Her new wing talons and claws had the color of day-old icicles. She stretched her whole body as if fitting her new skin to it. Wow! I've never seen her open her mouth so wide. She swung her head from side to side and wiggled her ears. Her tail caressed her neck and back and legs.

Danuka brought her snout down to her old skin then looked over to Nagora.

"It is promised to the Little People, Mother. The *Mêmêkwêsiw* will prepare it to create another dragon that looks like you."

Danuka moaned as she slipped back into the lake. She swam around the island a dozen times and then climbed out near Nagora. Already, Danuka's skin on her back and wings was changing to its natural color, taking on a deep, sky-blue hue while the red at her lips and along her wing's edges was darkening. Her belly took on its lush green hue. All over the dragon, the multicolored, iridescent hues were beginning to show. Is it because her skin is drying?

Danuka brought the tip of her snout to Nagora's brand. By the stars! Da was right. You've grown. By how much? She reached up to pet the skin between Danuka's eyes and along her snout. Oh! My! Danuka's eyes sit farther apart by at least the width of two fingers! "Mother, you are so beautiful. You have grown.

"You are tired. You will sleep and then you will eat.

"I will watch over you, Mother. Sleep. I will prepare a hot pot of food for you.

"First you will check your eggs.

"Yes, Mother, I will help you."

At the entrance on Danuka's side of the cave, Nagora sat on the floor with her vest laid out before her crossed legs. She reached for one of the four-pocket pouches, pulled it closer to her, and removed one of the single-egg pouches. Danuka brought her folded wing talons down to the floor just behind her. Nagora removed the egg from the pouch. *The essence of The Dragon's Kiss is back, but it's not the same as before I was with child. It's taking hold of my body's muscles, kneading each one into awareness. It's most intense in the muscles of my hands right now. Is it because I'm holding and turning her eggs for her?*

By the time Danuka finished her inspection, Nagora was relaxed yet aware of all that surrounded her. The clutching torture between her legs was absent. *Is it because of Danuka's new skin, or because I gave birth, or because I gave my Sarah to her?*

Danuka pulled back her wings. Nagora stood aside on tip-toes as Danuka curled around her eggs to rest. She was aware of how every muscle up and down her legs connected. *It's strange. I feel strong and relaxed at the same time. It's like my body is telling me I'm ready to take on anything.* Now Danuka's huge back pushed against the leather curtain on her side of the cave.

Yes, you have grown, Mother. In a strange way, I feel like I have also. Have I matured as a Dragon Talker?

Nagora went to her firepit and lit the fire starter under the kindling. When it took, she added several logs, then added water to the pot of cut pieces of prepared meat before hanging it over the fire. *I feel tired. I'll lay down for two counts, then check the pot.*

Nagora had fallen asleep while counting. When she opened her eyes, she listened and looked, only moving her eyes. *I'm* being watched. I can feel tiny eyes on me. Let them watch. She stretched before throwing the blanket aside and getting up. Nagora stood and went to put another log on the embers. She was hungry. How is my dragon? I'll go see.

Nagora had just finished the pan-cooked bread with honey, dried fruit, and nuts, when Danuka poked her head past Nagora's leather curtain. "Mother, you must be hungry. I'll bring the pot of hot meat pieces you like. Then I'll give you the bigger smoked pieces. If you do not have enough, I can get more at the other end of the cave."

Danuka had taken her time to empty the pot of boiled pieces of meat. She seemed to savor the tiny pieces, but she devoured the big pieces Nagora had set out, and she wanted more. So Nagora had set off with a big burlap bag and her sled to get some.

But when she reached the end of the passage that opened onto the lake, a network of ropes crisscrossing the passage there stopped her. At her feet to her right, she found a pile of smoked and salted meat pieces like the ones she was on her way to fetch.

Beyond the ropes, a dim procession floated across the water and onto the island in the lake. Are those inflated bladders and animal hides being floated across the water? To be placed inside the dragon skin?

Then a soft whistle came from above her head. She looked up, but could see no one.

"Look all you want. You will not see me, at least not today. But I can see you. As you can see, we are busy. Just let us work and all will go well."

"I have a sick person to look in on."

"Later you will be able to. Right now, you cannot disturb our work. We have brought meat for your dragon. If she wants more, come back here. If the ropes are still here, you'll find more meat right where that pile is. We know what your needs are. Those we can take care of."

"Thank you." Nagora packed the meat into the bag, set it on her sled, and glanced over at the island. I would like to stay and watch, but I must let them do their work.

For three days, Danuka ate and then curled around her eggs to sleep. For each of those days, the Little People let Nagora past the ropes to give Pug his medicine. Each day Danuka's old skin took on a more lifelike appearance. The invisible one at the ropes said, "Come the final day, you'll not believe your eyes."

The morning of Danuka's departure had arrived. Nagora prepared the bridle, the harness, and the leather bags that would hold her hatchling eggs. Once the Little People move Pug from my small cave, they'll transfer Danuka's feeding eggs there for safe keeping.

Nagora approached Danuka with the leather bags. "It is time, Mother."

Danuka followed each of the egg pouches with her eyes as Nagora carefully packed the pouches into the bags.

She fastened the flaps of the bags with their buckles and then picked up the bridle and the harness. She brought them over to the bowl of the entrance.

Nagora set the harness down and held up the bridle. She had set the pins of the buckles to the last holes. I hope I'll only have to tighten them instead of improvise extensions with lanyards. Danuka lowered her head to receive the bridle. Only one of the three buckles needed to be tightened. The other two were a tight fit.

Nagora climbed up onto the wing Danuka had lowered to the entrance floor. She cinched the straps tight. "Mother, you have grown so much. Soon, your harness and bridle will need to be adjusted for a more comfortable fit. Extensions will have to be added to them. Surely Geirador will notice."

Nagora went to get one of the leather bags. She buckled it in place on the harness.

"Mother, when you get to Geirador's, Da should be waiting to take you to the Dragonwood. Mum and Sagora should be there too. Pare will have given Sarah to Sagora. You will wait for me there. Tomorrow, when this is all over, I will go join you there and return your egg to you."

Once Nagora had attached the other two bags, Danuka looked down at her. Is she staring at my brand?

"Trust yourself, *Ka Peyakot Mahihkan*," said the dragon.

"Yes, Mother, I will trust in myself. What? Wait! Mother, you spoke to me without touching my forehead. Am I ... ? I guess I am." Just like Da said! It would just happen. It has! Today! I'm no longer an apprentice Dragon Talker!

Nagora reached up and scratched Danuka's chin until she moved her head back out of reach and looked into Nagora's eyes.

"The *Mêmêkwêsiw* know where I left my egg. They will have it ready for you," said Danuka.

"Thank you again, Mother. I will return it to you. I will make up for your stolen eggs." Even if it costs me my life.

Nagora stepped back so the dragon could turn and climb to the lip of the bowl. Danuka balanced there for a moment as she spread her wings forward and out. She pushed off with her powerful hind legs for her first flight in her new skin. The dragon glided away, pumped her wings once, then twice again before disappearing from view in the twilight.

Egg
Wâwih

Nagora packed a linen bag with the remaining clothes she had made for her baby over the winter and those she had made for herself. She wanted to pack the writing kit her mother had sent her, but could not find it. The Little People must've taken it. After all, I told them to take whatever was mine. Here I am packing as if I'm sure where I'll be going. Tomorrow is in the future. I can't predict what it holds for me, how my plan will play out, or whether I'll survive the day.

I'll know by midday. Raynhard and Aliza will arrive in the morning. Our battle will play out on the island in the cave.

If all goes well, I'll meet Lars at the valley entrance and Raynhard will leave by the main entrance, hopefully with the future of his dragon and his kingdom intact.

Hag, I will defeat you. I trust my plan. As for the unknown, I won't even consider it. Let it be unknown.

...

"Tomorrow, Pug, is our big day. Erin will get what she's always wanted. I hope you'll get healed and get your reward. And I'll get my freedom to choose my path. Sleep well, Pug."

Nagora had given him his last dose of medicine and his last drink of broth. Now the Little People waited to take over. Nagora crawled out of the cave and took up a position on the lake path opposite the replica of the dragon.

Pug's body floated along the path as if on its own. It was the Little People, invisible to her eyes, who carried Pug on their shoulders to the lake edge where they placed him on a hide that took the form of a shallow craft and ferried him to the island. More invisible Little People carried Pug over the island to the open seam in the dragon replica belly where they took him inside. Magically, the seam began to close as if being sewn up with an invisible thread by unseen hands.

Then before Nagora's unbelieving eyes, the dragon skin filled and stretched as muscles spread and took their appropriate places beneath the skin, giving form and life to the dragon that grew and took on the exact shape and color of Danuka's former body. The growth traveled out from the body to the legs, the tail, along the neck to the head, and finally to the wings.

The head moved, slowly at first. Nagora's eye caught the movement and saw it in profile. The single eye opened just as Danuka's did from sleep. The red eyeball rotated and its pupil found Nagora and stared at her. How do the Little People do that? I swear the eye is looking inside me.

The nostrils on the snout flared as the dragon took a great breath. Its head swiveled and now, as the dragon's neck rose from the island surface, both eyes focused on Nagora.

The dragon stood and reared its head back, keeping its eyes on Nagora's as it spread its wings wide. It lifted them until their open talons were an armspan from its head. The dragon flapped its wings twice, folded them in to its sides, and brought their talons to rest in front of it on the island.

Then the dragon swung its tail forward, so the finned, bulbous tip skimmed over the lake water and ashore to wrap itself around the dragon, as it leaned its head over the water to stare at Nagora and bare its teeth.

Tar piss! Teeth! It has teeth! True dragon's teeth! That is a living, breathing dragon before me. If I did not know, I would swear it was Danuka. By the stars! This dragon is real!

A now-familiar low whistle above her head caught Nagora's attention. She waited for the voice to speak.

"Watch and listen. This is what you must know for tomorrow."

On the island, the dragon folded its wings back and lay on its belly. A line of tiny lights formed up and took the shape of an upper body outline on the ground next to the dragon's belly.

"When the time comes, as your plan unfolds, you will fall there, at that spot," said the voice.

More tiny lights formed up with the body outline to show an arm with its forearm and hand holding an egg. "When you fall, hold the dragon egg there, nowhere else."

Another arm and hand holding a dagger of tiny lights formed up with the rest of the outline.

"Hold the royal dagger in your right hand."

The tiny lights of the dagger moved in unison to show a spot higher up on the dragon's chest.

"That is the target you aim for, those four dark scales. You'll only get one chance. Do not miss or the illusion will not work." Nagora swallowed. Only one chance. Do or die.

"The other items you need for your plan will be in place tomorrow. We have done our part with this dragon skin to make it come alive. The outcome is in your hands now."

Nagora nodded. "Thank you. I can't believe what my eyes see. I wish I could pay you more. Thank you, *Mêmêkwêsiw*."

"You have paid us well, Dragon Talker. You have paid us with what gold cannot buy. You have given us hope. If your plan works, we will be in debt to you. Go now. Sleep. We will watch over you. We will wake you when it is time."

The next morning, Nagora had washed her plate and bowl and was wiping the bowl dry when the whistle sounded. Should I look up? I won't see the one who speaks to me anyway. She was wrong. A tiny man was sitting on the stone shelf where the bowl in her hands was kept. He was as tall as her hand was long. He wore his hair in a single braid that fell over his left shoulder and down his chest to his waist. It was the color of gold. The man wore a brown leather vest and matching pants. He was barefoot. He had one hand on his knee and the other behind his back.

"Now you see me. Later you will not. Think about what you will tell people someday if ever you decide to talk about meeting me or what you have seen us do for you. People will ask for proof. We have nothing to give you as proof, except for this." The little man twisted around and pulled with both hands at what was behind his back. He rested it on his knees.

It was the gold coin she had used to call the Little People. "Wear it around your neck. It could bring you luck." He held it out to her.

Nagora reached out and took it. "Thank you." She looked at the coin which still had a leather lace threaded through its holes, though now the two ends were tied together with the four-eights knots. When she looked up, the little man was gone. Just as Nagora slipped the necklace over her head, with the dragon visible just below her neck, the low whistle came again from behind her at the lip of the cave entrance. It's time.

Nagora stood on the ladder and peeked over the edge of the bowl. Will I be able to spot them through the trees below? Will Raynhard come alone?

She had her answer moments later. In the distance on the slope below, Raynhard, with sword in hand, was leading a black-hooded figure. Their pace was without haste. Best take your time; the steepest part of the climb is to come. Your black cloak will be decorated in last year's dead thistles by the time you reach the entrance. Nagora's hand went to the handle of the dagger that hung in its sheath from the belt at her right hip. I'll be waiting to greet you.

After washing her face and hands, Nagora brushed her hair and tied it into a braid that hung down her back. Before sitting at the table with her eyes on the crack of the bowl entrance, she made sure the neck of her linen shirt exposed the coin necklace.

The tip of Raynhard's sword poked through first. Then the gloved fingers of a hand grabbed an inside edge of the crack.

Next, the pommel of a sword took position on the opposite edge of the crack, allowing the king to pull himself up and in.

"Nagora!" Raynhard spoke her name upon spying her, obviously trying to show surprise with his tone.

Nagora stood, took a step forward, and spread her arms. "Welcome," she paused, "to our lair. Have you come alone?"

"No, Nagora." Raynhard smiled. "I bring a guest," he said, raising his free hand, "and good news for you. I'm sure you'll be most pleased."

Nagora returned his smile and took a step closer. Will he return his sword to its scabbard? "Good news? For me? I can wait to hear it. Please, bring your guest in first."

Raynhard stepped closer, obviously taking all of her in as he did.

The dagger is the only weapon I wear. You see what I'm wearing at my neck. And what I'm not wearing. And I'm not carrying our child. Wait until you find out what I did with the baby. Checking before bringing Aliza in? I expected no less.

"You make me proud, Nagora. I'm happy to see you're wearing my father's dagger."

His grip on that sword says something else. "I take pride in wearing it. It's your gift to me. A symbol of the trust you have in me—that I will be faithful in my duty to you. That I am today, as I will always be, otherwise I would not wear it." He's relaxed his grip, but only for a moment. What are your intentions, Raynhard?

Nagora stepped to him with arms open. "It's good to see you. I've heard how busy you've been."

He quickly reversed his grip on the handle of his sword and embraced her with his free hand and the forearm of his sword hand. "Busy for you and Danuka. I can't wait to tell you."

Nagora leaned back, but kept hold of his forearms as she looked up into his face, doing her best to give him a sincere smile.

Raynhard's eyes traveled to her neck. "I see you now wear a gold dragon at your neck. Where did you get it?"

She kept her smile and held his eyes. "A friend gave it to me—for luck."

"But, your amulet? You'd worn it since birth. What have you done with it?"

Nagora let go of his arms and waved a hand. "I must've been destined to lose it. The lace was wet. I set it there in the sun to dry," she pointed to the stone lip of the entrance behind Raynhard, "and a crow dropped down, picked it up, and flew away with it. In a way, now I feel free without it."

Raynhard slipped his sword into its scabbard and pulled off one of his gloves. "That's strange. Could the crow have thought it was a young snake?" He reached out to Nagora, pulled her close, and placed his bare hand on her belly. "The child?"

She let her smile fade, then brought it back. "If I tell you now, I'll ruin the surprise."

He nodded briefly. "I'll not keep my guest waiting any longer." He returned to the crack and bent into it.

Did I detect regret?

He must be reaching for Aliza's hand.

The raven-haired beauty had just pulled the hood of her cloak back with her free hand as she stepped into the cave entrance, holding onto Raynhard's hand. Immediately she extended an immaculate white hand to Nagora. "I am Aliza. Nagora, King Raynhard has told me so much about you."

Nagora took the proffered hand. "Then I need no introduction."

Aliza smiled, let go of it, and looked to Raynhard. "Have you told Nagora the good news yet?"

Raynhard pulled on the fingers of his gloved hand. His smile was awkward. "Not yet, but I will now."

Nagora held up her hands and shook her head. "No, don't tell me yet. I think I can guess what it is. I'll find out after I've shown you what I invited you for. But first," she smiled at Aliza, "can I make you some tea? You must be thirsty after your climb up here."

Aliza returned her smile and unfastened the clasp at the neck of her cloak so it fell open to rest on her shoulders, revealing the red silk scarf she wore at her neck. "How gracious, but truly, I'm not thirsty. Are you, King Raynhard?"

Raynhard had just folded his gloves and slipped them behind the belt at his waist. Their leather fingers hung limp. He shook his head. "No tea for me, Nagora. Thank you."

"Are you sure?" asked Nagora.

For a moment his thumb played with the amber stone of the ring on his finger, and then he put his hand on her right arm. "In your invitation, you did say you were inviting us to witness a legacy. Nagora, does that have anything to do with Danuka shedding her skin?"

Nagora gave him a smile and looked directly at Aliza who adjusted the strap of her black leather scrip on her shoulder. "There's no keeping a secret from this man, is there? I guess you can say it has everything to do with Danuka's shedding."

Nagora glanced briefly at Raynhard, but kept her gaze on Aliza. "Today, you are going to see Danuka like you've never seen her before. Raynhard, you'll probably not believe your eyes. Aliza, what you will see will bring back mixed memories of the time when Queen Raganora ordered the slaughter of the dragons. I think today you will rejoice for having worn your red scarf all this time." Nagora gave Aliza a knowing look and a sly smile. Aliza's eyes widened and her hand clutched her scrip. What weapon have you concealed there?

Raynhard frowned. "You've truly piqued my curiosity. Can you show us now?"

Nagora held up a hand. "First, I must warn you. Danuka is in a weakened state." She paused to give Aliza a sideways wink. "She's resting now, but is willing to receive you. She's on the island on the cave lake. I've kept the lanterns to a minimum so she can rest. I'll swim across with one and light some others on the island so you can see. She's truly a sight to behold." Nagora shot another wink to Aliza who seemed to be fighting back a huge grin with a pinched smile, as she released her grip on her black bag

"This way, Aliza." Nagora led Aliza by the hand. Raynhard followed.

Light from lanterns on the opposite side of the lake created a halo of light behind the dragon so the back part of its tail and the ridge of its backbone all the way to its down-curved neck appeared as a silhouette.

Nagora stopped on the path along the lake where her bow rested against the wall of the cave. Three quivers lay empty on the ground. She held a finger to her lips as she slipped the curved tip of her bow through the lantern handle and lifted it from the peg it hung on. "Stay right here. I'm going to swim across."

Holding the lantern in front of her, Nagora waded into the lake and pushed away when she was waist deep in the water. She stroked with one arm and kicked with her legs until she reached the shore, setting down the lantern about two strides from the base of the dragon's tail.

Nagora climbed onto the island, picked up the lantern, and began to light candles from it along the shoreline. Will Raynhard and Aliza clearly see what I want them to? Not yet. Only when I light the tapers and hold the lantern closer.

After lighting the last of twelve candles, she returned to the first one near the base of the dragon's tail. With her free hand, Nagora picked up the taper and held it to the bare candle on the shore. As it sputtered to life, she walked closer to the obelisk-shaped pillar and held up the taper to show the chain that was wrapped around it. She followed the chain, showing it with the torch light as she went.

Nagora stopped at the large shackle locked to the dragon's hind leg. Then, she lit three of the nearby tapers that stood half an arm's length from each other. They lit up that rear side of the dragon. Is Raynhard believing what he sees?

"Nagoraaaaa?" Raynhard said, sounding panicked.

Yes, those are arrows you see, at least a dozen of them. There are more.

Nagora moved along and lit another set of three tapers to reveal more arrows stuck in the dragon's side.

Raynhard's mouth hung open as he shook his head.

Next, Nagora lit six tapers that stood in a row around which a dozen dragon eggs sat with arrows sticking out of them. "See these, Raynhard?" She held a torch close to one. "That's the gleam of gold you see. Dragon-young eggs for my target practice today." She pulled the arrow from the egg and held it above her head as she kicked the egg to pieces into the lake.

"Nagoraaa! Wha … ?" Raynhard stepped toward the lake, but Aliza held him back.

Nagora laughed and skipped along, kicking the other eggs into the lake.

When she stopped, she bent to the blue baby at her feet. She picked it up by its foot and shook it. "Look at this, my king. This is your bitch child. I ripped it from me with the help of your new friend."

Raynhard held a hand over his mouth as he looked from Nagora to Aliza and back to Nagora.

"Yes! Aliza provided me with poison to do it. Your little princess died in me. She never tasted my milk. Yes, Raynhard. Look! I used it for target practice too!" She held the torch next to it to show the half dozen arrows sticking from it.

Raynhard stood, reaching out with one hand while the other grabbed at the hair on his head. His mouth hung open. He was speechless.

Aliza clung to his vest.

Nagora flung the infant into the lake where it floated on its back, the arrows pointing up like misplaced masts on the tiny corpse. "Say good-bye to your bitch!"

Raynhard struggled to pull away from Aliza.

Nagora pointed. "Raynhard! Look here!" She bent and picked up Danuka's egg, cradling it to her chest with one arm. "It's the last one! The last of Danuka's dragon-young eggs! Watch me kill your dragon, then destroy her last egg. That, Raynhard, is the legacy I give you today!"

Nagora pivoted and jabbed the taper to the dragon's side. The dragon reared its head and came alive, bearing its teeth. It moaned a low sickly moan, reared its head higher, and raised its wings. Its belly and chest lifted off the ground. The shackled hind leg pulled on the chain. Nagora held out her dagger to defend against the strike from the dragon. She fell as planned when the dragon struck at her with its wing.

The dragon came down on Nagora pinning her legs under its scaly belly.

Nagora waved the dagger and cradled Danuka's egg to her side.

"No! Danuka! Stop!" It was Raynhard.

"Nagora! Don't! Stop! Don't harm the dragon!"

Nagora twisted to see her king. "Damn you, Raynhard for what you did to me. The last dragon is going to die and so is her last egg." Nagora lunged upward with her dagger and plunged it into the mark on the dragon's chest. Pug's blood spurted out over Nagora's hand and ran down her arm. The dragon's chest came down onto Nagora's so her elbow was bent as she held onto the dagger, just above her forehead.

"Noooo! ... Nagoraaaa! ... Nooo ... "

Nagora looked to Raynhard's screaming face.

Aliza cut his screams short with a swift blow to the back of his head. She had swung her scrip which must've held something heavy.

Aliza raised her hands and looked upward as she yelled out, "Heqet! Oh! Heqet! Come witness me end the curse you put upon me. Witness my destruction of the last egg of the last dragon in the Land of the Danu. Witness too, the dead dragon. And then grant me the eternal youth promised me! Heqet! I call upon you to come witness what I am about to do."

"Alizarine." The ancient voice echoed loud off the cave walls.

Nagora twisted to find the speaker. Where is it coming from?

"Alizarine, I have come to witness what you do not see. I have come to grant your due, eternal youth for as long as you find beauty in that which you wish to destroy. Mark, Alizarine, this will hold true until the day a queen and her daughter join their hands on their king's golden-handled dagger to pierce your heart. Only on that day, Alizarine, will you truly see what now you do not."

As Heqet spoke her new curse, Aliza threw her cloak and scrip to the floor of the cave and stepped from the shore into the lake. Aliza's eyes were open wide and focused on Danuka's egg. Tar piss! She wants to get to the egg. I'm ready. I'll pull the dagger from Pug's heart and kill you.

Nagora's eye caught movement on the path behind Aliza. It was Raynhard trying to pick himself up.

Aliza swam and her lips trembled as she spoke. "The egg. The beautiful egg. How lovely it is. I must have it."

Something's not right.

Aliza swam a stroke then reached out with her fingers spread wide. "The egg. I must have the egg." Her face disappeared underwater and resurfaced as she swam another stroke.

Tar piss! It can't be just the water. She looks younger.

Again Aliza had her arms outstretched, the fingers of both hands spread, grasping in the direction of the egg. "I must have it! The egg will be mine!"

This can't be! Not only younger, but she's smaller! Or can it be? She's a cursed witch.

"My egg! Oh! My beautiful egg! I will hold you and never let you go." Aliza's progress in the water slowed.

"Aliza! Stop!" It was Raynhard.

Aliza glanced over her shoulder, but she did not stop. She swam on toward the egg. "My egg. I promise I'll hold you forever. No harm will ever come to you."

No! It won't be your egg! Not while I'm alive! Nagora pulled on the dagger, but her hand slipped from the blood-covered handle. She tried pulling it free again, but Pug's blood wouldn't allow Nagora a proper grip.

Nagora let go of Danuka's egg, twisted at the waist, and clamped her left hand on the dagger's handle. As she did, she felt her side brush against the egg. With a quick glance over her shoulder, Nagora saw the egg roll toward the lake. It stopped at the water's edge. Tar piss! I have to get up!

Nagora pulled the dagger from Pug, and then she tried to pull herself back with the help of her forearms and the heels of her hands. She twisted her hips and pushed with her hands against the dragon's chest. Her legs were coming free of the belly's weight.

Nagora glanced over her shoulder.

Aliza continued to swim and gasp whenever she reached out toward the egg. Now she could only sputter the words, "I want you!"

Damn it! Drown, you witch! Nagora continued with her struggle to free her legs. Aliza's splashes were getting closer. Tar piss! Soon she'll touch bottom.

Nagora twisted and pushed with all her might. Her knees came free of the dragon's weight. She pushed again and looked to Aliza, who was standing in the water reaching for the egg, not an arm's length away. Nagora lifted her knees and gave a final shove against the dragon and pulled her feet free.

Aliza had reached the egg. She was kneeling next to it and caressing it with her tiny hands. Nagora couldn't believe what she saw. Aliza was no older than six, a little girl with big, dark eyes in a soft, round face. The child brought her cheek to the egg and closed her eyes as she sighed and spoke to the egg. "Now I have you, my egg. You are mine. I will never let you go."

Nagora took a step toward Aliza.

Raynhard screamed, "No! Nagora! Don't!"

I want to. I know you're a witch. I will my hand to raise this dagger, but it will not. I can't stab you. I'm cursed too.

Nagora went to her knees and shoved the dagger into its sheath.

Raynhard had waded into the lake and was swimming over to them.

Nagora stood.

Aliza cradled the egg in her lap and hugged it to her cheek over and over again.

The dragon toppled over onto the island, limp and lifeless. Its open belly seam exposed Pug's dead body.

Nagora reached a hand down to Raynhard to help him up. "See? Do you see? Do you believe me now, Raynhard?"

He stared into the face of the six-year-old at his feet. His eyes opened wider and his mouth dropped open as he tried to speak inaudible words the child would never hear.

Nagora pointed. "That's the shed skin of the dragon, Raynhard. And that's Pug. He came back to get more eggs for Aliza. I didn't let him get away this time."

Raynhard held a hand to his head and looked around, his face creased with incomprehension. His eyes settled for a moment on the tiny, arrow-pricked body floating in the lake. When he looked to Nagora, his mouth moved and his eyes teared.

"It's a skinned rabbit. Not your child."

Raynhard blinked back tears as he looked to the dragon carcass.

"Don't worry. Right now Danuka is safe. And so are you, except for a sore head."

Raynhard looked all around, as if trying to make sense of everything he had seen and been told. His mouth moved again, but not a word came out. He pointed to the child, Aliza, and looked at Nagora. You're dumbfounded, Raynhard. You can't even speak your question.

He looked back at the child and then back to Nagora.

Nagora put her hand on the gold handle of the dagger. "Go away from here. Leave her with me. I'll take care of her once you're gone. Then I'll send the dragon to you in a day or so."

Raynhard looked away from Nagora to the child, bit his lower lip, and nodded. He paused to say something before stepping back into the lake, but again, no words came. He put a hand to his head, stepped into the water, and when he was chest deep, he swam over to the path on the other side without looking back.

Nagora reached down to Aliza and touched her shoulder. Aliza looked up at her. "I think your beautiful egg deserves a good basket so you can carry it wherever you go. What do you think?"

Young Aliza nodded.

"I know where we can find one for you, not far from here. Do you want to come and get it with me?"

Aliza nodded and stood up with her arms around her dragon egg. "Let's go get the basket."

As Nagora looked up, a frog croaked, hopped into the lake, and disappeared. Strange, I've never seen a frog in here before.

Nagora led Aliza out of the cave through the valley entrance. Lars was waiting as planned. He held his arms open to greet her, and Nagora walked into his warm embrace. "Lars, I've been waiting for this moment for months now. I'm so glad you're here."

"I'm glad to be here too." He smiled one of his biggest and brightest smiles for her, and then bent to one knee to speak to the child. "What is your name?"

"My name is Alizarine."

"What do you have in your basket?"

"I have a beautiful egg in my basket."

Lars looked to Nagora and then back to the child. "Will you show me your egg?"

"Yes." She set her basket on the ground at her feet and pulled aside the red silk cloth that covered the egg.

"Oh! My! You are right, Alizarine. Your egg is truly beautiful. The sheepskin in the bottom of your basket is a good idea. It will help protect your egg and keep it warm."

Alizarine nodded. "That's what Mother says." She looked up at Nagora.

"Lars, I want you to take us to the Land of Skulls. First, you'll set us on the road to go there. Then you'll go to the Dragonwood. Tell my parents I won't be coming to join them. Tell Sagora to open the letter I sent her. After she has read it, you'll catch up with us. I'll tell you all about it on the way."

"Are you sure about this, Nagora?"

"Trust me, Lars. I am.

"Where are Aydan and Lyam?"

Lars whistled and moments later Aydan appeared. "Lyam's with the horses and the unicorn."

"The unicorn?" Nagora scratched her head.

"It was grazing next to the stream where I tied our horses."

Alizarine tugged on Nagora's sleeve. "Mother, that's Hope. She's mine."

Nagora bent to her knee. "Alizarine, Hope is your unicorn?"

Alizarine nodded as she held onto her basket. "Hope will carry me and my egg."

Aydan pushed his face into Nagora's to give her a face wash and, for those few short moments, she forgot what awaited her.

As Nagora stood, her hand came to rest on the golden handle of the royal hunting dagger. I promised it in payment. I'll go back in and put it in my small cave. The *Mêmêkwêsiw* will find it.

But a voice, clear as a tiny bell, spoke in her ear. "Keep it, *Ka Peyakot Mahihkan*, you will need it."

†

†

Dear Reader,

Thank you for reading *BRED*. For the benefit of future readers and to help me as an author, you would truly warm my heart by leaving an honest review at:

www.hnhenry.com/testimonials

OR wherever you purchased this copy of *BRED*.

Sincerely,

H. N. Henry

P.S.: Here's a **SPECIAL OFFER** for you:

Get the first chapter of *BLAMED* for **FREE**:

Find out how on the next page.

First Chapter for FREE

A dragon rules Nagora's future.
Her submission is total ... no matter the cost.

These are the ingredients of the blame lone-wolf warrior Nagora carries:

A newborn child, years ago abandoned in the custody of a dragon in the Land of the Danu.

One witch's malediction upon another.

A map to an ancient maze drawn in destiny's blood.

An ageless child witch love bound to the most precious egg of a dragon.

An unbelievable royal insult.

Superstition's thirst for revenge.

The only chance of survival for a race of dragons.

A kingdom on the brink of having the blood of all its people spilled and all its land scorched to ashes.

The legacy of a nation's heroine.

The onus of a curse's execution.

Are these a recipe for the fatal disaster Nagora's nemesis wishes to serve on her and those she loves? To find out... Come. Escape with Nagora into her dragon's world.

To learn more about the books in this series, visit the author at: www.hnhenry.com.

ISBN 978-0-9958419-6-3

9 780995 841963

BLAMED

The Dragon's Game

Book V

H.N. Henry

Go to the link below to get the FREE first chapter of BLAMED The Dragon's Game BOOK V:

https://www.hnhenry.com/blamedchapteronefree

ABOUT THE AUTHOR

Other than writing, his passions include kayaking, baking bread, and trying to learn how to play guitar. He shares the profits of his work with a local community cause, Point de Rue. They help the homeless people of his hometown find meaning and passion in their lives. Learn more about it here: http://www.pointderue.com/point_de_rue.html

To learn more about the author and the other books in the series, please visit: http://www.hnhenry.com.

Titles in **THE DRAGON'S GAME** series:

BANISHED BOOK I

BRANDED BOOK II

BETRAYED BOOK III

BRED BOOK IV

BLAMED BOOK V

H. N. Henry

ACKNOWLEDGMENTS

The Dragon's Game books wouldn't have come about without the generous and invaluable support of these people throughout the creative process.

From the beginning, Staecy-Lee, my editor, gave my manuscripts tough, honest critiques. Her hard questions made me see my stories with fresh eyes for the benefit of my readers.

Randi, my proofreader, closely read the final formatted-for-publication texts, finding inconsistencies in details, descriptions needing clarification, and grammatical errors my own eyes could no longer see.

Staecy and Randi, avid readers of this genre, also offered truly valuable and insightful comments that have made me a better writer. Learning from them has been a pleasure and a privilege.

My passionate beta readers of the first original brick, in first name a-b-c order, Ann, Daniela, Danielle, Maria, Marie-Josée, Randi, and Staecy-Lee generously delivered invaluable feedback and constructive criticism that helped spawn *BANISHED*, Book I, and from the volume they read, give birth to Books II and III of the series. I am forever in their debt for their support and encouragement.

I am grateful to the stained glass window artist, Guido Nincheri (1885-1973), who over ten years (1924-1934) created the beautiful windows in the Cathedral of the Assumption in Trois-Rivières, QC, Canada. From the photographs of those windows that I took on February 27, 2006, I was able to digitally manipulate images from two of the panels to create the unique dragons that appear on the covers of the first edition of my books, a humble homage to Nincheri's masterful work.

Though not referenced as Cree in the context of my stories, I have used Cree, in Roman orthography form, for the chapter titles and chapter numbers throughout the books in the series. More importantly, it is the " ... strange yet familiar language ... " Nagora, the main character, a.k.a. *Ka Peyakot Mahihkan*—Cree for *Lone Wolf*, hears in her mind and eventually uses to communicate with her dragon and other characters. At those times, when used, Cree is referred to as the *Language of the People*, in reference to the *First People* of *The Land* where my story is set.

The *Language of the People*, or "dragonspeak" as some readers of The Dragon's Game books call it, in a way, reflects the status of the Cree language in our land today. Though Cree is the most widely spoken Native language still spoken in Canada, it has yet to be recognized as one of this country's official languages. Similarly, in the fictional setting of *The Dragon's Game* books, the *Language of the People* is now only spoken by a few in a divided and renamed land where two different languages (those of the invading Outlanders) have become dominant in use.

To the Online Cree Dictionary Team: *Kinanâskomitin. Thank you*, I am grateful to you for making this resource available to all. It has been indispensable in helping me lend realism to that second language in my stories. I hope my readers will have as much pleasure as I do in discovering the living Cree language.

In the end, what appears on the pages of my books is mine, and I take full responsibility for any errors that show up in the final versions.